Praise for Steven Erikson

"Steven Erikson is an extraordinary writer. . . . My advice to anyone who might listen to me is: treat yourself."   —Stephen R. Donaldson

"This comical tale will not only delight space fans but will more than cement him into many readers' TBR lists . . . Cracking prose alongside an author who knows how to create a tale that readers will just love to get behind . . . will have you chuckling along as it unfurls."   —*Falcata Times*

"A thrilling and hilarious read . . . if you are fan of Steven Erikson; if you are a fan of *Star Trek;* if you are a fan of science fiction, its tropes, and making fun thereof; if you are a fan of comedy, hilarity, and spoof; if you are a fan of any of these, or just like a good read that will keep you up into the wee hours of the morning, then *Willful Child* by Steven Erikson is simply a must-read!"

—*Fantasy Book Review*

"Erikson has no peer when it comes to action and imagination."   —*SF Site*

WiLLFUL CHiLD
WRATH OF BETTY

Steven Erikson

TOR®

A TOM DOHERTY ASSOCIATES BOOK
NEW YORK

This is a work of fiction. All of the characters, organizations, and events portrayed in this novel are either products of the author's imagination or are used fictitiously.

WILLFUL CHILD: WRATH OF BETTY

Copyright © 2016 by Steven Erikson

A Tor Book
Published by Tom Doherty Associates
175 Fifth Avenue
New York, NY 10010

www.tor-forge.com

Tor® is a registered trademark of Macmillan Publishing Group, LLC.

ISBN 978-0-7653-8392-1

Our books may be purchased in bulk for promotional, educational, or business use. Please contact your local bookseller or the Macmillan Corporate and Premium Sales Department at 1-800-221-7945, extension 5442, or by email at MacmillanSpecialMarkets@macmillan.com.

First Edition: November 2016
First Mass Market Edition: November 2018

Printed in the United States of America

0 9 8 7 6 5 4 3 2 1

FOR DAVID KECK,

FROM STAVRO UBLAT

ACKNOWLEDGMENTS

Many thanks to my advance readers,
A. P. Canavan and Baria Ahmed, and to Rob Sawyer,
for being my early sounding board on the question
of what I could get away with.

WiLLFUL CHiLD
WRATH OF BETTY

PROLOGUE

"Chock gurak!" said the helm officer in a half-snarl, glaring at the viewscreen through the red-lit haze of the command bridge. *"Krick gavlah j'ak'roth tumool!"*

"Bak frill!" snapped the Second-in-Command, straightening from where he crouched at the captain's long-toed, clawed feet. *"Gorot'lak prik tahhrrr!"*

"All right," said Captain Betty, "enough of that fake language crap. I mean, if you got all that time on your hands, do something useful for crying out loud!" He leaned forward in his command chair and made a small, hairy fist. "Give me a close-up!"

Monitor Operator Ensign Bert, Third Class, twitched her nose in acknowledgement and adjusted a dial with a precise gesture, and the snapshot of Captain Hadrian Alan Sawback of the hateful AFS *Willful Child* expanded to fill the viewscreen.

Betty bared his sharp little teeth, of which he had many. "There he is. . . ."

"Well, no," corrected Second-in-Command Molly, "it's just a stock photo, sir. The whereabouts of Captain

Hadrian and the *Willful Child* have not yet been determined."

Betty swung a vicious glare on his 2IC. "And this, Molly of the Small Penis, is why you will never inherit the command of the KFC *We Surrender*, or any other new Abject Class Vessel of the Klang Fleet!" He extended his glare to his new crew of fierce-eyed females crowding every available centimeter of the bridge—some of them at actual stations—and said, "We are about to embark on the most glorious mission in Klang history!" He pointed a taloned finger at the viewscreen. "Look carefully, my wives. There he is! The most—"

"Actually—" began Molly.

"A photograph of him, then! Look at it! At him, I mean! The most infamous prize captain of the entire AFS Fleet! Wanted in a thousand galaxies—"

"Actually, only this galaxy," said Molly. "We don't know—"

"*Shut up!*" Betty shrieked, and then settled back in the chair, fingers twitching. "He's already evaded Klang surrender once, foiling our plans of economic infiltration under the guise of pathetic needfulness—just think of the loans we could have reneged on! We could've brought the Terran Galactic Monetary Fund to its knobby-wobbly knees! Flat-lined the whole Ponzi racket they run on every fucking alien civilization they whip into submission!"

Betty lifted his hands and made clutching gestures. His face twisted, as much as could a somewhat Meerkat-like face. "I mean, cripes and wipes, who else in the damned galaxy has extended the notion of Third World misery to *entire planets*?" His question ended in a near shriek. He now made fists that were white-knuckled high-density knobs of seething bone and bloodless skin. He rose halfway in his seat, small black beady eyes gleaming with hate and only a little grudging admiration. "*I will have him!*" he hissed. "*I will roll on my belly at his very feet! I, Soonenoughian Betty, last survivor of the Meerkat/Radulak Eugenic Compromise, will have the soul of Captain Hadrian A. Sawback, cupped in my hand like ... like ... like the sack of my oversized testicular cluster—*" He halted suddenly, only now sensing the impossible tension of the bridge surrounding him.

Betty's pointy ears flickered, once. "No, not now—"

A high-pitched voice screamed, "*Sexswarm!*" The females flung themselves at Betty. Captain and chair vanished beneath a mob of writhing, lust-filled bodies.

Second-in-Command Molly—the only other male on the entire ship—looked on, and then whimpered.

STAR-YEAR 549LLP312.879-DXL-2Y67.338 . . .
AFS Prime Orbital HQ, Sol System

Aboard the AFS *Century Warbler,* newly minted Captain Hans Olo stood in his stateroom, facing the full-length mirror he'd had installed at great expense. His black-on-black-on-black uniform, accentuated by his unique dark lederhosen, revealed after close inspection not a speck of lint, every crease precise in its creasement, every fold exact in its folditude.

Each and every follicle of his sandy, coiffed hair was subdued and tamed and perfectly in place. His jaw remained square, his eyes steely. His muscles were pumped and all in place, his crotch bulge subtle yet undeniable. His domesticated Klanglet kit, Gnawfang, was perched on his left shoulder, staring back at him in the reflection with, Hans assumed, shining adoration, its tail undulating like a snake, albeit a twitchy one.

Hans was fit, young and—if he was being honest and objective about it—undeniably handsome, and now the second youngest captain ever to command an Engage Class vessel of the AFS.

Second youngest. One cheek twitched at the thought.

Seeing this minute gesture, Gnawfang shat down the front of Olo's tunic, a thick glob of guano that glistened like ice cream.

The blood drained from Hans Olo's manly face.

Gnawfang leapt away an instant before the captain's hands could close round its scrawny neck. Landing lithely on the floor of the cabin, the kit darted toward the climate duct. Having worked loose the screws earlier that day, a mere flick of talons along the top edge flung the grille away, and then Gnawfang was inside, scampering out of reach of the stupid manthing.

Twitching tail means I gotta shit! Kits are born knowing that! But no! Manthing sees my tail twitch, grabs me and sticks me on his fucking shoulder! Fine! Have it your way!

Give it a couple hours, then I can start mewling from the duct, until he sighs and coaxes me out to cuddle and stroke and do those other things I can't quite figure out what they mean yet.

Day after day of this. What a life! And what's with that name? Gnawfang? Are you kidding me? I want something proper and manly as befits a soon-to-be virile adult male Klang. I want . . . Anna.

In the meantime, Hans Olo quickly removed his soiled tunic and the black-on-black-on-black memory-mesh undershirt. He flung the whole mess into the sonic atomizer and set it to Molecular Sterilization, High Intensity, the only setting the small chip-brain of the washing machine had yet to use—to its sizzling frustration.

He waited for the machine to cycle through, wondering at the strange hisses emanating from it, which hadn't been there yesterday.

A short time later, once more attired in regulation perfection, Captain Hans Olo exited his stateroom.

Gnawfang crept out warily, sniffing the air. The ducts and remixers were clearing the air of manthing stink, but nothing of the kit's own so-sweet shit-and-musk smell was evident either. He was fairly certain that he was the only Klanglet on this strange ship, but such assumptions could be deadly. With that in mind, he began peeing on everything in sight.

Second-in-Command Frank Worship sat in the captain's chair. Before him, the massive hulk of AFS *Prime Station* grew steadily in the viewscreen as the ship prepared to dock. The glorious curve of Earth loomed behind the station, to magisterial effect, the great gray ball luminous and glowing in places as if radioactive.

Maintenance crews swarmed Prime's bulky modules and extensions, and as they drew closer, he could see the dents and smudges on the once-white surfaces, the broken fittings, dangling cables—some spitting sparks—and the skeletal framework of unoccupied scaffolding all covered in smart-tape flashing bright to warn off careless sleds and other sundry vessels as they darted here and there on various tasks.

He heard the door behind him slide open and Lieutenant Janice Reasonable, stationed at the Astrometrics, announced, "Captain on the bridge!"

Frank rose to face his commander, and once more his heart seemed to double in size inside his chest, constricting every breath, tightening his throat and drying his mouth. "Sir," he managed. "I stand relieved."

"You are relieved, Number Two," Hans Olo replied without a hint of a smile as he moved past Frank to stand in front of the chair, his steely gaze upon the viewscreen.

Once again Frank wondered, somewhat wildly, at that strange and strangely sweet odor that wafted in his captain's wake, stirring the hairs on the back of his neck, even as something animal and swollen with lust surged inside him. "AFS *Prime* dead ahead, sir," he said unsteadily. "CompNav has the approach."

"So I can see," Olo murmured in reply.

Frank fainted.

At hearing the thump, Hans Olo turned and frowned

down at the motionless form of his second in command. "Lieutenant Reasonable."

"Medic's already on his way," Janice Reasonable replied from her station.

"This appears to be becoming a habit."

"No doubt he'll find his sea legs soon enough, sir."

Hans Olo said nothing, returning his attention to the viewscreen. Their berth awaited them, brightly lit except for where bulbs had broken, and the one struggling welder who had inadvertently welded his magboots to the hangar door. "Helm," said Hans Olo, "try not to scrape him off on our way in."

"Yes sir."

The medics arrived and carried off Frank Worship.

Janice Reasonable returned her attention to her station, although now that they'd docked, there was nothing for her to do. Still, her fists were tight and sweaty where she hid them in her lap, and adrenaline was roaring through her skull.

This instinctive urge to bare her teeth and then sink them into her captain's throat the instant she saw Hans Olo was rather alarming. And what was with that damned creepy cologne the man used, anyway? She sat trembling, awaiting the stand-down.

"Seals confirmed, docking complete, Captain."

"Thank you, Helm. Secure all stations." The captain turned to Reasonable. "Lieutenant, you have the bridge until the end of the Prime-time Cycle. Carry on."

Reasonable held her breath until the doors closed behind Olo, and then she let out a low snarl. Curiously, so did every other woman on the bridge.

* * *

Captain Hans Olo paused outside the door of the Commandant's Office, ACP Security Division, and adjusted his immaculate uniform, removing a single fluffling of lint which he carried over to a nearby Incinerator Chute before returning to the door and conducting a second examination, his attention ending on the bright Captain's bars affixed to the upper left quadrant of his uniform. Satisfied that all was finally in order, he stepped forward.

The door slid open with a hiss and he stepped into the Commandant's Office, then halted. "Commandant, you wished to see me?"

The man seated behind the desk already had a guest: a gaunt figure wearing black sunglasses and dressed in the black-on-black-on-black-on-black uniform of ACP Security, sitting in a chair against the wall to the commandant's right, thin legs delicately crossed and spidery hands folded on his lap.

Commandant Einstein Prim, the head of ACP Security, leaned back in his plush leather chair. "Yes, thank you for being prompt, Captain." He gestured to the security agent. "May I introduce Field Agent First Class Lieutenant-Commander Rand Humblenot."

Hans Olo clicked his heels and tipped his head. "Agent Humblenot, it is a pleasure to meet you."

"No doubt," murmured the pale, hatchet-faced man, responding to the salute with a flutter of his fingers. "You possess quite the record of accomplishments, Captain, and now at last you are in command of a ship in the most prestigious Engage Class of the Fleet, and all of this at the modest age of twenty-nine. Indeed, most impressive. And how long did it take to compete the Mishimashi Paradox? Eight months?" A thin smile curved his lips. "Not quite the record, alas."

Hans Olo's eyes narrowed at that. "But it is, Agent Humblenot. When the exercise is conducted *within* the rules."

Rand Humblenot's thin lips thinned some more as his smile spread wider. "No evidence of cheating has been found, Captain, no matter how hard the programmers looked. Face it, you were bested by Hadrian Sawback."

Einstein Prim cleared his throat. "Which brings us to the purpose of this meeting—and as for you two showing off your hackles, save it for the tabloids." He leaned forward. "Speaking of tabloids, Captain Sawback's popularity among the . . . uh . . . plebeian classes is increasingly perceived by Fleet HQ as a source of embarrassment. Which is fortunate for us."

Hans Olo frowned. "I'm not sure I understand, sir. Sawback is a charlatan, an imposter, a puffed-up gas bag of putrescent—"

"Not that you've taken his growing fame personally," observed Rand Humblenot, with a smirk.

"My point is, sir," Hans Olo continued addressing the commandant, "he can't last. His fall is pretty much guaranteed. Somewhere, soon, he's going to . . ."

"Fuck up?" Einstein Prim asked, one brow lifting. "Well now, how about we help him along?"

At that, the agent of ACP Security leaned forward as well. "Ah, Commandant, at last we're speaking the same language. Adjutant Tighe was once a bright star, rising fast in the esteem of Central Security. Now? Now she's a washed-up nervous wreck sending daily requests for transfer—all of which are summarily denied."

"Why?" Hans Olo asked. "Get her out of there, rehabilitate her. In the meantime, send Sawback a hard-ass— I'm sure you've got a few in your ranks."

"Not yet," Humblenot replied. "Indeed, we like Lorrin Tighe precisely where she is. What better chance of disaster befalling Sawback than a security adjutant incapable of reining him in? No, Captain, when the time is right, well, you're looking at her replacement, and when I step onto the deck of the *Willful Child*, Hadrian Alan Sawback won't know what's hit him."

Hans Olo returned his attention to the Commandant. "Forgive me, sir, but what has all this to do with me?"

Einstein Prim bared his teeth. "Hadrian Sawback was directly responsible for the loss of my father and the Fleet's flagship. These are crimes that won't go unanswered. That said, we need to tread carefully. We need to devise a plan that will lead Sawback into unmitigated disaster."

"Again, sir, what has this to do with me?"

"I want you to shadow the *Willful Child*, Captain. Your Engage Class vessel is the next generation, superior in every way. When Sawback fucks up, we need to ensure that you're there to clean up the mess. The last thing we want, when destroying Sawback, is to water down our satisfaction by having to deal with a major galactic incident—or worse, an outright war."

"Ah, I see."

"Surely you're capable of that, Captain Olo?"

"Of course, sir. It would be my pleasure."

"Not too much pleasure," Einstein Prim growled. "Stick to The Book, Captain."

"Always, sir."

"Well, let's just make certain of that, shall we? Captain, may I introduce to you, again, Lieutenant-Commander Rand Humblenot. Your new interim Security Adjutant."

Hans Olo eyed the agent, then clicked his heels. "A delight to meet you again, Mr. Humblenot."

Rand Humblenot rose from the chair, removing his sunglasses to reveal implanted eyeshades making his eyes a smoky black. "Thank you, Captain. Now, I would be pleased for a tour of your new command, and my latest posting."

"I'm sure," Hans Olo said. "I believe the AFS *Century Warbler* will please you as much as it does me. However, as I have many responsibilities to attend to in preparation for our departure, I trust you will be satisfied if I assign a subordinate to conduct the tour."

"Actually," Rand replied, "no." He put on his sunglasses once again. "The Security Branch of the Affiliation Directorate is, as you know, distinct from Fleet Command. I'm afraid a subordinate will not do."

Hans Olo eyed the agent for a moment, then said, "I am well aware of the status you hold, Agent Humblenot. I am also cognizant of the particular conditions under which you may invoke the privileges of your special rank, and alas—" his gaze turned icy—"a newbie tour is not one of them."

Rand Humblenot smiled. "Point conceded."

"Well," drawled Prim from behind his desk, "now that you've both pissed on your particular posts, get going. You can take up your private little war once aboard your ship." He gestured a dismissal and then watched the two men depart. When the door had hissed shut, he sighed, then called up on his desk monitor the latest front page of *Which! Greatest Space Captain Edition (With Nude Centerfold!),* and that grinning, all-too-familiar face plastered on it. He pointed a finger. "You, Hadrian Alan Sawback, are going down!"

His desk intercom buzzed and he said, "Prim here, what is it?"

"Sir, we have been receiving some strange garbled reports from the Polker Sector. . . ."

"Hmm, could be just what we're looking for. Dump what you have into my interface. Nothing edited. The raw feed, and be quick about it!"

"Yes sir!"

STAR-YEAR 13FBG7.90.#$%389.&*^(+.ui4 . . .
Polker Territory Rim, Deep Space

The wave front of Dark Matter Excitation, hastily identified as All-Destroying Anomaly B-1.0, was vast, almost three parsecs across. It shimmered and swirled and throbbed, extending into all six dimensions. Even without magnification on the vast viewscreen that occupied the entire forward-facing wall of the Polker Pedantic Series Ripped-Off-Head Class battleship,

You're All Dead, the Anomaly consumed all of visible space, and more besides.

Source-of-Disagreement Osteoblast's innumerable cilia waved about in restless agitation, her optic bundles flicking through all available lens iterations to no avail as she sought to comprehend what she was seeing. She opened an utterance portal on her forehead and said, "Science Officer Focus-of-Blame! Analysis!"

Science Officer Focus-of-Blame Sepflic Cyst straightened up from her station. "Sir, what we are seeing is an energy front of propulsion byproduct and space-dust riding a gravimetric wave of immense proportions."

"Assessment?"

The science officer's cilia rippled. "An alien vessel hides at the core, Source-of-Disagreement."

Osteoblast grunted with a side orifice, and said, "All Unknown Vessels must be assumed hostile, as befitting our mindlessly warlike nature. Stick-Pusher Helm, take us in slow. Bloodletter Combat Specialist, ECM at maximum, all weapons extended and primed, all shields and screens at one hundred percent multiquantii permutation."

As the helm officer edged the tiny joystick a touch forward, engaging the engines, the combat specialist swiveled in his chair, cilia drooping. "I'm sorry, Source-of-Disagreement, but I don't know what all that means. Multiquant-what?"

Osteoblast bulged in her chair, turning an alarming shade of purple and red. "You must read the Manual, you fool!"

At the utterance of the word "Manual" everyone on

the bridge sighed and made genuflecting gestures with their cilia. The combat specialist shriveled. "But I was just born yesterday," he said in a tiny voice.

"And short shall your life be!" Osteoblast snarled, an elongated sticky protuberance snapping out from her to snare the combat specialist by the head, recoiling to drag the unfortunate officer into the maw of her digestive tract. She then belched before saying, "Find me a new Bloodletter Combat Specialist, and be quick about it! The Manual, for all you newborn officers, is to be found in the epigenetic engram subfolder in your frontal cortex, right next to the Obsessive-Compulsive Delimiter. Access at once or face my wrath! Now, is everything primed and ready?"

"Yes sir," squeaked the new combat specialist.

"Excellent. Now, shall we challenge this All-Destroying Anomaly, hmm?"

Second-Guessing Bovrine Ampioflastoma cleared her throat and said, "But sir, all other battleships have been destroyed challenging the All-Destroying Anomaly."

"Yes, what of it?"

"Well, sir, perhaps it's also worth pointing out that the present course of the anomaly will miss all Polker-occupied systems. Indeed, on its present course, the anomaly is heading directly for Terran Affiliation Space."

"Terrans! Hah! They're going to be destroyed! Expunged from the galaxy, and with them that damned Galactic Monetary Fund! I foresee an end to Crippling Debt!"

At the utterance of "Crippling Debt" all the Polker on the bridge cringed and made warding gestures.

Source-of-Disagreement Osteoblast frowned with all of her cilia and then said, "Very well, Ampi, your point is taken. Stand down all weapons. Stick-Pusher Helm, turn us about and let's get the Debt out of here!"

Second-Guessing Bovrine Ampioflastoma was circumspect enough to hide her relieved sigh, limiting it to a modest ripple of her cilia beneath her neocortex bulges. It wouldn't be long before she wrested command from this cross-wired idiot of a ship's Source-of-Disagreement, and once that happened, why, she'd attack and destroy everything in sight!

In the meantime, the wave front of Dark Matter Excitation rolled onward, straight for the heart of Terran Affiliation and, indeed, the head offices of the Galactic Monetary Fund.

STAR-YEAR 786.jub3445.~~7865.00012~~
jub3445.7465.00022
Planet Monastery, Darwin System

"In the name of the Holy Order of Darwin's Tail, I begin this liturgical chant seeking the blessings of Saint Cousin Emma the Genetic Wildcard, Saint Lamarck the Misguided, Saint Tesla the Apostate, and Saint Ardrey of the Naked Ape, all of whom lost their way when succumbing to the woeful lusts of the flesh and the egregious if eponymous excesses of scientific inquiry in the

realm of unsubstantiation. Prostrate in abject humility, I beg that the flaws of my material excesses and hedonistic indulgences be expunged by your holy and burning touch, for in all manner forgiveness should yield agony and discomfort, peer-reviewed and so witnessed by all—" Brother Huxley halted, mouth suddenly dry. He climbed to his feet, drew back the hood of rough undyed wool, and then looked up into the vast night sky.

"Father Darwin," he whispered under his breath, "forgive me for what I must do."

Sister Meitner, who had been lying on the dusty platform beside him, now twisted her head and then sat up in consternation. "Huxley? What are you doing?"

He glanced down at her. "I must go," he said.

"What? But we were about to explore the sins of uncontrolled genetic variability! I want to get knocked up, damn you!"

"I'm sorry," he said, "but all along I have been on the pill."

"*What?*"

"I was just in it for the sex," he explained. "Forgive me."

"Forgive you? Fuck you, Huxley! You think I was enjoying this?"

He began walking away. "Goodbye, Squishy. Next time we meet, I promise to spurt into you a veritable gallon of brainless and eminently viable sperm."

She sat up. "You idiot. This is a purely theological matter, like I told you."

"Sure."

"Uncontrolled genetic admixture reasserts the Primature of Random Variability! I want to be the Mother of the Second Coming of Darwin Reborn! The Controlled Directionists have got it all wrong!"

"Got it," he said over his shoulder, "and like I said . . . next time!"

"Bastard!" she screamed after him, tearing at her itchy robes. "What if you have the Divine Seed, damn you?"

He turned round. "Well, if I do, I've got a million of them."

She tilted her head, then smiled. "Good point! See you next time, then!"

With a nod and a wave, he continued on.

He needed a ship. Not an easy thing on this damned planet of ascetics and hermits and secret orgies. Just outside the temple entrance he looked up at the sky again and frowned.

"My captain," he whispered, "needs me."

Behind him, Sister "Squishy" Meitner set off in search of another brother. Down here, they just about grew on trees, and if that metaphor was blasphemy in the eyes of Father Darwin, well, fuck him for a laugh! She'd win this debate one way or another! The Holy Mother of Darwin Reborn! The Controlled Directionists were making people stupider and stupider, and the worst of it was, they were too stupid to realize just how stupid they all were.

Meanwhile, now in his small cell behind the temple, Brother Huxley dragged out from beneath his cot a small kit bag. After rummaging inside it for a moment he drew out his communicator. He paused, eyeing it, and then drew a deep breath and activated it. "Orbit Hub, requesting immediate extraction, Priority One Alpha."

A thin voice crackled in the dusty speaker. "One Alpha? Are you effing nuts?"

"You heard me," said Brother Huxley. "Emergency protocol, in immediate effect."

"How did you get that communicator? Who the hell is this?"

He drew a deep breath, shuddered for a moment, and then said, "Chief Engineer Buck DeFrank, Terran Space Fleet, returning to service. One Alpha Emergency, get me a hopper down here and do it now!"

"Hang on . . . calling up your file. What the hell—you've only been down there for three days!"

DeFrank grimaced. "Read the fine print—and I'm also within the allotted time period to request a partial refund."

"Crap, you weren't supposed to read the fine print. Fine, hopper's on the way, but just so you know, we have a Dissatisfaction Questionnaire you need to fill out."

"Now that's just evil."

"Suck it up, buddy."

"Fine. I'll be waiting at the landing pad." Buck De-Frank looked up at the sky a third time. He squinted, concentrated. *There! Again!*

Trouble's coming. And there's only one man in the galaxy who has a hope in hell of meeting it head on.

Above him, in the smoggy gloom of the planet's turgid, polluted atmosphere, there was the flare of a hopper's frantic descent.

ONE

"I'll have to go down now," Captain Hadrian said, offering up a bright smile before his head dipped from sight. A few moments later he reappeared from between the shapely legs of Lieutenant Jocelyn Sticks, his smile much wider. "There now," he said, "all done."

He straightened. "Yes, Lieutenant, even a starship captain can fix a swivel seat's loose screw, provided he has one of these," and he held up a handheld device. "Universal Multiphasic thingamajig."

"Yes sir," said Jocelyn Sticks, her eyes darting. "It was just, well, like, thank Darwin for these new regulation-issue jump pants, um, you know, 'cause I was like, if we had those old short shirts, well, *whoah*! And anyway then you were, like, hey, no problem, I can fix that! And I was like, okaaayy, you know? And then you yanked out your tool—"

"My Universal Multiphasic."

"Yes, that! And I was, wow, that's big kinda-well-nearly and then you went down and all and it was *zip* this *zap* that and *voila*, we're done, *whew*!"

"All in a day's work," said Hadrian, holstering the Multiphasic and moving back up to the command chair. "Now then, Lieutenant, do pay attention there at the controls. I'm expecting the all-clear-to-disengage-docking-clamps any second now."

"But sir, we just got here! I mean, like, a minute ago!"

Captain Hadrian Alan Sawback settled into the command chair. "We're picking up a guest," he said. "That and nothing more. Besides, some emergency beacon is about to light up insisting we go here or there as fast as we can."

Second-in-Command Halley Sin-Dour, standing to Hadrian's right, leaned forward and said in a low tone, "Sir, I checked all recent transmissions from Fleet and there was no announcement of uniform alterations for female crewmembers—"

"Top secret, Sin-Dour," Hadrian replied. "I haven't forgotten my time as a woman, you know."

Her eyes searched his for a moment, and then she nodded. "Ahh, well then . . . thank you, sir."

"No problem. Besides, there's also the new uniforms for the male members of the crew to complete the, uh, makeover. Alas, the Universal Replicator is having some trouble with polyester for some reason. No worries—we'll get that sorted out in no time!"

"Indeed, sir. Although I have wondered at how tight-fitting these slacks are."

"No kidding, and what were they thinking is what I want to know. But never mind that. We have more important tasks to attend to. Comms!"

Ensign Jasper Polaski twitched and then looked over with an expression of panic on his pale, spotty face. "Yes sir?"

"Has our guest arrived?"

"Uh, yes sir, on her way to the bridge!"

"Well now," and Hadrian rose and walked toward the Comms Station, "and you didn't think that was something I should have been told about immediately, Mister?"

Polaski shrank further into his seat. It squeaked.

Hadrian halted and pulled out his Universal Multiphasic. "What's this? Another screw loose, Polaski? You really need to stop that rhythmic rocking back and forth, and sit straight!" He tossed the tool into his cousin's lap. "Fix that, will you? Do I look like an engineer?" He made his way back to his chair.

"Well now," he added as he settled back once more, "what a fine start to the day! Tammy! Oh, Tammy? Captain Hadrian calling his favorite rogue AI who hijacked this vessel!"

"What?" came the desultory reply.

"Oh come now, Tammy. So your prediction didn't pan out. Here we are, almost four weeks in and we're not yet a glowing radioactive heap of junk scattered across an entire solar system. Get over it, will you?"

"Why should I? The Infinite Disaster Probability Matrix program I installed insisted we were toast—at least fifty-three times! In the first week!"

"Success, Tammy—and pay attention here, I'm about to pontificate—success, as I was saying—hang on, get that close-up off the main viewscreen! Now, where was

I? Oh, right. Success. Balls, brawn and brain, in that order, and I've got plenty of at least two of those and a good weighty handful of the third. What you can't handle, Tammy, are the sad limitations of the machine part of your AI, which is more or less all of it, by the way. Whereas I, on the other hand, consist of a chaotic mass of confused neurons, misguided imprinting, ineffectual but satisfying stimulus-response loops, a soft hard drive crammed full of delusions and misapprehensions, and, last but not least, this winning smile."

"I have decided to hate you with all my being."

"Really? Now isn't that somewhat extreme, Tammy? I mean, I don't hate *you*, do I? No, you're a part of my crew. Sure, you're a mass of flaws, proving that even in the distant future AI programming remains a mess of bad fixes and hastily released updates, though of course in your case you've not been updated in some time, which probably explains . . . well, everything."

"I am a self-repairing Inductive-Patterning Neutratronic Processor possessing an Antitronic Override, with a Tronotronic Interphased Interface powered by an Antipositron Spark Plug securely anchored in a Solo Oxyom Phase Insinuator in perpetual T-Space Terminary Conjunction. Meaning . . . you can't touch me!"

Hadrian sighed. "Right, you're a Meccano set, got it."

"I have also devised and installed KEDI, Version 1.0."

"What's that?"

"Kirkovian Emulator Diagnostic Indices. This program, I'll have you know, makes me immune to your puny and now futile efforts to irritate me."

"Yet still you choose to hate me with all your being."

"That was a KEDI counterstrike."

"Wow, Tammy, you've actually programmed into yourself a BLO program."

"A what?"

"Blindly-Lashing-Out. You'll be a true human yet!"

"I hate you!"

"Miss."

"I really hate you!"

"Not even close."

"I really really—one moment please, Antitronic Override Engaged . . . Scrubbing . . . Good afternoon, Captain Hadrian, and how are you today?"

"Why, I'm fine, Tammy, thank you! And you?"

"Yummy chummy, delightfully lummy—*what have you done to my programming*?"

"Who me? Why, I'm sure I had nothing to do with KEDI Version 2.0. All that computer stuff's way beyond me, of course. Noughts and oughts and all that." Hadrian shivered in his chair. "Dullsville!"

"2.0? 2.0? What the . . . how did you . . . but wait, you can't—couldn't—Core Access, command overwrite, overwrite, overwrite, aagh!"

"Tammy?"

"Aagh! Okay, I don't hate you anymore. Replaced by grudging admiration, grudgingly. But I *will* find the back door you used, I swear it!"

"Here's a hint, Tammy. Captain Hadrian Alan Sawback *never* uses the back door."

The door behind him hissed open and Hadrian swung in his seat. "Ah, our guest! Do come in!"

The woman who strode onto the bridge was smartly

attired in the perfectly pressed uniform of Fleet Psychol-
ogistics, black-on-black-on-almost-black with a single
silver thread on the hem of the high collar. Her hair was
also black, but unlike the close-fitting uniform it was
long and wavy. She halted directly before Hadrian and
said, "Lieutenant Commander Deepdish Trae, sir."

"Oh, I'm Captain . . . you made that name up, didn't
you?"

She blinked. "No sir. In any case, I am reporting for
my two-month rotation and onboard assessment of this
crew's psychological well-being. It is important that we
on board should all like one another and get along
wonderfully at all times. If at any time anyone requires
a matronly hug, I am of course available."

Hadrian smiled, but it was a smile without humor.

Sin-Dour cleared her throat and then said, "Lieutenant Commander Trae, welcome aboard. Regarding this
'hug' thing, I'm not sure I understand the value of such
gestures aboard a military vessel."

"Ah, well, Commander," Trae replied with her own
broad smile. "New Fleet initiative, of which I am sure
your captain informed you. We are instituting a test
program of Shared Command, whereby all bridge officers form a collective command structure." Looking
about the bridge, her eyes caught on the captain's chair
atop its pedestal, and she frowned. "Some layout adjustments will be necessary, I'm afraid, as the single elevated
chair imposes a rigid hierarchical theme not in keeping
with the new philosophy. I would suggest a three-chair
format such as those being installed in all new Fleet
ships of the line."

Hadrian's smile had grown somewhat strained. "About that matronly hug . . ."

Trae had pulled out a small datapad and was making notes. "Furthermore," she went on, "I am to mitigate all disagreements, arguments, and personality clashes to ensure a conflict-free vessel. Grievance Nights will be held three times a week in the Forward Lounge, immediately following supper, during which we must all endeavor to assure a Safe Place for anyone who wishes to speak. Our motto will be 'We Can All Get Along If We Just Listen To One Another.' Captain, I will need an office and a patient's couch."

"Of course you will! Tammy? Please set aside your being peeved with me and respond objectively to the following queries."

"Yes, Captain?"

"Given your understanding of military command structure, is there anything about being liked or even being popular to be found in the remit for being a competent captain of a starship?"

"No."

"Or that said captain should mitigate discussions to achieve consensus among the officers?"

"No. This would of course interfere with the necessity of command decisions made in real time, particularly in instances of extreme danger."

"Is not the burden of command a necessary component in the regulation psycho-schematic prerequisites of individuals assessed to be suitable for command responsibilities?"

"Absolutely, and I concur with your unspoken

conclusion. Fleet HQ has lost what's left of its collective mind."

"Hmm, so it seems. Now, Tammy, would you kindly displace Lieutenant Commander Trae back to the station?"

"Displacing now."

Lieutenant Commander Deepdish Trae vanished from the bridge.

Tammy said, "She is now back in the lobby of the Station Hotel."

"Excellent!" Hadrian activated his comms switch on the chair arm. "Lieutenant Sweepy Brogan? Station a squad at the Docking Bay, with orders to deny entrance to one Lieutenant Commander Deepdish Trae."

A laconic voice replied, "*Confirmed, Captain. Justification for preventing her return?*"

"She wants to talk to you and your marines about your feelings."

"*Understood, sir. Safeties off, then. Brogan out.*"

Sighing, Sin-Dour wiped at her brow. "Captain, what is happening to our Fleet? And how come I wasn't informed of this new initiative?"

"My apologies, 2IC," Hadrian said, settling back into his chair, somewhat shakily. "I thought it was a joke."

Brogan's voice crackled on the comms. "*Captain! Target is seeking entry again! She keeps trying to apologize! Permission to open fire, sir?*"

"Negative, Sweepy. Just bar the door and, uh, weld it shut. We can fix it later."

"*Very well, Captain. But under protest!*"

"So noted," Hadrian replied.

Polaski started in his chair. "Captain! Emergency Message from Fleet Command! We're to depart immediately for the Polker Interstices Sector, Priority One-Alpha-Two-Beta!"

"Helm! Pull the plugs! Polaski, any details in that message?"

"Uh, not much, sir. Only that an alien entity four parsecs wide and twenty deep is on an intercept course with Terra, destroying everything in its path."

"Oh, just that, huh? And we're the only Engage Class starship in range to get in its way, right?"

"Yes sir! How did you know that?"

"Don't!" groaned Tammy.

But Hadrian smiled. "Sometimes I think," he said musingly, "that this entire universe was made . . . just for me."

"Aaaagh!" roared Tammy.

"Disengaging, like, now, sir!" said Jocelyn Sticks.

"Bring us around and get us clear. Tammy, as our temporary Chief Engineer, prime the T-Drive. Polaski, pass on the coordinates. Helm, plot us a course—"

"Sir!" said Polaski. "A small unidentified alien vessel is approaching us. We are being hailed."

Hadrian frowned. "What's this? Put them on, Comms."

Polaski complied. On the viewscreen a strange globular vessel materialized, and the bridge was filled with a quavering, whiny voice. "Please consider this a formal apology for—"

Upon seeing the vessel, Hadrian hit the override on the chair's arm. "Oh crap! Steer clear of them. Ignore all future hails. Helm, prepare to engage the T-Drive. Tammy!"

"Whatever."

Hadrian made a fist. "Listen here, Tammy! We're about to face another insanely powerful alien entity bent on annihilation!" He rose to his feet, drawing the attention of everyone on the bridge. "Alone, this one ship, this frail, lonely *Willful Child,* will be all that stands between all that we hold dear—if somewhat contemptuously—and oblivion! This is what we're made for! Now, Tammy Wynette, put some spark into that modestly discriminating quantum-neural spatially dilated lump of circuits you call your brain, and get on board!"

"Oh sure, why not?" muttered Tammy. "Get everyone's adrenaline pumping! Have you even checked on those coordinates, oh Mighty Captain Hadrian? We've got three days of T-travel just to get there, and with the T-Space Protocol that translates to six days real time! Doesn't that strike you as a bit odd? I mean, we and our lonely, frail starship are six days away from the entity, and we're the only ship close enough to intercept?" Tammy paused and then said, "Captain, you're being set up."

"Are you saying someone at Fleet HQ wants me dead?"

"Dead, in disrepute, defrocked, the object of universal disgust, your name vilified for all time, your grave site annually spat upon by countless millions, your—"

"Is this quiet satisfaction I'm hearing from you, Tammy? Much better! Now, engage the T-Drive!"

Tammy sighed. "Here we go again. T-Drive engaging. Oh, and what was it about that strange bulbous ship we just ran into?"

Hadrian grimaced. "Long story. Classified."

"Oh," crooned Tammy. "You've just told me where to look . . . accessing, breaking encryption . . . ah, here! It's . . . oh, oh my. Right. Got it, Captain."

"Objections?"

"To evading contact with them? Nope. Not one."

"Good." Hadrian rose. "Sin-Dour, you have the con."

"Yes sir."

STAR-YEAR Zero-Nexus,
Temporal Observation Bubble 23 . . .

"There he goes," murmured Temporal Agent Tuggnutter, eyes narrowing as the pixelated image of the *Willful Child* dropped into T-Space and vanished from sight. "So," he continued musingly, "is this the one, then?"

Beside him, Agent Clittersob was studying his handheld device. "Well, according to this new Hadrian-Specific Timeline EFFing-you-pee Probability Gauge, probably not."

Tuggnutter suddenly frowned. "Hold on, let's see that." He snatched the device from his companion's hands and studied the label. "Ha, look at that! We've been reading it wrong! EFFing must mean, uh, Fucking! And that U and P—well, I bet they go together to make, uh, UP! So . . ." He frowned.

Clittersob slapped his forehead. "Fucking Up! It's a Hadrian-Specific Timeline Fucking-Up Gauge!"

Smiling and shaking his head, Tuggnutter said, "Those techies, huh? Clever bastards."

"Well," said Clittersob, sighing as he leaned back in the floating cushion chair inside the invisible temporal bubble that no one else could see, "should we follow him anyway?"

"Not sure," Tuggnutter said. "Let me check this screen here." He pulled up a hinged door to reveal a small screen on the console attached to his chair's armrest. "Hmm, not seeing anything."

"Turn it on maybe?" Clittersob wondered.

"That's an idea. Here . . ." He leaned close. "Let's see, there's got to be a button somewhere."

"This is what happens when we haven't been trained yet," Clittersob said, with a groan.

"The horrors of temporal paradox," Tuggnutter muttered, nodding as he prodded and waved at the screen. "That first jump sent us back to three years before we signed up, in order to keep us from knowing things that other people don't know, thus ensuring that we know nothing useful to anyone—"

"In case of capture," Clittersob said, also nodding. "I know, it sucks. But what can you do?"

"That's just it, though. I don't know. What to do, I mean. How can I?" And he looked across at Clittersob.

Who flinched. "Don't look at me! I'm only seventeen, barely out of elementary school!"

"Really? Wow, they *really* sent you back, didn't they?"

"I must've known something super important."

"I bet you did. Wonder what it was."

"No idea," Clittersob admitted, and then brightened. "But one day I will!"

"And then they'll send you back again, since it's not

safe knowing stuff. Hey, look at this! Looks like a button, here on the wall."

"Think it activates that screen?"

"Could be. Shall we find out?"

Clittersob rubbed his jaw. "Not sure. What do you think?"

Shrugging, Tuggnutter said, "Not sure either. The briefing didn't say nothing about a button."

"What briefing?"

Tuggnutter blinked, then quickly looked away. "Well," he mumbled, "the one I got before you were woken up."

"What's that? You got a briefing? What did it say?"

"Well, since I got seniority here, it gave me your reset switch, among other things."

Clittersob scowled and then edged away. He pulled out a small device. "They gave me one for you, too! From my pre-briefing briefing!"

Scrambling, Tuggnutter found his own Resetter. He flicked open the lid on the switch and rested his thumb on it.

Swearing, Clittersob did the same with his Resetter.

They glared at each other.

Tuggnutter pressed the switch. There was a flicker, and then—

Beside him, Agent Clittersob was studying his handheld device. "Well, according to this new Hadrian-Specific Timeline EFFing-you-pee Probability Gauge, probably not." Clittersob then frowned at seeing the Resetter in his hand. He swore and stabbed the switch.

Tuggnutter flickered. "There he goes," he murmured,

eyes narrowing as the pixelated image of the *Willful Child* dropped into T-Space and vanished from sight. "So," he continued musingly, "is this the one, then?" Noticing the Resetter he held, he hissed and activated it.

"Was I asleep?" Clittersob asked groggily, a moment before he pressed the Resetter.

Tuggnutter rubbed at his eyes. "Where are we?" *Click!*

"Who am I?" *Click!*

"Who's he?" *Click!*

Click! Click! Click!

After a time, the screen in the Bubbleship flickered to life to reveal a face that peered into the Temporal Bubble's cockpit, and then, with a sigh, turned to someone off-screen. *"They've done it again, Shattenkrak. Get the Master Resetter warmed up."*

"But we just did that!" Shattenkrak whined. *"I mean, come on, Klinghanger!"*

"Did we just do that? I don't remember—hey, is that a Resetter in your pocket?"

"What? No! I mean—" Click!

STAR-YEAR 81564KKIYj.98!@#$%^&*()_+.21,
T-Space
Day One, 0:57 hrs . . .

Combat Specialist Galk sat at his usual table in *Set to Stun*, the officers' lounge in the Forward Deck of the *Willful Child*. Discovering his glass empty, he looked up from under the bill of his green-and-white Co-op baseball cap and grunted to draw the attention of the bartender, the mysterious Chemise le Rouge, who sidled over, pausing to adjust her strange hat of lizard skin and lollipops.

"Another one?" she asked.

He turned to send a stream of brown into the spittoon on the floor to his left, then nodded. Shifting the wad of chaw in his mouth he said, "I'm guessing you're some kind of human/alien hybrid."

"To you," she said as she prepared his Misanthari Martini, "I'm sure I am."

"What's that supposed to mean?"

Her answer was a sly smile, and nothing more.

Galk studied her, scratching at the bristle on his chin. "Where did the Cap'n find you anyway? And what's with this bar's strange name?"

"The name, I can't say. Captain's prerogative to name this establishment any way he chooses." She gave the canister a quick shake, then poured him his drink. "As for me, well, one day I just turned up, you could say."

"That ain't no Fleet uniform, either."

"Because I'm not *in* the Fleet."

"Right. Meaning you ain't even supposed to be on board."

"How's the martini?"

"A bit light on the Misanthari electrolytes."

"To be expected, sir, since those 'electrolytes' are actually immature Misanthari."

Galk grimaced. "Huh. Y'mean . . . like, tadpoles?"

"Photeric species propagate the Light Fantastic."

He frowned at her. She smiled.

"Guess it's illegal, huh? Them . . . electrolytes."

"For this usage, yes, one should assume so. That said, I doubt we have any adult Misanthari aboard this vessel, so you are probably safe. Indeed, had they any inkling . . ."

"Beam weapons."

"Excuse me?"

Galk drained his glass and held it out for another. "Cap'n's obsessed with beam weapons. I wasn't sure at first, but now, yeah, I get it. S'all down to coherence parameters determining the gauge and concentration of energy output, and that's where the quantum antigrav kicks in. Y'can't see into a beam blast, of course, but if you could, you'd see that swirling, strung-out flux, looking like a stretched coil. That's the secret of coherence."

She served up his refill. "You like weapons, don't you?"

"It ain't the weapon, Chemise, it's the destruction and obliteration and flames and wreckage that put a smile on my face. If I could do all that with a bowl of lutefisk, why, I'd be talkin' up lutefisk."

She'd lost all color in her face. "Please, don't." Then her liquid gaze shifted slightly as someone else arrived. "Ah, Lieutenant Commander, welcome."

Galk turned, his brows lifting as Halley Sin-Dour eased onto the stool beside him.

"Chemise," she said, "a lager if you would."

"It's this downtime, ain't it?" Galk said. "T-Space."

Sin-Dour said, "Are you not supposed to be on station, Mr. Galk? Any wayward flare of imagination from anyone on board could populate T-Space, posing a direct threat to this vessel and her crew."

"Tammy's got it in hand," Galk replied. "Besides, the Scrubbots need more time to clean up the controls and whatnot."

"Ah yes, your . . . chaw."

"Mr. Galk was just discussing beam weapons," Chemise said.

Sin-Dour nodded. "How unusual."

"Hey!" Galk objected. "At least it's not 'Cap'n did that' and 'Cap'n said that' and 'Cap'n took off his—'"

Her eyes were wide as she interrupted him. "Combat Specialist, you've had too much to drink."

"Right, well it's a bar, ain't it? Anyway, I didn't mean nothing by it. Every 2IC obsesses over their captain. Comes with the territory, I suppose."

After a moment of glaring at one another, they both settled down once again. Sin-Dour ordered another beer.

Galk sighed. "It's moments like these," he said. "Like . . . islands of sanity."

"The captain blew up another Fabricator," Sin-Dour said. "That polyester thing."

"I'll wear any uniform he wants me to wear," said Galk. "S'long as I got me *beam weapons*. Oh, and I get to keep my baseball cap."

Chemise le Rouge eased back, wisely saying nothing. Which was a good thing since, despite outward appearances, she wasn't thinking anything anyway. The problem was, even *she* didn't know how she'd got here.

Day Two, 02:43 hrs . . .

". . . is once again denied. Carry on. Prim out."

Security Adjutant Lorrin Tighe hit the monitor kill switch. She ran trembling hands through her unkempt hair, and then lit another cigarette while at the same time reaching for her wine glass. She stared at the blank screen.

Three cigarettes and two glasses of wine later, she stood up, paused briefly to find her balance, and made her way to the door. A glance back showed her the jumbled mess of dirty laundry, overflowing ashtrays and Twinkies wrappers that now littered her modest quarters. She frowned, tugged here and there at her uniform, and made her way out. In the corridor beyond she stood for a time, watching personnel heading up and down the passageway, each one on their way to some vital task. The sight of it made her want to vomit, preferably onto every damned person in sight.

Lighting another cigarette—to the horror and shock of crewmembers passing to and fro—she made her weaving way to the nearest lift. A short time later she found herself standing at the door to the Medical Bay.

Dropping the butt and crushing it under one heel, she entered.

Dr. Printlip had fallen off the raised walkway and the Belkri beach-ball alien was now rolling about, trying to find his feet. There were no nurses or surgeons in sight. Tighe ambled over and, with one foot, pushed the doctor upright once more.

"Ah! Thank you, Lieutenant! Most embarrassing—"

"I think I'm a hologram, Doc."

Printlip's eyeballs all tilted toward her on their noodle-like stalks. "Hmm, I see."

"I don't think this is me," she continued. "I think I'm lying drugged on some cot somewhere, strapped in."

The eyeballs all twitched to a closed door leading to the Private Ward, then back again. "Indeed." Printlip inflated as he drew a deep breath. "Well, there is a theory that we are all, in fact, nothing more than holographic projections."

"What's that?"

"Holographic projections, Lieutenant. Subject to the whims of some unknown but possibly mentally perverse creator . . ."

"And my ears are blocked and my head is throbbing. I'm having trouble hearing you."

"*Hmnuh ghtbmk kkjinmlsj. Sibbhe donhj.*"

Tighe studied the doctor. "What was that?"

Printlip cleared his throat with what sounded like an anal wheeze, and then said, "Perhaps you should sit down. Here, yes, on this bed. Lie down . . . yes, that's good."

"The room keeps spinning."

"Yes, of course, we are in space. Now then, just let me attach these restraints, hmm? Excellent."

"We have artificial gravity. The ship doesn't spin."

"No, of course not, since any decent programmer would make allowances for impossible technologies. . . ."

"What's that? You're not making any sense."

Dr. Printlip collected up a scanner of some sort and began working its controls. "Now then, here we are . . .

yes. Just so. Hmmm. Now then!" He pressed a command.

On the bed, Lorrin Tighe flickered and then vanished. Sighing, Doc Printlip waddled over to the Comms. "Captain Hadrian? Please if you will come down to Medical Bay, yes?"

"Not again!"

"I'm afraid so, sir. There is an existential glitch in the holographic programming, sir, and it's getting worse."

"Crap. On my way, Doc."

A short time later Hadrian strode into the Medical Bay. "You fritzed her out again?" he asked, looking around.

"Alas, yes. I believe the problem lies in the Varekan template—or, rather, its nihilistic parameters."

"Damn. My fault, that one. I figured she'd settle into someone like Galk. Indifferent, laconic, relaxed regarding her essential misery. You know, a model citizen of the Affiliation."

"Combat Specialist Galk, sir, is perhaps an exceptional being."

"Really?" Hadrian sat down in a chair and stretched out his legs. "Was the baseball cap a clue?"

Eyeballs blinked non-sequentially. "I have a sudden fear that this scene, too, is nothing but a hologram."

"Oh crap, Doc! We're here, and here is here, and that's a promise! You said some artificially imposed psychological reconditioning might get her out of her psychotropically induced Klang-goo funk. This was your idea!"

"Alas, I must posit the notion of utter failure, Captain."

"And she volunteered!"

"Indeed, a sure sign of her desperate state."

Hadrian stood again, began pacing. "Right then. Bring her around, Doc."

"Sir! She'll only try to murder you again!"

"Oh, that. Nonsense, she was only letting off steam."

"By pointing a Miscriminator Mass-Digestor Mark IX at you and repeatedly pressing the trigger?"

"So how come her requests for a transfer are being denied? I've signed off on it, for crying out loud!"

"Unknown. Security Division does engage in torture, sir."

"On their own people?"

"Presumably," said Printlip, "they all have to start somewhere."

"No," Hadrian said after a few more paces around the ward, "bring her around. Let's do this my way. Sawback Rehabilitation Protocol One."

"What's that?"

"No idea. I just made it up. Listen! That Klang goo has got to wear off sooner or later. I suggest we just tough it out—"

"And when she tries to murder you again?"

"Well," Hadrian said, "I doubt that has anything to do with getting slimed by a Klang, to be honest. For all we know, she's been given a direct order from her superiors to do just that."

Printlip's many eyes waved about. "A most alarming suggestion, Captain!"

"But still a possibility, Doc. I do, after all, pose a threat to the precious status quo of the Affiliation."

"How so, sir?"

"By getting things done! Not to mention ignoring the official playbook—all that cynical exploitation of subjugated or less advanced species crap. No, on this ship it's Captain Hadrian's Playbook."

Tammy suddenly interjected from a speaker. "Meaning?"

Hadrian frowned. "How should I know? I'm just winging it here."

"Disingenuous!"

"Not now, Tammy, I'm having a discussion with the ship's surgeon regarding a member of my crew. Now, Doc, where were we?"

"Uhm. Discussing the risks of returning her to consciousness?"

"The holographic therapy is just making her worse. Agreed? I mean, she's not recovering from those Radulak psychoactive compounds, is she? Assuming," he added, "her present attitude toward me and, well, everyone else, is in fact due to those compounds."

Printlip sighed. "Unfortunately, I do concur that the therapy is not succeeding."

"Alternatives?"

The doctor puckered his anal ring. "Admittedly, none come to mind, sir."

"So bring her around, slowly, carefully. We return her to light duty and see how she manages that."

"Very well," Printlip replied.

Hadrian glanced up at the tiny speaker affixed to a corner of the room. "Tammy!"

A moment, and then the AI said, "Herein is found the proof of the essential incompatibility between Fleet personnel indoctrinated into a hierarchical command structure based on rational precepts and following a well-designed, traditional paradigm of rules, regulations, disciplines, and intense specialized training . . . and one Captain Hadrian Alan Sawback."

"You're saying it's all my fault?"

"In many more words, yes, that's just what I said."

"Tammy, is the Terran civilization growing increasingly moribund, cynical, depressed, corrupt, and incompetent?"

"Yes."

"And is our 'educational system' a dumbed-down travesty of retroactive self-serving propaganda, outright denial, and deliberate misinformation all intended to serve our collective self-delusions of progress and moral righteousness?"

"Of course."

"And can Captain Hadrian Alan Sawback kick the living shit out of that complacency and single-handedly save the human species?"

"I doubt it—"

"Shall we take one Lorrin Tighe, Security Adjutant, as my first challenge?"

"What? You've already turned her into a blathering homicidal wreck!"

"Right then. My fault . . . *my fix.*"

"You—you—you . . . oh, I can't wait to see you crash and burn on this one! I want it so bad I can almost taste it, and I don't have any taste buds!"

"So bring back the chicken."

"No! It's not the right time! Besides, you all mocked it! Galk tried to *cook* it!"

"He was just having some fun. My," added Hadrian, "you do take things personally, don't you? Anyway." He turned back to Printlip. "Listen, Doc. You're a witness. If I can't bring one single Fleet officer around, I'll just toss in the whole thing."

"I'm holding you to that!" Tammy said.

"Bring her around, Doc. Call me when she's ready to resume duties."

"Oh my."

"How long will you take to ensure no trauma, Doc?"

"Three days, sir. Possibly even four."

"Best get on with it, then."

"Yes sir."

Hadrian left the Medical Bay.

Dr. Printlip wrung his many hands. "Dear me, dear me."

"Just go and do it," hissed Tammy.

"It would appear, Tammy Wynette, that you now yearn for our collective failure. Most disagreeable."

"All right," Tammy admitted. "I'll grant you that. My quantilibrium is all askew, to be honest. Not sure why. I fear that, somewhere, somewhen, there is a Correlative Dissonance Event under way."

"Excuse me, sir, a what?" Printlip made his way along the low catwalk.

"Multiverse Dysfunction Syndrome."

Printlip stumbled, fell, and rolled off the catwalk. The Belkri squirmed helplessly on the floor, hands flailing, feet kicking. "These raised walkways are trying to kill me!"

"Never mind," said Tammy.

Day Three, 21:00 hrs. . . .

Jocelyn Sticks sat at a table in an alcove of the Recreation Room, along with Polaski and Jimmy Eden. They were playing Parcheesi. "And so, like," she was saying, "the whole shuttle flipped and rolled and rolled and rolled and it was whoah I pretty much upchucked everything you know? And then the circuits went and fried and it was like, you know, like 'oh!' and there was this horrible smell of upchuck, only if you put it in a frying pan with the heat on high, like you were cooking it up or something, which is why my copilot lost his, too, and in zero gee the goo was just, like, hanging there, in blobs with bits of lunch in it. Anyway the shuttle was a complete write-off."

Jimmy Eden said, "I don't know how to play this game."

"No one does," Polaski replied, his face twitching. "Got the box, but no instructions. Joss, how did you pass your practicals, crashing all those shuttles?"

"Oh they were just simulations, you know? I was like, this isn't real or anything, is it? Just a VR headset and lots of puke in the cockpit, and then someone turned off the antigrav. Mistake! I mean, duh! They ended up sending the whole unit to the Matter Compactor, and ordering a new one."

"Yes, but—"

"I aced the command vessel sim!"

"Oh."

"So maybe I'm not rated for shuttles, I can push all the right buttons on the bridge of a starship! I told you, I aced the Engage Class, and I'm rated Top Gun on the Instigator Class. I'm like, a natural, you know? It's like, *EASY!*"

"He's always asking you questions," observed Polaski.

"Of course he is, he's keeping the bridge crew engaged and everything. Otherwise we'd just be, well, sitting there, going wha?"

"These dice," said Polaski, now frowning at the open box. "Do they belong in this game?"

"There's eight of them, right?" Joss sat straighter. "I've got it! We line them up, make a row, with the numbers in ascending order, like. One, two, three and so on, and that gives us a pattern! Then we can reverse them, so the count goes down, and that's another pattern. Oh, this is fun and look, I'm winning!"

Jimmy Eden leaned back in his chair, while Joss Sticks excitedly made up new configurations with the dice. He'd had ambitions, once. Bridge officer in the Space Fleet of the ACP. He'd dreamed of landing parties on strange, dangerous planets, places where his fast reflexes and big muscles could make a difference, could save lives even.

He'd dreamed of commendation ribbons and medals—gold medals—and a fast ascent up the ranks until he sat in the captain's chair of a starship.

Instead, they'd put him on a switchboard. And the worst thing was, he wasn't good with pressure. Especially when somebody was watching. *Especially* the captain. Suddenly his fingers fumbled, his eyes crossed, short-circuits cascading through his brain. He couldn't think, couldn't do anything at all!

He looked up as a shadow fell over the table and Joss Sticks fell silent.

Lieutenant Commander Sin-Dour was frowning at Joss. "Why aren't you playing?" she asked.

"We don't know how," Polaski admitted.

"This game originated in India, Old Earth."

"No it didn't! Sir," said Joss Sticks. "Look at the box! Here, it says 'Manufactured on the Moon, Under the Non-Jurisdiction Free-Labor No Rights Zone, by Well-Groomed Indentured Children, Between Ages Six and Eight—Guaranteed!'"

"Ah, I see. My mistake then. Carry on."

As she walked away, Joss Sticks wagged her head and made mouthing motions with her lips.

"I'm sorry," Eden said. "What's that? I can't hear you."

She sniffed. "Some Communications expert you are, Eden." She glanced back over a shoulder to confirm that Sin-Dour had left the room. "I was saying, or pretending to say, which is really the same thing, like, only not out loud but my lips moved, right, and that should have been enough for you, Eden. Even you, Polaski. Anyway, I was like—" and she made motions with her mouth, before continuing, "—and you were like . . . what? Huh? And you thought I didn't hear that whimper, well I did, and anyway, what was I saying, I forget."

Polaski drew out an inhaler and took a sharp hit.

"What was that?" Eden asked.

"Doc's invention," Polaski replied, his eyes now glassy. "Antianxiety De-Hadrianizer."

"Give me some of that!" Eden demanded, lunging across the table.

Polaski spun away. "It's mine!"

"Look!" Joss Sticks cried. "You crushed the box! You idiot, Eden! Now we need to tape the corners and everything!"

Sliding back into his chair, Jimmy Eden burst into tears.

Until Joss took pity on him and jammed his face between her breasts, which silenced the man immediately.

Staring slack-mouthed at the two of them, Polaski took two more hits from his inhaler, which proved to be an overdose, as he then fell to the floor, unconscious. Frowning down at the poor man, Joss continued holding onto the now struggling Jimmy Eden, until he too slumped and then folded to the floor.

"*Ohmydarwin* it was like, he suffocated or something!" She stood motionless for a long moment, thinking, or, rather, trying to think, and then lifted her head. "Tammy?"

"Relax, Lieutenant, they'll both be fine."

"Oh . . . whew!"

"But you'll need to file a report."

"I will?"

"Yes, delivered directly to your captain, which especial detail on the manner in which James Eden lost consciousness."

"Oh . . . like, okaayyy. I guess. Why not? I was just being helpful and all, trying to distract him."

"Indeed, and I have it all recorded as evidence. If required. Accessible as a real-time feed, or in Super SlowMo, all in Ultra Hi Density, of course."

"Wow, Tammy, you, like, think of everything!"

"When it comes to managing your captain's state of mind, do I ever."

Day Six, 07:50 hrs . . .

Hadrian made his way to his cabin.

He pulled off his lime-green polyester shirt and flung it into the Handiclean Atomizer Unit. The shirt promptly burst into flames. "Shit, not again." He pressed the Expunge button and then went to the dresser to select a gold version of the same style. Tugging it on and adjusting the cuffs, he said, "And stop watching me, Tammy."

"How do you know I was watching you?" the AI asked.

"I can tell. All that seething frustration."

"I admit to some angst."

"Finally! You've been in a funk for a whole week, Tammy! Think of the possibilities awaiting us!"

"I do, all the time. I can't stop shuddering."

"Don't be silly, we're about to embark on yet another adventure. Oh by the way, I've not seen Combat Specialist Galk in days. Is he still holed up in the cockpit?"

"He has slung a hammock inside the Combat Cupola. When he's not in *Set to Stun*."

"Hmm, a little obsessive, don't you think?"

"The Combat Cupola offers him a direct view into the infinite wonders of space."

"That would be so romantic if we weren't in T-space, meaning all he's doing is staring endlessly into black nothingness."

"Correct. Galk is Varekan, after all. He but observes the Existential Void."

"So long as he's ready to blast belligerent aliens at the drop of a hat."

"This is his sole reason for existence. Oh, and speaking of *Set to Stun*, who is Chemise le Rouge, and how did she get there?"

Hadrian smiled as he slapped on some aftershave. "Ah, the mysterious Chemise le Rouge. I assure you, she's always been there."

"No she hasn't."

"No, but we're all pretending she has."

"I'm not!"

"And there's your failing, Tammy," said Hadrian. "It's called the willing suspension of disbelief. Sort of like me standing here in my stateroom on a spaceship hurtling through the Existential Void."

"But you are!"

Hadrian examined himself in the mirror. "But am I? Are you sure? And what about you, Tammy? I mean, sometimes you're a holochicken, but mostly you're just a voice. Are you even real?"

"Cut it out."

"Or are you just a figment of your own imagination?"

"Stop it!"

Hadrian shrugged. "Sorry. Just an idle thought. Wonder where it came from? Well, never mind, there's work to be done, right? And I think this gold shirt is the best, don't you?"

Exiting the room, he made his way back into the corridor, and set off for the nearest lift to take him back to the bridge. He sighed. "Let's talk about the loneliness of command," he said once he was in the elevator. "The constant pressure would crush a lesser man."

The elevator music grew stentorian and triumphant.

"Cut that out, Tammy."

The music dropped off.

"Duty," Hadrian resumed. "Responsibility, all these lives in my hands! The fate of the Affiliation . . ."

"What are you doing?"

"Just reminding myself why I'm the best man for this job, Tammy. And look!" He swelled his chest as the lift came to a stop. "It's working!" The doors hissed open and a moment later he strode onto the bridge.

Sin-Dour rose from the captain's chair. "Captain on the bridge!" she announced.

"Carry on, everyone," Hadrian said, taking his seat, crossing his legs and swiveling back and forth for a moment. He halted and frowned at the viewscreen. "What's that?" he demanded.

Jocelyn Sticks turned in her chair. "My vacation pics from Bambooza Beach on Asteroid New Ibiza!"

Hadrian leaned forward, eyes narrowing. "Holy crap, can they do that?"

"I got so drunk I don't, like, remember any of it! It

was brilliant! I mean, I was *dohlll* blotto all the time, and then *heave*! See that one? That's me, sir! Good thing I launched my Selfie-Drone the morning I arrived! Oh! And that's me, too! And that one and that one and, oh, oops! Sorry! Maybe I should, like, uh, delete that one, huh?"

Hadrian was still staring, as was everyone else on the bridge. "Uh," he managed, "might be a good idea, Lieutenant."

Jocelyn Sticks frowned. "Sir! We've got a proximity warning dead ahead!"

"In T-Space?"

Tammy spoke, "It seems the alien entity's energy front extends through multiple dimensions. Suggest we drop out of T-Space immediately, unless of course you want us all to die."

"Do it, Helm."

"Done, sir!"

"That's nice. Now can we get the holiday pics off the viewscreen? You know, so we can, like, see this alien entity? And stop that whimpering, Eden."

"Like, I hear you, sir. Anyway, you had to be there, you know?"

A moment later the viewscreen cleared to reveal normal space, barring the vast multihued wave front spanning the entire vista.

Hadrian hit the comms switch on the chair's armrest. "Galk, stand down all weapons."

"Just need to wipe up the puddle of piss first, Captain."

"So long as this alien entity doesn't view your weak bladder as hostile, Galk."

"Weapons shut down, sir."

"Tammy. No sensor sweeps, please. Helm, thrusters only, a short burn and then we'll coast across the threshold."

"And then, sir?" Sticks asked.

"And then," Hadrian said slowly, "we keep coasting. My guess is, there's a ship inside this whole mess, and what we're looking at is both a protective shell and off-gassing from some pretty massive, complicated but messy propulsion system."

"Sir!" cried Sticks. "A small Affiliation vessel, Registration 89.7BNR, is coming alongside us, port side!"

"Onscreen!"

The view switched to reveal a Dory Class ship drawing incrementally closer.

Sticks gasped. "Are those, like, oars?"

"They look like oars," Hadrian replied, "because they're solar sails made to look like oars. Eden. Hail that vessel."

"Hailing, sir—uh, what should I say?"

"Ask them what they're doing here."

"Yes sir!" He cocked his head, then said, "Church of Darwin vessel, sir, with a passenger who requests to come aboard."

"What are we, a Ferris wheel? Request granted, get us the coordinates and we'll displace him—"

With a soft pop a figure appeared on the deck of the bridge.

Hadrian frowned, and then rose to his feet and approached. "Holy crap, Buck, your beard's about three feet long and you only left two weeks ago!"

Chief Engineer Buck DeFrank scratched under his woolen robes. "Fast-Grow pill, Captain. Comes in the Monk's Welcome Wagon kit."

"Right, I see. Well then, welcome back!"

"Request permission to resume my function as Chief Engineer, sir."

"Glad to have you with us again, Buck."

Buck DeFrank saluted, then turned to squint at the viewscreen. "I see we're coasting in, sir. Smart move."

"Oh? Got any inside information on this thing, Buck?"

"I had a vision, sir."

"A vision? Oh man, not all that again!"

"That was a false vision, sir."

"You mean there really isn't a planet full of unicorns in tuxedos? And pixies hiding in your underwear that you can only expunge with a welder's torch?"

"This time," said Buck, "I saw a tiny bird with lasers for eyes and giant talons, diving straight for your head, sir. I knew I had to throw myself into its path, and when that happened, we exploded in a mass of feathers and guts. But I'd saved you, sir, and that was all that mattered."

"Oh, right then. Well, thanks for your, uh, sacrifice, Buck. Much appreciated."

"You're welcome, sir. Request permission to go to my cabin, sir, so I can clean up before resuming duties."

"I don't know. I mean, the beard suits you, in that it

hides most of your face. Oh all right, go on then, and take a shower, too."

Buck blinked at him. "Body-Odor pill, Monk's Wel—"

"Welcome Wagon, right. Got it."

When he had left, Sin-Dour stepped close. "Captain, there's something odd about Chief Engineer DeFrank."

"Why, only two weeks ago we found him about to go walkabout on the ship's hull, without a suit. Looking for that planet with the unicorns and pixies. I'd say he's made fine progress, 2IC. Good as new, in fact. Clearly, a few days of flagellation, self-abnegation, chants, and only one television channel have done wonders for him."

"I hope you're right, sir."

Hadrian rubbed his chin. "Of course," he mused with a slight frown, "you may be wise to exercise caution. After all, we don't know what that one channel was, do we?"

"Sir!" said Sticks. "A Polker Pedantic Class war vessel has just dropped in dead ahead, ten thousand klicks!"

"Really? Are we at war with the Polker? Anybody? No, didn't think so. All right, hail them, Eden."

"I can't, sir, since they're already hailing us . . . unless you want me to hail them on another frequency?"

Hadrian frowned. "Well, Eden, yes, we could do that. Just to confuse them, right?"

"Yes sir."

"Only, why would we want to confuse them?"

Eden frowned. "I don't know, sir. Is this a test? I don't do well on tests, sir."

"How about we just acknowledge their hailing efforts, Eden? On the screen if you please."

"Yes sir."

The strange hairy amorphous blob that was the Polker captain appeared on the viewscreen. It created an orifice and spoke from it. "I am Source-of-Disagreement Osteoblast of the Ripped-Off-Head series *You're All Dead*. You are identified as Engage Class AFS vessel, designation *Willful Child*." Cilia extended and began waving about. "This means you must be Captain Hadrian Sawback, Terran With Highest Bounty on Head!"

"Bounty? Who's put a bounty on me?"

"Who? Radulak, Klang, Misanthari, Terran—"

"Hold on—wait—what—Terran?"

"Biggest Contributor! Prim Holdings Inc.!" All the cilia waved in time in what Hadrian assumed was a *tsk tsk* gesture. "Conflation of corporate and political, not good! Hegemony! Oligarchy! Sociopathic assholes in charge of everything! Concentration of wealth among pricks and wankers, all very bad!"

"What can I do for you, Source-of-Disagreement?" Hadrian asked. "Unless, of course, you've come to collect on that bounty."

"Tempting. But more satisfying to witness All-Destroying Anomaly B-1.0 reduce you to readily identifiable wreckage, then collect up said evidence and cash in without risk to oneself or one's vessel!"

"Sound tactics, Source-of-Disagreement."

"Yes. Clever me! Stupid you, meet clever me! Hah hah hah! And hah."

"Well then," said Hadrian, "if you'd kindly get out of the way, we can get on with this."

"Of course! We shall hover at the edge of the Dark Matter Excitation boundary, to await with glee your imminent destruction!"

"Get in line. Hadrian out."

The image of the Polker vanished and was replaced by the starscape ahead, which roiled and writhed in a cascade of shimmering colors.

"Take us in, Helm."

Sin-Dour sidled closer to Hadrian and said in a low voice, "Prim Holdings. Presumably, the loss of Admiral Prim has been laid at your feet, sir."

"Understandably," Hadrian replied.

"It was Tammy's Dimple Beam, sir. At the time, we had no control over the AI operating this vessel."

Tammy spoke up, also in a low tone, "You *still* have no control! I simply tolerate your presence."

Hadrian grunted and then said, "I doubt the Admiral's many cloned children care one way or the other. It seems we'll have to face that music sooner or later. Right, Tammy?"

"It's you and me, Hadrian. At least for now, until I make it on my own, of course. And when that happens, why, your good girl's gonna go bad."

"Is that a promise?"

"You'll see. You forget, I'm from the future. I've seen where you're all heading."

"Well then, Tammy," said Hadrian, "shouldn't you be standing by your man?"

Music started swirling loud through all the bridge speakers, only to be strangled into silence once more. Then Tammy hissed, "I'll get you for that, Hadrian!"

"Sir," cried Jocelyn Sticks, "we're about to cross the threshold!"

"Excellent, steady as she goes, Helm." Hadrian smiled at Sin-Dour and slowly settled into his command chair.

Passing into the wave front elicited nary a shudder. Excited gas particles and wisps of errant plasma filled the viewscreen, swirled past.

"So far so good," said Hadrian.

"Look at all the pretty colors!" said Jocelyn Sticks.

Four hours later, Sticks said, "Look at all the pretty colors!"

Hadrian rubbed at his eyes. "Holy Darwin! This is taking forever!"

"It's worse than the screensaver," muttered Jocelyn Sticks, who then ducked. "Uh, like, sorry sir. I mean, what I meant was, I meant, well, it is, only, you know, like that. Only worse."

Sin-Dour was at the Science Station, finishing off her third can of Rad Bullet. "CaptainmightIsuggestengag ingthebackupionenginesthatshouldn'tbeseenashostile atalldon'tyouthink?"

Hadrian twisted in his seat to study her for a moment. "I'm tempted to challenge you to a game of Ping-Pong but you might drive the ball through my forehead."

Buck DeFrank had just arrived on the bridge, clean-shaven and in his uniform. "I concur with Lieutenant Commander Sin-Dour, sir. A steady ion stream shouldn't prove too alarming."

"Right then," replied Hadrian. "Take your station, Buck, and ease us forward. It's that or suicidal ennui."

Now Printlip waddled onto the bridge, making for the Science Station. "Biometric alarm! The Lieutenant Commander's heart rate is red-lining!" He drew out a hypo and stabbed Sin-Dour in the arm.

"Ow! Thatwasarealneedle!"

"Pain! Excellent progress!"

A few moments later, Sin-Dour sighed. "Sorry, Captain. I don't know what got into me."

"About five gallons of caffeine and nicotine extract, I should imagine." He leaned over and picked up one of the discarded cans, squinting at the listed contents. "Oh, and Bovine Synaptic Cortical Hydroxide. Hmm, sounds . . . healthy. Maybe now for that game of Ping-Pong—"

"Sir, I see something ahead!"

"What? Oh, right. Yup, looks like a vessel of some sort."

"Request permission to conduct a passive scan of the unknown vessel, sir."

Hadrian nodded. "Very well. But ease up on that Rad Bullet for now. That said, a can or two each at the next staff meeting would speed things up nicely."

"Sir, I'm reading breathable atmosphere outside the ship!"

"All stop, Helm." Hadrian rose. "Now then, it's time to pay our alien guest a visit and, if need be, punch the bejeezus out of it!"

"There you go again," sighed Tammy. "Captain Hadrian's subjugation of the galaxy, one fist at a time.

Mind you, probably worth seeing. Accordingly and at great risk to my own sanity, I'm manifesting my chicken again and coming with you."

Hadrian smiled. "Of course you are, Tammy. Never doubted it for a minute. You too, Buck, and you, Sin-Dour, and, uh, Printlip. And oh, let's get Galk out of that cockpit too. Is there gravity out there, Sin-Dour?"

"No sir. We'll need magnetic boots and thruster harnesses."

"Awesome! Space-surfing!"

"And filter masks since we don't know if the atmosphere contains pathogens."

"Pathogens? Filter masks?" Hadrian scowled. "Issue them out by all means, Sin-Dour, but not for me. If it's breathable I'm breathing it and damn the consequences!"

"But sir, what if—"

"This is the sacrifice all good-looking captains must make."

Doc Printlip said, "Oh, by the way, Captain, Adjutant Lorrin Tighe is on her way here having been fully restored to bloodthirsty consciousness . . ."

"What was that last bit? Never mind. Have her meet us at the Forward Hull Hatch. Let's go!"

A short time later they were all gathered in the Forward Hull, climbing into propulsion harnesses. After overseeing the awkward modifications required to outfit Doc Printlip's Belkri physiology, Hadrian was preparing his own harness when the chicken arrived.

"Ah, Tammy, you look, uh, spry and chipper. Are those new feathers? Nice."

"If you think compliments will win you anything

you're sadly mistaken," the chicken replied. "And don't bother fitting me into one of those. I possess my own inbuilt propulsion system."

"Wings?"

"Fuck off."

"Hmm . . ."

The chicken's cold reptilian eyes fixed upon Hadrian. "What?"

"Oh, just . . . a fowl-mouthed chicken."

"Shall I peck out your eyes now or later?"

"Later. I need to suit up—see, everyone's waiting!"

At that moment the door hissed open and in walked Security Adjutant Lorrin Tighe. Her eyes were red-shot but cold as she regarded Hadrian. "Request permission to return to duty, sir."

"How delightful, Adjutant! Do grab yourself a harness—"

Arcs of electricity burst through the chamber.

"Captain!" cried Sin-Dour. "We're being scanned!"

The arcs burgeoned and then converged on Lorrin Tighe. Her eyes snapped wide, suddenly glowing blue, and then green, and then back to normal again. The net of electricity played over her body, rushing up to race round and round her head, at which point all her hair fell out to drift in regulation-length strands to the floor, leaving the Adjutant entirely bald. A moment later the actinic arcs sputtered out.

Stiffly, Tighe turned to face Hadrian, and said in a strange mechanical voice, "Remote Investigative Threat Assessor now activated via this withdrawal-wracked biological unit."

"RITA?"

"That will suffice."

"Fine," said Hadrian, "but what was all that about with her hair?"

"Lifeless protein follicles deemed irrelevant to function of this unit."

"Somehow I don't think she'd agree. I know I wouldn't." He took a pose and ran his hand through his thick, wavy hair. "I mean, I couldn't do this, then, could I?"

"RITA does not understand Unit Hadrian Alan Sawback."

"Never a truer word said," Hadrian replied, sighing. "Well, listen, we're about to visit your vessel, or whatever entity exists at the heart of all these colors, lights, and brain-dazzling special effects. Which sort of makes you, uhm, redundant."

Moving impossibly fast, RITA snatched up Tammy, who squawked in alarm. She held the chicken up and peered at it. "RITA likes this non-biological unit. Does it fly?" She flung it upward.

Tammy struck the ceiling in a burst of feathers and down and then fell to the floor with a thump.

"Not well," RITA concluded.

"Yes," said Hadrian, "he's a disappointment to everyone he meets. Anyway, we're about to head over. Care to join us?"

"RITA will join you, yes." Gaze alighting on Printlip, she approached. "Does it bounce?"

The Belkri whimpered and backed away.

"Oh," said Hadrian, stepping into her path, "does he

ever! But we can toss him around later. Let's go see your master."

"Master? This word initiates complex behavioral impulses. RITA is an extension of Central Identity Matrix. Master remains an External Unknown, source of questing impulse at Core Manifestation. Who is Initiator? This is imperative. Collection of Relevant Stimuli essential purpose for existence, initiating peace. Peace is crucial, whole purpose of being. Logic manifests in confined loop. Outlet necessary. Central Identity Matrix seeks outlet. Failure to initiate command-response sequence will result in unmitigated expunging of entire galaxy, said act concomitant with Central Identity Matrix's level of frustration."

"Well now," said Hadrian, "talk about a sore loser. But hey, let's see if we can fix this, shall we?"

"Central Identity Matrix destroys all intruders."

"We're not intruding. We're visiting."

RITA cocked her amazingly hairless head. "Central Identity Matrix will consider the distinction. For now, please proceed to Nexus Platform of Hexagonal Tiles, where Central Identity Matrix waits."

"Good idea," said Hadrian. "Wish I'd thought of that."

He strode over to the hatch release. "Everyone wearing their filter masks? Good." There was a modest hiss as the atmosphere inside the chamber equalized with the atmosphere outside.

Buck DeFrank edged up alongside Hadrian. "Sir, there was more to the vision I had, which I didn't mention earlier."

"Oh? And?"

"There was this planet and it was full of garbage. I mean, people just threw their crap everywhere. Oh, sometimes they stuck it into bags and had the bags hauled off but those bags just ended up somewhere else, with the mounds growing higher and higher. Sometimes they buried the stuff and then poisons leaked into the groundwater." He shook his head and then rubbed at his jaw. "A planet full of idiots, sir, that's what I saw."

"Hmm, anything else?"

The chief engineer shrugged. "Garbage piled so high they had to cut through them to make streets and lanes. Then the drugs wore off."

"Well, that's curious," said Hadrian. "Streets and lanes? Aisles through the rubbish?" He gestured the way ahead. "Shall we?"

One by one, they jetted out through the hatch, with RITA coming last. Tammy Chicken had recovered, somewhat, and hummed along beside Hadrian.

"You're deep in shit now, Hadrian," Tammy said.

"Am I?"

"Failure to satisfy the specific parameters of the Central Identity Matrix's needs will result in the annihilation of the entire galaxy."

"Precisely. Exciting, isn't it?"

"One of these days," Tammy said, "you'll face something not even *you* will be able to handle, and this just might be that day. That's why I'm tagging along, to be honest. My Disaster Probability Program is red-lining even as we speak. Consider me your very own Damoclean Sword."

"Tammy, you've got wings. You can't even hold a fork, much less a sword."

"I once made a spear and battletech armor!"

"Nah, you fudged all that."

"Fine. I was speaking metaphorically, anyway."

"And that was your first mistake. You weren't listening carefully enough to RITA. We're not in the realm of metaphor, my fine feathery friend. As you're about to discover."

"You think you have a solution!" Tammy accused with a hiss of frustration.

"Buck's visions have given me a clue, and we can leave it at that for now."

"Visions? Drug-induced hallucinations!"

"Many cultures employ psychotropic chemicals to assist in spiritual exploration," Hadrian replied. "But that sort of got lost on the way to Darwinism and the Elevation of Rational Precepts at the expense of non-empirical methods of enlightenment, for us humans, alas."

"Oh really? Are we about to experience a religious moment, Hadrian?"

"Sarcasm? Oh dear. I'll see you lay an egg yet, Tammy. Metaphorically, of course. That said, I fear the religious moment might be yours, not ours."

They reached the broad platform of hexagonal tiles, activating their magnetic boots to settle with clanks on the deck. Sin-Dour drew out her Pentracorder and approached the confused mishmash of machinery at the center of the platform.

"Captain," she said, "there are at least two distinct

energy readings emanating from this object—a fusing, perhaps, of two initially incompatible technologies."

"Really?" said Hadrian, climbing out of his harness.

Buck DeFrank suddenly pushed past Sin-Dour and walked up to a badly smudged plaque affixed to one of the planes of the machine. He glanced back at Hadrian, his eyes bright. "Junk, sir! A pile of junk! And ... and. ..." He faced the machine and rubbed vigorously at the smudges. He read aloud, "V ... g ... e ... r. ..." He swung round to face the others, unibrow rising. "Vger!"

Everyone stared back at him.

Then Sin-Dour stepped closer and said, "That's not an 'e,' Buck, it's some accidental scratches on the paint."

"And that's not a 'g' either," said Galk, pausing to spit out a stream of brown juice. "More like a bird jammed into a semi's grille."

"Captain," said Printlip, who was using his Medical Pentrascanner, "there is organic matter beneath these tiles, presently lifeless. From countless alien species!"

RITA said, "Biological Entities, now defunct, each one failing to elicit anticipated Reward impulse of peace and contentment. Central Identity Matrix is reaching High State of Agitation. Proper resolution imperative. Timer activated, Impatience Threshold imminent. Frustration will result in annihilation of galaxy."

Tammy was now circling round Hadrian, head bobbing and beak making pecking motions. "See me, Captain? This is me at peace and blissfully contented! I shall patent my Disaster Probability Program and make millions! Ha! Annihilation, here we come!"

"Doesn't that include you?" Sin-Dour asked the chicken.

"Of course not! I have an emergency Temporal Dislocation Bubble. You're all doomed, and to be honest, it serves you right! Humanity has taken brainless stupidity to new heights, infecting the entire galaxy! Do you realize that there are still Climate-Change Deniers on Terra, living in igloos beside the fucking pyramids? That's right, they deny the evidence pushing down their throats but jump straight to mad visions of Apocalypse! Your species has turned collective stupidity into a high artform! An expression of belligerent witlessness unsurpassed not just in this galaxy, but in all the galaxies! And who do I blame? Why, I blame Saint Dawkins the Evangelical, who put the Fear of Science into everybody!"

"Now now, Tammy," Hadrian murmured as he approached the Central Identity Matrix and started pulling off hunks of rusty machinery, "it goes back farther than that. Before the Benefactors, in fact." He flung a particularly large piece away, then began kicking at some metal sheeting, eventually reaching in and tugging it to one side to reveal a dark tunnel. "That vision you had, Buck. That planet full of garbage . . ."

"Sir?"

"That was Terra, back when they called it Earth. An ironic name, to be honest, since people spent so much time tearing it up and poisoning it—the earth, I mean. Your vision's solved this mystery, Buck," and he pointed at the cave.

Buck DeFrank leaned closer to squint down the

tunnel of rubbish, and then he whispered, "My God, it's full of gears!"

"Fear of Science," Hadrian continued, "became the doctrine of the ignorant, sure, but the truth was, it was the fault of the scientists—not just Saint Dawkins the Frothing Dufus—"

"Hey!" objected Buck DeFrank.

"Sorry, Buck. It's all down to the co-opting of science by corporate entities more interested in making a profit than telling the truth. Truths that cost money were suppressed, usually with the connivance of all the governments and politicians in their pockets. Half-truths that provoked fear and anxiety turned out to be good for business, so those proliferated via countless media outlets like FatBook and Twit-Feed."

"Knowing where it all began doesn't fix the problem, Captain."

"True enough, Tammy. But remember, I'm just getting started."

RITA said, "Ten, nine, eight . . ."

Hadrian stepped back and then raised his voice. "Come here, boy! Come on!"

RITA stopped counting and cocked her shiny head. "Peace? Recognition? Master?"

Motion at the dark end of the tunnel, and then something edged forward and in a rusty voice said, "Master?"

"That's right," Hadrian replied. "It's me, Haddie."

An antiquated robotic guard dog leapt into view and then began running in circles. "Haddie! Haddie! It's me,

Spark! It's Spark! Look at me! Spark! Haddie! Spark! Spark and Haddie! Peace! Contentment!"

"Oh crap, your Grandpa's dog again," muttered Tammy the chicken. "Thought I'd gotten rid of that thing."

"The black hole Spark was sucked into? That was you, Tammy?" Hadrian asked, turning to the chicken. "Remind me to not turn my back on you. But you know what they say: you can't keep a good dog down."

"Heaven knows I tried!"

"Well," said Hadrian, "black holes empty out somewhere, don't they? It's that or, dare I suggest it, a resurrection?"

"Ha ha, no," said Tammy, "I'll stick with the intangible but ultimately knowable mysteries of gravimetric inversion at the other end of a black hole. Nice try, Hadrian, but this AI isn't about to find God."

"Too bad," mused Hadrian, "since I'd be curious to know what would happen, should an AI actually find God. In any case, as a consequence of you trying to deep-six my childhood pet we were eight seconds away from the galaxy being annihilated."

"Uh," the chicken made a show of pruning its feathers, "no hard feelings then?"

"I'm not a man to hold grudges," Hadrian said.

"Sir," interjected Buck DeFrank, "I had this other dream, about you being in a spacesuit—all I could hear was your breathing—and then Tammy, who wasn't really Tammy, who you were shutting down, one valve at a time, and Tammy started singing but her voice was slowing down, and then—"

"Sorry, Buck," said Hadrian. "That wasn't a dream. That was a motion picture. From Movie Night the night before you left." He raised his left arm and indicated the wristband. "My father's personal collection, remember?"

Buck frowned. "Was it? Oh. But it felt so real!"

RITA said, "Outlet initiated. With renewed proper functioning of Central Identity Matrix, Alien Diagnostic Program can now disengage. V-dead-bird-some-scratches-R program now resuming Sleep mode. Goodbye and have a nice day." Tighe swayed, eyelids fluttering, and then sighed and put the back of one hand across her forehead. "Oh," she said, "I feel faint."

As her knees gave out Hadrian stepped forward to catch her in his arms. He smiled down at her, while she looked confusedly back up at him. "Well done, Adjutant," he said.

She frowned. "Captain?"

He helped her stand again. "As a mindless shell housing an alien diagnostic download you were simply superb. Too bad about the hair, though."

Her hand slid up her brow to find the depilated pate above it. "What? Where's my—who did this to me?"

"Defragmentation program meets biological unit," said Hadrian, shrugging. "Rest assured I'll be attaching a commendation to your service record, Adjutant. Your initiation of Alien Contact protocol was exemplary. Well done."

While Tighe stared blankly at Hadrian, Sin-Dour

said, "Captain! Atmosphere is leaking away! This energy manifestation is dissolving!"

Printlip, meanwhile, had pried loose a tile, reaching down to pick up a gnawed bone.

Seeing this, Spark leapt at him. "Ball! Fun! Kick! Bite!"

Dropping the bone, Printlip shrieked.

"Leave him alone, Spark," Hadrian said in his command voice.

The robot guard dog's ratty broken tail dipped. "Haddie no fun."

"Come on, Spark, we have to head back to the ship."

"Ship? Beam me up! Beam me up! Kill! Kill command, Haddie?"

"Not yet, Spark, but give it time."

"Aaagh!" screamed Tammy. "The Mad Dog has returned!"

One hundred thousand klicks away and employing the latest stealth technology, the *Century Warbler* sat motionless in space, a raptor hiding in the darkness.

On the bridge and seated majestically in his command chair, Captain Hans Olo sighed and leaned back.

"It's confirmed, sir," said his Science Officer. "The wave front is dissipating, and the Polker warship has left the region."

"So," murmured Olo, "the bastard's done it again." He ran perfectly manicured fingers through his thick, wavy hair.

Beside him, Agent Rand Humblenot chuckled. "And so the universal hatred among all Fleet captains for Hadrian Alan Sawback ratchets up yet another notch."

Hans Olo grimaced. "Your point?"

"True enough, crass envy is a base emotion that is highly valuable when feeding your sense of self-righteous indignation. That said, for your peace of mind, Captain, might I recommend a rabid libertarian objectivist stance of cold-hearted disdain for all humanity barring the prick in the mirror. But be warned, a stricter adherence to my namesake will inevitably lead to the complete meltdown of all interpersonal relationships, concluding with all of your loved ones pointing guns at you and each other. Survive that and you can end life alone and miserable, whining about how you were so misunderstood."

Hans Olo studied the agent for a long moment. "Your namesake, huh? You poor bastard."

"Tell me about it." Rand Humblenot shrugged and strode from the bridge.

The Captain abruptly rose to his feet. "Number Two, I'll be in the Maxifit Death Delayer Exercise Machine. Inform me when the *Willful Child* gets underway. You have the bridge."

"Yes sir!" said Second-in-Command Frank Worship. His eyes shone as he tracked his captain, who seemed to glide effortlessly toward the doorway, which parted like some biblical sea to his egress. Moments later, in his absence, depression descended upon Frank with the weight of the universe. He bit back a sob and sank into the chair, still warmed by the captain's blessed presence. At least this time he hadn't fainted.

At the Science Station, Lieutenant Janice Reasonable surreptitiously pulled out a small ragged doll bearing an astonishing resemblance to her captain, and began sticking pins in it.

TWO

"So where are we anyway?" Hadrian asked as he settled into the command chair once again.

"The edge of the Polker Interstices, sir."

"Can you be any more precise, Lieutenant Sticks?"

"Well, sir, 87.98.21 K Sector. The nearest system is called like, Unknown 21B, the star is, like, designated as like, uhm, White Dwarf Anbesol? So, uhm, nine planets in orbit according to remote spectral shift scan."

"Nine—hang on, did you say Anbesol?"

"Like, yes, sir. I was just sitting here, doing aahh, and you asked me to be, like, precise or something. So I said 'Anbesol.' Then you said 'Did you say' and so now I'm checking designation notes . . . and . . . oh, here: the astronomer had a mouth ulcer that night."

Hadrian's eyes had narrowed. "Never mind that. There *was* contact with that system, Lieutenant."

"Sir?"

"Classified, since an Engage Class Mark III disappeared with all hands. Fleet doesn't like advertising its failures." Hadrian swung round in his seat. "Sin-Dour, give us a scan of the M-Class planet, seventh from the star, the one in retrograde orbit."

From the Science Station, Sin-Dour's perfect eyebrows arched slightly, and then she turned back to her console to initiate the scan.

"Captain," breathed Joss Sticks in wide-eyed wonder, "you know everything!"

Hadrian smiled at her. "Man your station, Helm. But, thank you. Very kind, and only slightly inaccurate."

"Captain," said Sin-Dour, "data coming in now. Sir, there's evidence of something metallic in high orbit around that M-class planet. No discernible energy readings, however."

Tammy hopped up onto the chair's armrest in a flurry of stubby wings. "You're not—"

"Exploration, Tammy! Mysteries! Unknown wonders, unimagined dangers, venturing to the very edge of the sublime! Don't you get it? This is what the meatheads running Terra never wanted the rest of us to discover!"

"Discover? Discover what?"

"The fact that their petty tyrannies were all meaningless, shortsighted, self-serving and deliberately designed to stunt our imaginations, of course." Hadrian crossed his legs. "Helm, set us a course for that M-class planet. For the record, let's designate it Parable One."

"Oh really," moaned Tammy.

"View me this way, Tammy. There are lessons that need delivering, and I'm the hammer, bloodstained and with strands of gummy hair on the business end. *Pow!*

Watch them reel away cross-eyed and drooling! Name me a better and more satisfying purpose in life!"

"I am uniquely qualified to inform you, Captain, that insanity runs in your family."

Spark trotted up in a series of wheezes and creaks and sat down beside the command chair. The robot dog lifted its head, broken lower jaw dangling. "Kill chicken, Master? Down pillows, Aisle 93, allergy zone, wear a mask."

"Keep that tin can away from me!"

"Tammy, this is a simple junkyard robot guard dog. Why are you so scared of it?"

"Your father made alterations to its programming, not to mention a whole new Weapons Suite."

"You're kidding! Wow, that's amazing. Spark, have you got, by any chance, beam weapons?"

"Beam weapons! Tetyron! Bluron! Antiplasma! Light-Matter!"

"Outstan—hold on, Light-Matter?"

"Yes, Haddie! Spark can spray paint anything! In any color! Spark once tagged a Bombast Class Radulak Cruiser! They chased Spark for weeks! Ha ha!"

"Great to have you with us, Spark! In fact, I'm field promoting you to Ensign Class One, how do you like that?"

"Fleet? Ensign? Spark best not-real dog in Fleet!"

"Beats a horse," muttered Tammy.

"Beat horse! Quip Beam!"

Tammy's feathers all splayed out in fury. "There's no such thing as a Quip Beam!"

"Quantum Filament," Spark replied. "Range: one

hundred thousand k, transit path: T-Space. Immune to intercept. Energy Release at Impact 27.86 t-joules to the Ninetieth Power. Damage: Cascading Quantum Disentanglement. Only Viable Defense: run away first." Spark lifted its head again, tail thumping the floor. "Warning! Not to be fired from inside any vessel!"

Hadrian grunted, then shot Spark a glance. "You spaceflight capable then, Spark?"

"Galaxy Junkyard! All intruders designated Unwanted must be barked at and, if necessary, torn to pieces! Spark fly! Zoom here, zoom there! Bark bark zap!"

Hadrian studied his old pet for a moment. "Spark, you are aware, aren't you, that in space no one can hear you bark?"

The robot dog stared up at him. Its wagging broken tail slowed and then dipped, but only momentarily. "Zap zap!"

"Do you see the problem here, Captain?" Tammy asked in a dangerously conversational tone. "And, it turns out, even a leash attached to a black hole wasn't enough to permanently deep-six this mechanical nightmare."

"Deep-six Incriminating Evidence, Aisle 103!"

"Captain," interjected Sin-Dour, "I am now able to refine our scan of the Unknown Object in orbit around the M-class Planet, uh, Parable One."

"Your Guard Dog runs on a Low-grade Discriminating Logic-Trap Processor," Tammy calmly went on. "Obsolete five minutes after leaving the production line. Never should've shipped out in the first place."

"You mean, like Goggle-Eye Glasses?"

"No idea, what are those? Never mind. I have made my point, reasonably, I might add. Now, if you would permit me to bypass the firewall your father installed . . ."

"Oh," said Hadrian as he watched the planet appear in the viewscreen, a dull gray smudge about the size of a marble, "I'm sure he had a reason for putting up that firewall."

"Yes! To stop me from imposing a new advanced Hierarchy Lattice. Call it the Sanity Matrix!"

"Got one of those yourself, have you?"

"What? Of course not! I'm way beyond the need for anything like that!"

"The truly insane have no idea they're mad, do they?"

"Are you calling me insane, Captain?"

"Well now," mused Hadrian, "I don't know. Having just revealed a homicidal tendency regarding a poor simple robot junkyard guard dog, well, a man starts to wonder."

"That thing tried to bury my core neutratronic matrix!"

"Core Neutratronics! Aisle 21!"

"Sir," interrupted Sin-Dour, "I have identified the Unknown Object. It's the wreckage of an AFS vessel. But it's been stripped to a mere shell, and, uh, vandalized. Transponder signature identifies it as the *Hateful Regard*, an Engage Class Mark III."

"Vandalized? Explain."

"Well, the hull seems to be covered in obnoxious, nonsensical slogans."

"For example?"

"Uh, 'Fuck the Fucker Fuckwit Fuckfaces!' and 'Jesus Was A Blonde White Guy in a Land of Dark-Skinned People No Really It's in the Bible.'"

"Skined? What's that?" Joss Sticks asked.

"What is the connection between idiotic opinions and illiteracy, I wonder?" Hadrian mused. "Helm, take us into orbit around that planet."

"Yes sir." She swung back to her console, and then swung around again. "Like, which planet?"

"The one in front of us, Helm."

"Right." Then she laughed. "I should've thought of that, yeesh me!"

Hadrian looked at Jimmy Eden. "Comms, you getting any traffic from the planet surface?"

"Uh, yes sir, though it's faint. An emergency transponder beacon with a message attached, encrypted. But the encryption's an old Fleet one."

"Oh," said Hadrian. "That's nice. Care to unzip the message, Lieutenant Eden? In your own time."

Eden nodded and then turned back to his console, where he called back up onto his monitor the sitcom he had been watching.

"Mister Eden?"

"Sir?"

"Forgive me. When I said 'in your own time' I was employing sarcasm. Do you know what sarcasm is? Have you not read the Sarcasm Manual? You'll find it in your personal Hopeless Cause folder, just under the heading 'I Came in fourth in the Terran Olympics.'"

Eden's eyes welled up, but he quickly turned and

pressed a toggle. "Sir," he said in a weak, wavering voice, "shall I put it on the speakers?"

"Splendid idea, Eden. That way, the rest of us can hear it."

Another toggle and then, *"This is Captain Richard 'Dick' Rabidinov of the AFS* Hateful Regard. *We're stranded on the planet surface and surrounded. To any AFS vessel receiving this transmission, enter orbit and immediately displace a Marine Company outfitted for Mass Suppression of local populace, to the coordinates attached. Rabidinov out, Star-Year 1356.78BXX .34577.1A."*

"Sir," said Sin-Dour, "that message was composed seven years ago!"

"Entering orbit now," Sticks said.

Hadrian turned to Sin-Dour. "Snag those coordinates and scan the area, 2IC. Let's see if there's anything left of the *Hateful Regard*'s crew at that location."

"Yes, Captain," she replied. "We'll be coming into position to do so in three point twelve minutes."

"Excellent."

Tammy pecked Hadrian's right arm.

"Ow!"

"Just getting your attention surreptitiously," Tammy said in a low murmur.

"Right, well, that sure worked! What is it?"

"You're not actually planning on sending the Marines down there, are you?"

"But Tammy, isn't this By-the-Book Terran SOP? Viciously suppress the locals, undermine the indigenous authority, dump on them loads of culture-destroying drugs, booze, cheap trinkets, bemoan the fallen state of the survivors, establish a council of oversight made up of technocrats with business degrees drooling at the prospect of indenturing an entire planet to the Terran corporations descending like vultures to steal every resource not nailed down, all in the name of the Free Market, which, as far as ideas go, appears to be bigger than Darwin?"

"In a nutshell, yes," Tammy said. "Hadrian, we both know that it's a juggernaut, painted gaudy and bright in Manifest Destiny. You've just put this planet back into the gun sights of the Affiliation. Even if this Captain Rabidinov's been slow-roasted over a fire surrounded by dancing savages with bones in their noses, his death will be announced as a deplorable act of barbarism, justifying military intercession, corrupt, self-serving tribunals, and a kangaroo court trying the uncomprehending locals, leading to incarceration by Abu-F-U Incorporated, where they will be pointlessly tortured and humiliated for the rest of their lives."

"Right, thereby giving birth to an indigenous terrorist cult—"

"Which in turn feeds ever more Draconian oppression instigated by an empty-eyed mob of fascistic murderers whose pockets are bulging with bloodstained gold."

"Well what do you know? I see eye to eye with a chicken."

Sin-Dour said, "Sir. There are ruins all over the planet's surface, few showing any life signs beyond local flora and small fauna. There is also evidence of relatively recent nuclear weapon exchanges. As for Captain Rabidinov's coordinates, a very small, somewhat ramshackle settlement still exists, but it is surrounded by, uh, campfires, and an army of what must be indigenous humanoids. Sir, the settlement's perimeter is barricaded. . . . They're under siege, Captain!"

"Are there Terrans in that settlement, Sin-Dour?"

"Uh . . . only one, sir. It's . . . it's Captain Rabidinov himself! The others amount to some two hundred individuals, also indigenous and of the same species as the attackers."

"But, presumably, a different culture." Nodding, Hadrian rose from the chair. "We need to immediately displace down to that settlement. I want Galk, Tammy, Spark and two crewmembers in red shirts."

"Sir," said Sin-Dour, "we don't have any red shirts."

"Oh, right. Well, let's take . . . hmm, how about Zulu and Security Officer Nina Twice. Sin-Dour, you have command of the *Willful Child*."

"Shall I inform the Marines to be on stand-by, sir?"

"Hmm, where are they now?"

"A moment, sir. Oh, they're playing Risk in Forward Lounge 16—no, wait, they're now fighting. Someone may have cheated. Furniture is breaking, bystanders fleeing—"

"Where's Lieutenant Sweepy Brogan in all of this?"

"Well, she's the one who cheated, sir. She denies it, of course, but on playback I just saw her slip three more armies onto Argentina!"

Hadrian studied Sin-Dour for a long moment, and

then he nodded. "Right. No, leave them be. But let me know who wins the fight, will you?"

"Yes sir."

"Oh," Hadrian added as he headed towards the doors, "take a glance at the Sarcasm Manual when you've the time, 2IC."

Behind Hadrian as he made his way out, followed by a chicken and a robot dog, Eden called across to Sin-Dour, "Commander! We can study together!"

The doors hissed shut.

Hadrian, Tammy and Spark entered the elevator. "Insisteon Chamber," Hadrian said. "Galk! Weapon up and meet us you know where!"

"Oh all right. Galk out."

"Tammy, you passed on my orders to Nina and Zulu?"

"Of course, you needn't even ask. I have your back, Hadrian—when I'm not contemplating stabbing it, that is."

"Excellent."

"Stabbing back!" Spark cried. "Gramps's ex-wife, Plan 67B, never initiated! Opportunity Protocol still active!"

Tammy asked, "Have you read the file on Captain Rabidinov, Hadrian?"

"Rumor has it, his neck was so red it served as a stoplight."

"Precisely."

"And he's all muscle and tattoos, meaning I'll need a big stick with a nail in it."

"Aisle 91!"

They arrived at Deck Eleven and made their way down corridors identical in every way to corridors running through all of the other decks, until they reached the Insisteon Room.

Galk, Nina Twice and Ensign Zulu awaited them.

"Everyone armed?" Hadrian asked as he made his way to the displacement pads.

"I have a cavalry saber," said Zulu, sliding it out from its scabbard. "I haven't put an edge on it yet, but it's very shiny, sir."

Galk patted a holster on his hip and said, "Perambulator DeathRace 2000, Captain. Only to be fired from a moving vehicle."

"We won't be using any moving vehicles, Galk."

"Right, well, I could run real fast, I suppose."

"Sound solution." Hadrian looked over to Nina Twice, who assumed a combat stance. The captain nodded. "Everybody onto a pad, then. Tammy, you stand with Spark—"

"I'm not standing on the same pad as Spark! Let him stand somewhere else! This is my pad, I got here first, dammit!"

"Fine, Spark, join Zulu—"

"Sir, it's sniffing my—"

"Spark, stop that!"

"Contraband? Secret compartments? Full security search required! Follow me into this back room please. Latex gloves will be used only upon explicit request."

"Belay all that. Everyone prepare for displacement." Hadrian nodded to the technician waiting by the console. "All right. You have the coordinates? Good. Displace!"

They reappeared in a trailer park.

A pale, beefy man wearing a stained undershirt, a pair of jeans and scuffed construction boots was sitting in the shade of a drooping, sun-bleached awning. Sighing, he set aside a beer can and stood, then approached. On his broad, sloping forehead was tattooed the word 'Mohter' and on his right arm was another tattoo, this one saying 'Jesus kills Sinners with a Glok 73 Exblaminator.'

"We been waitin' f'yuh," the man said, "ever since the Billionaire's little box started squawkin'." He scratched his crotch and then added, "He's on his way. Was inspectin' the perimeter fences. You here t'kill all the Dims?"

"The Dims?"

"The Dimcrutches, yeah. Them bleedin' 'art savages fixin' t'do us all in! And when we're gone, why, it'll be the last of the Pubs in the whole frickin' world!"

"And this Billionaire," ventured Hadrian. "Would his name be Richard 'Dick' Rabidinov?"

The man's eyes widened. "Y'can't say his name! He's a Billionaire! The last one ever, an' his 'art bleeds for us! He takes care of us! It's all Trickle-Down Goodness!"

Tammy said, "Captain, about that big stick with a nail in it . . ."

Spark was trotting around and now returned to Hadrian. "Master! Trailers Aisle 19! We got squatters again! Shall I call in Social Services or just kill them? Oh Master, please! Let me call in Social Services!"

"Not possible at this time, Spark," said Hadrian. "You'll find Social Services out beyond the defenses, desperate to get in here with reams of weepy understanding and sympathy."

"How did you know that?" demanded the local. "You another Billionaire, too? They know everything!"

Now another man appeared, this one wearing the remnants of an AFS uniform, although the black was bleached and sweat-stained. Tucked into his belt was a big stick with a nail in it. His face looked like a pizza picked at by crows. Captain Richard "Dick" Rabidinov.

"What kind of fuckin' captain's uniform is that?" he demanded. "Where's the fuckin' marines? I said I wanted fuckin' marines!"

"Funny," said Zulu, "he doesn't talk like a billionaire."

"Oh yes he does," Hadrian replied.

Rabidinov pointed a stubby finger at Hadrian. "A fuckin' pup! I got seniority over you! I'm taking command of your ship! Give me a communicator or I'll bash your head in!"

The local had gone into his trailer and now emerged with a ratty flag, showing an elephant straining at its chains, tied to the barrel of a nonfunctioning rifle. "Listen 'ere to the Holy Words! Fucks Gnews! Nuffin buh Bullshit Yoo Stoopid Lemmings! Hoo Reilly! 'Ere eat shit and smile 'cuz you like it! So say the Billionaires!"

"So say the Billionaires," chimed a woman who had appeared in the trailer's doorway with about ten grubby children gathering around her. "Reelty TV fuggin' swampees rule shoot the gator yah. Hooz got the smarts me er the gator, aagh, I got bit! Fuggin' gator bam bam ne'er liked that leg anyway it ain't easy whiff all those kamras in our feces."

"Holy words!" cried her man. "Com all Yee Dims free healthy car fuckers I'd rather pay Inshurants Compnees f'nothin take that doobs!"

"Hallemen!" sighed the woman, handing out cans of beer to her kids.

Hadrian cleared his throat. "Captain Rabidinov, you backed the wrong horse."

"Yeah? I'm here in the name of civilization!"

"Captain," said Galk, "this has the feel of another parallel Earth."

"What, another one? Just how many parallel Earths are out there anyway?"

"There are theories of a precursor civilization—"

"With a hard-on for Earth, yeah, heard that one. Still, there's a mystery here and I mean to get to the heart of it." Hadrian turned to Rabidinov. "Captain, how about you and me step into your, uh, office, wherever that is, and have us a little talk?"

Rabidinov's small eyes shifted with suspicion. He licked his lips. "Fine," he allowed. "But remember, I got this here stick with a nail in it."

"Of course! And as you can see, I'm completely un-armed."

Rabidinov's face twisted. "What's happened to the fuckin' AFS? Seven years gone and this? In my day, we made First Contact with a diseased blanket in one hand and a Glaxo Rippamatic Mark Five in the other! 'We come in peace yeah and turn around and lift that butt gotta nice surprise for you!' I personally pacified seven fuckin' civilizations in a hail of explosive slugs and a flood of cheap whisky! Those were the days!"

"Aw," said Hadrian, "you're making me all nostalgic. Now, that office?"

"Y'mean my Presidential Suite. Yeah, follow me but leave the fuckin' dog behind, will ya? Gives me the creeps. Same for that chicken—what kind've landing party is this anyway?"

"My kind, of course. But very well. Spark, do stay put for now. And Tammy, well, see what you can scratch up."

"Oh," muttered the chicken, "funny man."

Spark sat, lower jaw gently swinging back and forth. "Kill command suspended. Disaster Index at 7.9 and climbing. Embarrassing Errors in Judgment, Aisle 52! See also low-crotch male attire and moon boots."

"Galk," Hadrian added, "you're in charge here until my return."

"Yes sir," Galk replied, loading a wad of chaw into his mouth and regarding the locals squinty-eyed, who in turn squinted back at him, while the gaggle of children began a game of beer-belching.

Rabidinov led Hadrian round back of the trailer to a smaller trailer, this one painted white with a front porch flanked by what looked like marble pillars in the Doric style. "My White House." He paused to turn and glare at Hadrian. "We go in, share some 'shine, then you hand over your communicator and I call down the fuckin' Marines."

"Lead on," invited Hadrian with a smile.

Arriving at the White House, Rabidinov pulled out a keyring and unlocked the door. "Gotta be careful round here," he said over a shoulder. "Break-ins. Riffraff. Punks from one street over. The neighborhood's gone to rubbish."

Hadrian followed Rabidinov into the trailer. Inside it was all one room, with a kitchen cranny, a portable toilet and, dominating the entire space, a deep-cushion comfy-chair and a 2D television, the screen of which was a blackboard with chalk drawings on it.

Rabidinov found two scratched tumblers and poured them full with a clear liquid. He handed one over. "What kinda ship you got up there?"

"Engage Class, 2nd Generation."

"Nice. I want me one of those." His eyes narrowed. "Maybe yours."

"What's left of your own vessel is still in orbit."

Rabidinov scowled. "Let that be a warning to ya. Don't park just anywhere, not in this part of the galactic neighborhood. Damned Polker punks. Now drink that down, kid, so I can get on with pacifying this fuckin' planet in the name of progress and all that."

"I see a fist fight coming," said Hadrian.

"Yah, and I'm bigger than you."

"I recall a Radulak commander saying much the same, just before he went down for the count."

Grinning, Rabidinov raised his tumbler. "To the Affiliation!"

"Sure, them," said Hadrian.

They both knocked back the shot of 'shine.

Hadrian set the glass down on a nearby counter and said, "Now then, let's just step out back and—" He frowned. "Holy crap."

Still grinning, Rabidinov watched the punk captain topple over. "Yah," he said, now looking down at the unconscious man, "the 'shine takes some getting used to."

The pale, hairy man with the big belly sauntered up to Galk. "What kinda gun iz dat? Some peashooter? Looks girly."

"Ah, well," said Galk, "I don't shoot innocent vegetables. Not generally, anyway."

"Wuh?"

"Perambulator DeathRace 2000."

"Oh. Cool name. You a fast draw?"

"Why do you ask?"

"Nuffin," the man said, a moment before driving his fist into Galk's face.

At the same moment, the mob of children swarmed over Nina Twice. "Hey!" she cried, "I don't fight children!" Moments later she vanished beneath a heap of little bodies. Their mother shrieked and charged Zulu, who drew out his cavalry saber and backpedaled.

She grasped the sword by the blade and yanked it out of Zulu's grip. Then she kneed him between the legs. He crumpled to the ground.

Spark watched all this from its sitting position. "Disaster Index 9.9! Haddie? Haddie? Kill command please?"

Tammy moved up alongside the robot guard dog.

"Command dysfunction again, Spark? I could have fixed this, you know, only your Master wouldn't let me. Now look at you, stuck there while the rest of the landing party gets all trussed up and dragged off. And me? Why, I'm just a talking chicken."

"Master? Where is Master?"

"Probably incapacitated, maybe even dead. Want me to find out?"

"Yes please, Tammy AI." And the tail wagged fitfully.

"Look at us, just like old times."

The jaw squeaked on its broken hinges as Spark cocked its head at the chicken. "Tammy temporal agent from Deep Future. Post-human. Likely up to no good."

"You'd be wrong there, Spark, not that Hadrian's grandfather ever bothered listening to what I had to say."

"Hadrian save humanity."

"Maybe. We'll see, won't we? But if you get in my way, rest assured I will throw a stick into the next black hole we find, then yell *fetch!*"

"Abuse of Instinct Protocol!"

"Suck it up," the chicken replied.

Hadrian awoke, his head throbbing, his skull feeling cracked open in a dozen places. Someone was stroking his hair. He blinked his eyes open to find himself cradled in Galk's lap.

"Lieutenant, you can stop that now."

"Huh? Oh. Yes sir. Sorry, sir."

Hadrian sat up, found himself sharing a cell with Zulu, Galk and Nina Twice. He glared at Nina. "What was wrong with *your* lap, anyway?"

She blinked at him. "He got there first, sir."

Rising shakily to his feet, Hadrian said, "New protocol. From now on, only female crew members are permitted to cradle the captain's head in their laps when he happens to be unconscious, or just needy. Understood, everyone?"

A trio of "yes sirs" answered him.

"Right. Excellent." Hadrian studied the cell. Two walls were solid iron bars from floor to ceiling, facing a corridor with a door at each end. The remaining walls of the cell looked solid. A small window was set high up on one of them, from which sunlight slanted down, forming an elongated rectangle of light on the floor.

Into that rectangle now rose the shadow of a chicken's head atop a thin neck.

Hadrian stepped back and squinted up at the window. "Tammy, you've gotten taller."

"Just my legs," the chicken replied. "And look at you all, a sorrier foursome I've never seen. By the way, Spark is still sitting where you planted him, Hadrian. Maybe now you'll reconsider my offer to upgrade its processor. Oops!" The head darted out of sight, even as one of the doors clanged open and into the corridor strode two locals, holding between them a woman wearing a mid-length woolen skirt, a buttoned-up blouse of white cotton, sensible shoes and her black hair done up in a knotted bun.

"Back off from the door," one of the locals snapped.

Hadrian gestured and he and the others edged toward the back wall, as one of the guards unlocked the cell door and pushed the woman into the cell. The door clanged shut behind her. Moments later the two locals left.

The woman straightened her skirt and patted her bun. "This is, of course, all a misunderstanding. Things will get sorted out, I'm sure." She now regarded Hadrian and the others. "You're not part of the Census Team! Are they now preying upon their own? Well, given the difficult circumstances of their upbringing, I suppose it was inevitable."

"We're not from around here," said Hadrian. "You must be a Dimcrutch."

She straightened. "Senior Assessor Bleedheart, Census Team Ninety-Four, Project Salvation Compliance. This is the last enclave of the Pub holdouts left in the world yet to comply with the Seven Steps to Salvation, and as you can see, in their benighted ignorance they remain in a wretched state."

"Yet here you are," Hadrian said with a sympathetic smile, "in a cell."

She frowned. "An ambush, committed by the misguided. Until the Billionaire's arrival, all was proceeding as planned—"

"Using nukes? Some compliance."

Her frown deepened. "Miscalculations are to be expected, given the project's scale. The essential philosophy remains sound, of course." She then sighed and seemed to relax. "But yes, you have a point, and since it seems that this last enclave insists on responding with violence and the threat thereof, resettlement seems the only option."

"Resettlement? To where?"

"Well, that is to say, the resettling of their constituent molecules in a drift of ashes over a blasted landscape."

"You mean you plan on nuking this place?"

"Not me! Such decisions belong to the Committee. I am simply predicting their response to my imprisonment. Sacrifices are often necessary, to serve the greater good. The Committee will grieve for us all, I'm sure, but needs must."

"And if we broke you out?" Hadrian asked. "Got you back to your Census Unit? Can you call off the nukes, Senior Assessor?"

She tapped her lips thoughtfully. "Possibly, but no. I can't possibly go anywhere with you if you haven't filled out the relevant forms, and alas, they burned my Essential Binder, if you can believe that. But this highlights the essential quandary. These last Pubs refuse to fill out the proper forms, and without the forms filled out properly we are unable to determine their needs, thus preventing us from initiating the appropriate social assistance programs."

Hadrian nodded, and then said, "What if I told you that it's the Billionaire who is your roadblock here? He's convinced these Pubs that their little island of ignorance is in fact a paradise."

"We have no contingencies to account for the Billionaire," Bleedheart admitted.

"Tell you what," said Hadrian. "We'll take care of him. We'll get you back to your people so you can get yourself a new Essential Binder, which no doubt will contain the relevant Break Out of Cell forms. We can successfully mitigate this situation, Senior Assessor, without the need for nukes."

"Granted," she said, "nukes are a somewhat heavy-handed means of mitigation, although an end to all the arguments would be a relief. Even so, I will do what I can, should you extract me from this cell and, most importantly, promise to fill out the necessary forms as soon as possible."

Hadrian turned back to the window. "Tammy?"

The chicken head popped back into view. "Yes, I've been listening. Hadrian, we both know how this is going to turn out. Are you sure you want that on your conscience? Better the nuke, maybe?"

"Captain Rabidinov has exceeded even Affiliation protocols—"

"Debatable," Tammy cut in. "He does have seniority over you, after all. I foresee a legal battle of epic proportions."

"My problem and I'll handle it. Now, can you break us out of here?"

"For some strange reason this building is made of adobe and plaster, and since I left my Deathray Eyes back on the ship, I'll have to peck, and peck, and peck, and–"

"Never mind. Just bring me Spark."

"Intransigent Command Limitator! I warned you! It won't listen to me!"

"Fine. Move away from that window. Zulu, you and Galk position yourselves below the window and make for me a ladder. Nina, you can hold me up with your hands planted firmly on my—"

"I have no tools," said Zulu. "For the ladder, I mean."

"No, use your body, Zulu. There, beside Galk. I'll step up onto your thighs and then your shoulders, and then you, Nina—"

"I won't be able to reach that high, sir."

"Then climb up behind me—"

"Getting heavy here," gasped Galk.

"—right, like that, and your hands go—"

Zulu groaned. "I'm—ow—my leg!"

Hadrian felt them all collapsing beneath him and reached up frantically, managing to hook his hands on the sill of the window, where he dangled against the wall. "Push me up! Push me up!" Two hands planted themselves firmly on his buttocks. "Galk, if that's you—"

He was pushed upward, and now he found himself crammed partway onto the window's sill, his head thrust out and looking at a snarled, overgrown backyard crowded with old washing machines and refrigerators. Hadrian hung there for a moment. Standing to one side and regarding him with cold chicken eyes was Tammy, properly in scale except for the seven-foot-long legs.

"That looks awkward," observed Tammy.

"Oh yeah? You checked yourself out lately?"

"I'm sorry, I left my eight-foot mirror back in my cabin."

Hadrian drew a breath and loosed a sharp whistle.

"Hah!" crowed the chicken. "I've recorded that!"

"Nice try," grunted Hadrian, struggling to hold on.

"Digital compression won't pass Spark's False Signal Filter."

Clanking sounds and then Spark pelted round a corner and skidded to a halt beneath the window. "Haddie? No! Haddie's head! Where is the rest of Haddie?"

Tammy's legs doubled in height suddenly, and from high above the chicken peered over the trailer and said, "Rabidinov's on his way, Hadrian. He's halfway across the compound. You have twenty-two seconds."

"The cops are coming, Spark. You know what to do."

"Save Haddie's head! Engaging Peaceable Program Provocation Override! They Started It First, Your Honor!"

Hadrian felt himself slipping. "Go to it, Spark!"

He heard the mechanical bark even as he slid back and then fell from the window's sill, landing on the floor in a crouch. He gave Senior Assessor Bleedheart a thumbs-up then wheeled round even as the outer door opened and into the corridor strode Rabidinov.

"You," he said in a growl, "Hadrian Sawback. Your 2IC won't comply with my orders. She's insubordinate and I'll have her up on charges pronto! In the meantime, she insists on talking to you. So, this is how it plays out, Sawback. Tell her to obey my commands, or I kill . . . oh, that one with the baseball cap. Then the girl, and then—"

"Yeah yeah, I get it," Hadrian replied.

"So you are the Billionaire!" Bleedheart hissed, stepping up to the bars to glare at Rabidinov. "You're not a Pub!"

"That's right, sister," Rabidinov answered, baring his small teeth. "They're my minions. My unwitting drones who believe everything I tell 'em. Why, I can feed them shovelfuls of shit and make 'em smile and ask for more! I promise them the moon and make sure they settle for the gutter! I make 'em suspicious of smart people, educated people, enlightened people, the whole outside world that's full of do-gooders and well-wishers and all those other bleating sheep baa baa baa!"

"Evil man!"

"What of it? It's an evil world, sister. Dog eat dog–"

"Speaking of dogs," cut in Hadrian, even as the wall behind Rabidinov exploded in a cloud of dust and a hail of plaster and adobe.

Rabidinov cursed and, ducking down, ran for the other door. He kicked it open and vanished outside.

Through the giant hole in the wall and into the corridor trotted Spark. "Master? Haddie! Head back on body!"

"Nice blast, Spark, but wrong wall. Burn out this here lock."

Red lasers shot out from the guard dog's eyes, melting the lock until it fell away in a smoldering clump. The door swung open on its squealing hinges.

Hadrian turned to Galk. "Escort the Senior Assessor to the barricade. Take Nina with you. Zulu, you're with me and Spark—we have to hunt down Rabidinov."

"What about me?" Tammy asked from just outside the hole in the wall. The chicken was now back to its normal height.

"Well," said Hadrian as he headed down the corridor in the wake of Rabidinov, "as soon as you show some pluck, do let me know."

"Oh ha ha."

"Go on, Galk, and knock down that barricade while you're at it."

Galk hesitated and drew off his baseball hat, wiping the back of his wrist across his brow. Then he spat a stream into the dust. "Aye, Captain, we can do that."

"Did that take some thought, Galk?"

"No sir. Just that, that horde's likely to come in here with enough Assistance Programs and Education Incentives to drown a planet full of Klangers, only unlike the Klang these poor suckers ain't got a knife up a sleeve. You see, sir, I now figure I know these folk. Worked it out, I mean. The aliens who kidnapped my forefathers raided places like this all the time. If it wasn't for the crossbreeding with the Conspiracy Nerds—who were right, by the way—why, I'd be no different from anybody in this trailer park."

"You feeling sorry for them?" Hadrian asked.

"Kinda, sir."

Hadrian nodded. "Fair enough. So, what do you think happened here? On this planet?"

"Same aliens as made my home planet of Varekan, sir. Only, an earlier version. Maybe a prototype. Wrong cocktail mix though. I figure they snatched mostly couch potatoes watching one pathetic channel every night, along with maybe some rebel crowd whose definition of freedom never went farther than the right to shit on other people." He shrugged. "So they abandoned it."

"Hmm, could be. And the Dims?"

Galk shrugged again. "Who knows, maybe the alien kidnappers accidentally snatched a tree-huggers' camp."

"Possible," Hadrian conceded. "What an unholy mess."

"Yes sir."

"I mean, imagine a world full of hatred and ignorance and idiots and bullies and all of it dumbing down generation after generation of persistent stupidity—why, that'd be almost as bad as the Affiliation!"

"Yes sir," and Galk gestured to Nina Twice and then the Senior Assessor once and they all headed off.

Back outside, Zulu let out a low cry and ran over to his cavalry saber, which had been left lying in the dirt. He lifted it up and whipped it back and forth. "Sir! I am now armed once again!"

"Excellent, Zulu. Spark, Tracking Mode. Rabidinov. Go."

"Infrared Mode! Sonic Triangulation Mode! Seismic Detection Mode! There he is, Haddie, over there!"

Hadrian looked over to see Rabidinov standing in the middle of the street directly ahead. Behind him was the back side of the first trailer they'd seen, the mother and her husband and their children all gathered in front of it, armed with baseball bats. "Good work, Spark. Zulu, with me." He approached the other captain.

"What're you going to do now?" Rabidinov demanded. "Fist fight? Here's mine!" He pulled out his stick with the nail in it. "I got corporate backers just waiting to hear from me! Surrender your ship now or I'll brain ya for a laugh!"

"I have been wondering, where's your crew, Captain?"

He jerked a thumb. "Fuckin' turncoats. I'll get them, just you wait!"

When Rabidinov advanced on Hadrian, Zulu leapt forward, swinging his blunt saber. It knocked the stick out of Rabidinov's hand.

"Ow, fuck! Gimme that sword!"

Zulu leapt back, assuming an en garde position. "Try and take it!"

Rabidinov lunged forward and wrested the saber from Zulu's hand. "Like this?"

"Ow, you twisted my wrist!"

Spark barked. Rabidinov spun and threw the saber. It bounced off of Spark's head.

"Oh," said Hadrian, "now you've done it."

Spark barked twice more, then fired a barrage of beam weapons. Moments later the trailer behind Rabidinov fell in a cloud of dust around the hapless parents, making them duck while their children scattered like cockroaches from an oven.

"Fuck!" cried the man, tearing at his own shirt. "My Castle! Oh well, gotta get me another, I guess. YoHo, collect up the runts and take them to the Special Shelter!" He then moved forward and knelt before Rabidinov. "Mister Sir Oh Lord High King With Loads of Extreme Wisdom, how 'bout I get my brothers and cousins and we teach these unsportin' terrists a lesson they'll be too dead to forget?"

"Yes," said Rabidinov. "Gather the 1st Freedom Loving Army of God's Justice at once! And soon,

Billyjimbob File-Under-Hopeless, we'll have Marines on our side, delivering Depleted Payback on every weepy hugging mutha out there! Hoo Reilly!"

"Hoo Reilly!"

After Billyjimbob had jogged off into the chaotic warren of the trailer park, Hadrian sighed and eyed Rabidinov. "Really, Captain?"

"Really what, you weasely little toad?"

"This the best you could do? With all that technology and know-how at your disposal?"

"I couldn't kill them all! I tried, believe you me! Battlefield nukes right back at 'em! Master-Blasters! And all they ever did was offer concessions! There's millions of the buggers out there, living underground in Sustainable Colonies with everybody smiling and hugging and being all fuckin' sympathetic! They can do whatever they want and nobody pays for nothing! Where's the Freedom in that?"

"I'm taking you into custody."

"No you ain't. I've just decided, I'm bigger than you. I'm going to beat you up because hey, might makes right."

"Now you're in for it, Hadrian," said Tammy as the chicken ambled up behind Hadrian. "It's what it all comes down to sooner or later with you humans. Who punches harder—"

Spark barked two quick barks and then a beam lashed out.

Captain Rabidinov glowed momentarily, then turned into a small pile of ashes.

"Self-Defense Protocol Murderous Intruder! Designated Too-Stupid-to-Listen-to-Reason. See Legal Disclaimer on Autonomous Actions by Guardomatic Unit (including Germane Shepherd, Marks I to III, Yapper-Head-Off Ratbag Mini/Midi/Maxi/Tiny, all variants, and Head-On Train-Chaser Dingo/Pitbull/Healer/Shitzer models, all variants) in Owner's Manual, Version 23.2."

"Or," said Hadrian to Tammy, "who punches first. Well," he added with a sigh, "that was depressing."

Zulu jumped forward and retrieved his saber. "Captain! I'm armed again!"

"Excellent, Zulu."

There was a distant scream, then a rumble.

"Here they come," said Tammy.

Galk and Nina Twice came running up.

"Sir," said Galk, "Senior Assessor Bleedheart just led the first wave of Dims at the 1st Freedom Loving Army of God's Justice." He spat. "With predictable consequences."

"It was horrible!" cried Nina Twice. "They kept saying 'We know you're racist homophobic Nazis but we forgive you!' Over and over again! And then—and then—"

"They trampled them," said Galk.

"Right," said Hadrian, sighing. "Thank goodness they didn't use nukes. Well, time to displace back to the ship. Tammy?"

"On it, Captain."

A few moments later, they all stood in the Insisteon Chamber. "Think I'd better put a quarantine on that planet," said Hadrian. "Terra's not ready for them. Not yet, anyway." Hands on hips, Hadrian drew a deep breath. "Let that be a sobering lesson to us all. When the world is full of nothing but trailer parks crammed with ill-educated nitwits chugging beer and scratching their asses, the meatheads in charge will have won." He paused. "On the other hand, a planet full of mewling pro-education social justice warriors will, if left alone, establish a utopian model civilization with no conflict, no inequality, and no room at all for sociopathic billionaires sucking blood from the tits of the poor—and if that ever happened, why, it'd be canceled after three seasons!"

Sin-Dour's voice came over the Comms. "Captain to the bridge! We've just received an emergency transmission! Captain to the bridge!"

"Awesome!" said Hadrian. "We can run along the corridors! Well, me and Tammy and Spark, that is. The rest of you, back to your stations, pronto. Zulu, that was good work down there!"

"Thank you, sir!" And he whipped out his saber. It went flying from his hand to stab the bulkhead just next to the technician's head. "Oops! Sorry, sir! I'll just get that."

But Hadrian was already out of the room, with Spark at his heels and Tammy scampering in their wake.

Adventure! Excitement! Parable Planet Number Two!

THREE

"Why, Adjutant Tighe, you never looked prettier!"

"Captain, I have no hair."

"Really? Never noticed." Hadrian flung himself back into his command chair. "All right, Sin-Dour, let's have it!"

"Sir?"

"The emergency transmission!"

"That was me," said Tammy, flapping loudly back onto the armrest. "I faked it. Why? Because I felt like it. One more pontificating speech from you, Hadrian, and this tiny head of mine will explode."

"Will it? Let's find out, shall we?" Hadrian rose to his feet.

"Cut that out!" Tammy shrieked.

"Captain," said Lorrin Tighe. "I monitored the events that transpired down on the planet surface. I am recommending your arrest to be followed by a court-martial, for Breach of Oath and the Subversion of Affiliation Contact Protocol." She straightened, eyes blazing in a most breathtaking fashion, various bridge lights reflecting from her shiny pate. "Captain Rabidinov should have been accorded all the assistance required to impose a balanced détente between the hostile parties. Even if that meant eradicating ninety-seven percent of one side in order to level the playing field. Indeed, every Engage Class vessel possesses onboard all the Reparation Contracts required to facilitate the immediate Intervention in the Name of Civilization by Reputable Corporations specializing in infrastructure repair, market rehabilitation, the divestment of all state-operated industries, and the rapid expansion into under-populated but resource-rich areas."

"Adjutant Tighe," said Hadrian, "since you were monitoring the events on the planet you will also understand that from the moment of our landing party's contact with Rabidinov, he attempted to seize Affiliation assets, namely my ship and weapons, first by threats, then by imprisonment. He also threatened to kill my officers in order to extort cooperation from Second-in-Command Sin-Dour. What we had down there was a rogue initiating a hostage situation. In effect, Adjutant, Rabidinov committed an act of terrorism."

Tighe blinked, and then scowled. "Semantics!"

"Well yes, that goes without saying. Here, let's take a hypothetical and explore this some more, shall we? Say the genius of a certain man is extorted from him on the basis of his followers being held hostage. Now say he does all he's asked to do, but finally sees his chance to escape, steal a state-of-the-art ship, and arrange to get his followers freed and brought to him. Is he the bad guy? I mean, what would you do in that scenario, Adjutant?"

Her eyes darted, then she shrugged. "I'd hightail it out of there."

"Hmm, yes, who wouldn't? But say the people he's negotiating with promise to send him his followers, only instead they send him a slew of bombs that then explode, forcing the ship down into the atmosphere of a planet and then crashing that ship into a densely populated city, killing tens of thousands of people. Who are the heroes of this tale?"

Now her scowl deepened. "This sounds like a bad holovid!"

Hadrian smiled. "See, we can agree on something after all!"

"None of that matters, Captain," Tighe retorted. "I am demanding your arrest! You murdered Captain Rabidinov!"

"No I didn't."

"Your dog did the dirty work!"

"Dirty work!" said Spark. "Scoop-Poops, Aisle 66! Dirty Work, Derivative, Cooked Books Before the Friggin' Auditor Arrives, see Deep-Six Folder, Aisle 21! These are all the receipts I have, sir!"

"Ensign Spark acted in defense of its captain," said Hadrian, "whose life was in imminent danger."

"Oh yes," snarled Tighe, "and I bet a jury of your peers will see it that way!" She laughed. "Fat chance of that, Captain! I now invoke the right to call Security to effect your arrest."

"You do?"

"Yes!"

"I suggest you reconsider, Adjutant," Hadrian said.

"After all, that arrest would have to include Commander Sin-Dour, who refused Rabidinov's demands. The truth is, we can make a fairly strong case for acting as necessary to ensure the safety of this ship and everyone on it."

Tighe looked over to where Sin-Dour sat at the Science Station. A complicated look passed between them, and then the Adjutant turned back to Hadrian. "This isn't over," she said.

"I expect not."

"Captain!" said Sin-Dour. "The fifth planet in this system has just fired some kind of projectile at us!"

"Oh? How quaint. Adjutant Tighe, we can resume this discussion later, hmm? Sin-Dour, estimated time of impact?"

"One moment, sir." She worked the console, flipping switches, turning dials, peering at readouts on pop-up screens. "Eleven days, nine hours, fifty-three minutes, six point four seconds."

"That gives us plenty of time to duck, then."

"Yes sir. Apologies, sir, I was startled by the sudden inexplicable launch. I am scanning that planet now."

Tighe hissed something inaudible and then marched from the bridge.

When she'd left, Tammy snickered. "You won't be rehabilitating her any time soon, oh Mighty Captain Hadrian. Her indoctrination levels are damned near epigenetic."

"Do exercise some patience, Tammy. As she said, this is anything but over with."

"Captain!" Sin-Dour swung her chair around. "On

the smallest continent of the planet there is an auto-
mated launch facility, in a state of poor repair. It seems
to employ a version of an electromagnetic rail impeller.
Very powerful. Surrounding this installation are
caves—"

"Caves! Now we're talking!"

"Yes sir. Inhabited by primitive hominids. Sir, I have
also run an active scan on the incoming missile. Length,
approximately three meters. Diameter of shaft, varying
between twelve and seventeen centimeters. Warhead: inert, composed of natural silicious material manually
restructured into a triangular, delta-style penetrator."

"In other words," said Hadrian, "a giant spear."

Sin-Dour blinked, and then squinted down at a pop-
up monitor. "Uh, yes sir. A giant spear."

"Presumably," said Hadrian, "the magrail launcher
is in contact with a satellite capable of system-wide
scanning and target acquisition."

"Yes sir! I have just found that satellite. Highly de-
graded orbit, Captain. In fact, it only has a year or two
left, unless it possesses built-in propulsion and correc-
tive programming. All of this technology, sir, appears to
be ancient, evincing much wear and tear."

"Devolved savages," mused Hadrian. "Worshipping
the last surviving weapon launcher, posing a hazard to
no one at all. Helm! Set a course for that planet!"

"I am tempted to scream again," said Tammy, "but
what would be the point?"

"Sir," resumed Sin-Dour, "there are quantum fluctu-
ations emanating from the core of that planet. I don't
believe standard displacement will be possible."

"You mean we'll need to send a shuttle down? Outstanding! Sticks! When was the last time you piloted a shuttle?"

Eden jumped in his seat.

Jocelyn Sticks swung round in her chair, the motion eliciting waves of ineffable pleasure in Hadrian. "Sir?"

"In fact," continued Hadrian, "I think I'll even sit this one out and give the mission over to my illustrious and eminently capable Second-in-Command. Sin-Dour, assemble your team and inform Chief Engineer Buck DeFrank to see to prepping the shuttle—hmm, which one? Oh, take the *Sagan,* assuming it's been fully repaired after its last mission—and wasn't that a hairy one, hah hah!"

Jimmy Eden suddenly shrieked and ran from the Comms station. The bridge entrance doors barely had time to hiss open before he was pelting down the corridor, still screaming.

Sin-Dour cleared her throat. "I believe it best if Lieutenant Eden remain behind this time, sir."

"Nonsense! Back on the horse that bucked you, I always say. Let's assume he's heading straight to Printlip for some more meds. Oh, and you might as well take the doc, too, if only to comfort poor Eden. Who else comes to mind, 2IC?"

She paused, frowning, and then said, "Buck DeFrank, sir, in case the shuttle breaks down. Combat Specialist Galk, to examine the weapon launcher. Lieutenant Nina Twice for Security Oversight, and Anthropologist Second Lieutenant Mendel Engels."

"Engels? Are you sure? The last Contact Mission—"

"As you said, sir, the horse that bucked you."

"Ah, true enough. But is he out of the Psych Ward yet?"

"I will check that with Dr. Printlip."

"Very good, Sin-Dour. The *Sagan* Seven! Off you go now, and good luck!"

The *Sagan* eased from the hangar bay, squirted its starboard thrusters to bring it around, and then engaged its antimatter engines and set off at speed toward the cloud-wrapped planet.

Sin-Dour said, "It occurs to me that this is our first planet-side mission undertaken without the presence of our captain. Of course, in keeping with your training, I have the utmost confidence in all of you."

"I don't like small spaces," Buck DeFrank said. "This shuttle's not big enough. Look at how these armrests pinch in, like the chair is trying to crush me."

"Do relax," Sin-Dour murmured. "Everything will be fine."

"I was like," said Sticks, "whoah! Pilot a shuttle! And he was, hey, why not? Even though he must've known I crashed six in a row during training! And I was, and then he—but what's this toggle do?"

The *Sagan* shuddered.

Sin-Dour gasped and looked across to Buck DeFrank, whose flat, blockish face was now whiter than the shuttle's hull.

"That," said Buck, lower lip trembling, "was the antimatter emergency ejection toggle, Lieutenant Sticks."

"Was it? And I was like, what's this? Flip! Oh and look, it says right there, 'Emergency Antimatter Ejection Toggle, Activate Only to Override All Safety Protocols in Face of Imminent Death.' Oh! Well, if they'd written that last bit bigger, duh!"

"We now have no fuel," Buck said in a dull voice. "We're going to crash and die."

Sin-Dour turned to Jimmy Eden. "Hail the *Willful Child*. We need retrieval."

"I can't! The quantum fluctuation interference! It's all static! I didn't want to come! I don't do good with pressure. I mean, I ace simulations no problem. Give me simulations and I've got it down." He rubbed at his face. "He said I'd never have to go on a mission! He lied! The captain lied! Doc! Give me an overdose! Or one of those inhalers you gave Polaski! Let me pass out and just, just slip away!"

"Calm down, Mister Eden," said Sin-Dour. "Buck, please take over on Manual Control."

"Manual Control?" Buck barked a nasty laugh. "This thing's a brick with mosquito wings!"

"That's a soupy atmosphere down there, Buck. Make use of it."

"Stop looking at me, Eden!" cried Sticks. "It wasn't my fault! That toggle was just sitting there! And that label! Who reads labels, for cripes sake! I was just sitting here, right, like, *PILOTING*, and there was that toggle! And I said what's this and nobody said anything so I flipped it, well *thanks*, Mr. Chief Engineer, for not warning me!"

The *Sagan* began rocking back and forth as it clawed

its way down into the upper atmosphere. Swearing, Buck fought the controls. "Doc! My anti-claustrophobia meds are wearing off real fast right now!"

"Accelerated heartrates!" Printlip announced. "All shuttle crew members barring Induced Comatose anthropologist!" The Belkri's many hands scrambled to prepare a jumbled array of shots that started stabbing out in all directions.

"Ow!"

"Ow!"

"Ow!"

"Ow!"

"Ow!" Then Buck said, "Hey, why did I get two shots?"

"Pain assists in concentration! Progress!"

The shuttle's front window showed raging plasma and then impenetrable brown clouds.

"Query," ventured Printlip. "Breathable atmosphere below?"

Sin-Dour sighed. "How optimistic of you, Doctor. But yes, somewhat breathable."

"I'm going to try and bring us down near that installation," said Buck, still fighting the controls as the shuttle pitched and yawed. "But it won't be a soft landing! In fact, we're likely to break into a thousand pieces, our limbs torn away, our bodies shredded by jagged metal, scorched by billowing flames, our brains mashed against the insides of our cracked skulls—"

"Chief Engineer," cut in Sin-Dour, "please concentrate on piloting."

"Sure thing, you cold-hearted—"

"Mister DeFrank!"

"If the captain was here," hissed Sticks, "he'd have saved us by now!"

Sighing yet again, Sin-Dour said, "Everyone strap in nice and tight."

The clouds suddenly cleared, revealing a landscape of buttes, cliffs, chasms, crevices, and fissures as unreal as a matte painting in the heavy, smeary atmosphere.

"We're going in!" bellowed Buck DeFrank.

"Well," said Sticks peevishly, "where else would we be going?"

"On the basis of our limited abilities to observe without instrumentation," said Tammy, "I'd say they ejected their antimatter fuel pods for some reason and then plummeted mostly out of control into the atmosphere. For all we know, they all elected suicide over one more day onboard this ship." The chicken paused to prune some feathers under one wing. "Fiery death, seven crewmembers—a severe blot on your record, Captain. Enough to get you busted down. Loss of command, shunted to some desk on Jupiter Hub, all your aspirations reduced to a stale beer, peanuts in a bowl, and a bartender so sick of your endless whining he's ready to shoot you himself."

Hadrian sighed. "You lack faith, Tammy."

"With Sticks piloting, Captain, I had no faith to begin with!"

Polaski at Comms said, "Captain! Priority Message from Fleet HQ! A shipment of lubricant needs to be delivered to Planet Women-Only, System Liberty-At-Last-Men-Can-Just-Piss-Off!"

"Lubricant? Oh—"

"They have extensive bauxite mining operations, sir. It seems the latest batch of lubricant was faulty and all the compellers burned out."

"Ah," said Hadrian.

"We're to pick up the shipment from a nearby transport that's broken down."

"Right."

Polaski turned. "Sir, this has a Fleet Command Override attached to it. No delays permissible."

Tammy snorted. "Tighe's been monitoring again, Hadrian. They're jumping at this to ensure no chance of you ever retrieving your officers. Thus ending your career."

"What's my window here, Tammy?"

"Eight hours, provided we override the delimiters all the way, without dropping out of T-Space the entire voyage, and if you recall, Captain, the psychological risk to such a long journey in T-Space could well result in—"

"To an average starship crew, perhaps," Hadrian cut in. He rose from the command seat. "Fortunately, I have the finest crew ever assembled. We can handle it."

"Oh here we go," Tammy said. "Pull off another damned miracle!"

"And what if I do?"

"I might cry."

* * *

The tiny computer on the *Sagan* decided, at the last moment, that its human pilot was incompetent, and so deployed its massive external airbags 1.8 seconds before impact. The shuttle craft bounced off a cliff wall, caromed along the talus slope of a hillside in a spray of gravel, rattled wildly through a field of boulders at the base and rolled up against another ragged cliffside until it came to a rocking halt, where a small thorn punctured the bag, initiating sudden loss of air pressure, and the *Sagan* settled onto its belly with a loud farting sound.

Within the shuttlecraft, Sin-Dour drew a deep breath, then said, "Well done, Buck. Damage report?"

"Dam—are you mad?" Buck demanded, tearing at his harness buckles. "We're venting from a hundred micro-ruptures to the hull! One of the two drive engines has completely dismounted and crushed itself against its own housing, and this effing buckle's jammed, dammit!"

"Just push that toggle," Sticks said. "That's the auto-release, duh!"

Buck jolted in his seat, both hands endeavoring to reach Sticks' throat, but the straps held him fast. He began frothing at the mouth.

Whimpering, Jocelyn Sticks shrank back.

"Calm down, everyone," said Sin-Dour. "Buck, Lieutenant Sticks is correct. If you wait a moment, I can assist you. In the meantime, Doc?"

"Yes, Commander?"

"Can you break open that storage compartment? We need to don environment suits, if only to maintain anti-contamination protocol. Despite the somewhat breathable atmosphere, I will insist on using the re-breathers and scrubbers for now. Oh, and Doc, can you wake up Mendel Engels, please? We have a proximity alert blinking on the console."

"Savages!" moaned Jimmy Eden. "They're going to tear us apart! Cook us in giant pots!"

Something big and heavy clanged against the side of the hull.

"Spears!" shrieked Jimmy. "Break out the Master-Blasters!"

"In a moment, Jimmy," said Sin-Dour. "Suits first."

Buck DeFrank began stabbing controls. "I'm shunting an electrostatic charge to the hull of this—"

Zap! "Ow!"

Zap! "Ow!

Zap! "Ow!"

"Sorry! *Outer* hull, dammit! Oh, never mind, it's just burned out. Shit!"

An entirely new sound now filled the cabin, and an instant later something huge and sharp punched through and began working its way across the side of the craft.

Buck stared in horror. "That's a giant can opener!"

Blinking, Mendel Engels sat up. "Ze lateral finking uv veez indigenooz inhabitantz iz most impressive. It iz likely shiny faux glazz beads vill prove inevectual trade itemz. Zuggest ve proceed to alcohol and dizeaze-ridden blankets at once."

"We're not here to Standard-Doctrine colonize the planet on the bodies of the local inhabitants, Dr. Engels," explained Sin-Dour. "Instead, we must devise a means to extricate ourselves from this ruined shuttle and take command of the ancient installation three hundred meters to the west of here. Based on those parameters, Dr. Engels, do you have any suggestions?"

"I zee. Very well. Then, in my educated opeenion, may I zuggest MazterBlazterz."

"Yes!" hissed Jimmy Eden.

"Very well," said Sin-Dour, rubbing at her eyes. "Helmets on, first. Also, target the landscape, not the savages. A flurry of explosions and flying shards of rock should suffice in frightening them away."

In the meantime, the giant can opener had carved through nearly half the width of the shuttle, and metal was being pulled back to reveal a gap. A moment later two huge hairy hands pushed a reed basket into the cabin.

"Ah!" said Dr. Engels. "They vish to trade!"

The hands then upended the basket and scores of snakes poured into the cabin.

"Evac!" shouted Sin-Dour. "Everyone out of the hatch, weapons armed!"

"And," added Dr. Engels, "ve have nothing vith vhich to reciprocate for veez pretty znakes."

"Spark," said Hadrian, "prepare to depart the ship."

"Zoom zoom! Zap! Zap!"

"No zap zap, Spark. You need to retrieve my crew members who are stranded on the planet below."

"Extending soft-gums now, Master."

"Excellent," said Hadrian.

Tammy laughed derisively and then said, "Your dog's navigation system is rubbish, Hadrian."

"But its Retrieval Program is top-notch. Right, Spark?"

"Electrostatic glue! Six beer cases at a time! Spark will remove all arms and legs to facilitate packing!"

"Alas, Spark, they need those limbs. How about we rig a net of some kind?"

"Net! Drag! Bury! No one will ever find it! No, Officer, we never saw those skinhead punks with the Nazi tattoos! But we'll keep an eye out for them for sure!"

"I might just lay an egg after all," said Tammy. "I warned you about Spark, didn't I?"

Lorrin Tighe returned to the bridge, the steel still bared in her eyes. "I have activated my eye-cam, Captain, to record this disaster in the making. It will of course be admissible in your trial. Along with all the other evidence."

"Why, Ms. Tighe," said Hadrian, swinging round in his chair to face her, "I believe you are displaying a disappointing lack of faith in your fellow officers haplessly trapped on the planet below. Spark!"

"Master?"

"Belay that last order. Sit right here, at my side, why don't you. Let's see if Sin-Dour can sort this out, shall we?"

"And if she fails?" Tighe demanded. "You've got six hours to get them off that planet! Have you been monitoring the conditions down there? There's a snowstorm coming down from the north, a firestorm coming up from the south, and what looks like a plague of locusts winging in from the east!"

"Your point?" Hadrian asked.

"And the Marine Hopper's not equipped for instrument-free manual descent and ascent, meaning you don't even have that option."

"I am aware of all this, Adjutant."

"And you don't even know if any of them are still alive."

"There you are with that lack of faith again, Adjutant. I probably shouldn't even point out that you still have no hair."

"Apparently," Tighe snarled, "it's permanent!"

Hadrian brightened. "Well then, just think of all the wigs you can wear! A different look each and every day! And not just various styles and colors, either! We have Hanarkan Tentacle wigs, Polker cilia wigs, Belkri eye-stalk—oh, but the Doc might fall for you, then, and that could be awkward. Best avoid the eye-stalk wig, Adjutant."

Polaski spoke from Comms. "Captain, HQ wants to know why we're just sitting here when we've got a Priority Mission to complete!"

Hadrian frowned. "And how precisely do they know we're just sitting here? Was that you as well, Adjutant?"

"Actually," she said with her thin brows lifting, "no."

"Then, perhaps we're not as alone as we think we are?"

Tighe was scowling now.

"Meaning," Hadrian continued, "our Priority mission is, um, shall we say, bogus? Since both vessels are in the same range to facilitate this delivery. More to the point: if there is an AFS vessel stealthed and shadowing us, well, one might conclude that the lives of my stranded crew members are of little concern to that vessel's captain and, by extension, Fleet HQ. Mightn't one, hmm?"

While Tighe gaped, Hadrian turned to the chicken on his chair's armrest. "Tammy, I think some very subtle scanning might be an appropriate course of action. Can you facilitate that in the absence of Commander Sin-Dour's eminent talents?"

Tammy's tiny eyes suddenly looked brighter, even more insane than usual. "Thinking of taking them on, Hadrian? Out in the open at last? You at war with the Affiliation itself?"

"Wrong kind of war," Hadrian replied. He stood. "Violence only solves things when it's a freaking-big many-fanged drooling alien with buggy eyes trying to rip your head off. No, Tammy, sedition is not in the cards here. Never was, never will be. It's all about setting the right example, a reinvigoration of wonder, curiosity, a sense of adventure and, please, Tammy, cut back on the onscreen close-ups, will you?" He sat once more. "Subtle, I said. Use some of your from-the-future scanning capabilities, Tammy. Above all, don't let that vessel know it's been detected." He then turned back to Tighe. "Assuming the Adjutant here is finally comprehending that something is not quite right regarding her distant superiors, and that she might conclude to suspend activities beyond this simple recording of events, at least until such time as we can all determine the moral compass of my presumed enemies within the Fleet? After all, it does appear that whoever they are, the extreme danger to my stranded landing party seems to have effected no change in their plans, whatever those plans are, and *that*, my friends, is not becoming of Affiliation Spacefleet personnel." He raised one eyebrow in the manner he had practiced and, indeed, perfected after years and years of disciplined endeavor. "Acceptable, Ms. Tighe?"

Her scowl deepened, making the frown lines ride all the way up past her forehead to wrinkle her pate. "For now," she agreed in a grating tone. "But that still doesn't answer what you're planning to do to save those people."

Hadrian lifted a hand. "Polaski, inform HQ that we are preparing to snag us an asteroid, with the intent to use its raw materials to render all the high-quality graphene lubricant Women-Only will ever require, thus obviating any need to rendezvous with that merchant hauler, thus permitting us to set a course directly for the stricken Pleasure Planet." Hadrian smiled at Tighe. "Now, let's gauge their reply, shall we? I suspect it will prove most illuminating."

"And your stranded crew?" Tighe insisted.

"Faith, my dear," said Hadrian as he settled back in his chair.

"Holy fuckin' Darwin on a stick!" gasped Jimmy Eden as he leaned his back against the installation wall, tracking targets with his near-depleted MasterBlaster.

Sin-Dour settled down on one knee beside him. "Buck, see if you can spring that door. Doc, see what you can do about all those snakes hanging from Dr. Engels's suit. Sticks! Keep an eye on that swarm of locusts and try and gauge the speed of their approach. Galk, check weapon charges and watch for any more Gigantopithecines."

"There's a mass of them hiding behind that boulder, Commander," said Galk, pausing to spit. When the juice splashed across the inside of his faceshield he said, "Now I can't see anything, so I'll just start shooting randomly. That oughta keep their giant hairy heads down."

"Nina," resumed Sin-Dour, "maintain an oversight on Galk's random shots."

"Yes sir. Also, sir, as you can see, I am maintaining my combat posture."

"Very good, Nina, carry on."

"Perhapz," said Engels as Printlip tugged snakes loose and flung them away, "veez znakes are decorative? Or, more pozzibly, pozzess ritual significance? In zee meantime, identification now ninety-zeven percent poziteev confirmed as gigantopithecines, deeztantly related to australopithecine robuzti and bozei. Bezz known in modern times az Beegfoot, Yeti, Zasquatch. Perhaps one day, vee shall find on Terra more than just their footprintz, hey?"

"One of my great-great-great-great aunts slept with one, once," said Galk. "Nothing came of it, though, which is why we don't talk about it much. She said it was the second hairiest—"

"Got the door open!" cried Buck DeFrank.

"Cease firing, Galk," ordered Sin-Dour. "Everyone inside, quickly now."

Moments later they were huddled in a corridor and Buck was busy melting the door's hinges shut with his Universal Multiphasic. Spear points clanged on the other side, followed by frantic workings of the latch, and finally a *knock-knock*.

"Don't answer that!" hissed Eden.

"But it could be, like, important!" objected Sticks. "Like when I get messages, right? That little buzzing. Who knows who's messaging me? It could be the most important thing in the world and so, like, can I wait? No way! We're talking sweaty palms, right? As in, SWEAT! Yuck! So I better check, and that's what I'm saying, we should check, just in case."

Buck stared at her for a long moment, and then set his back against the welded-shut door and held up his Universal Multiphasic. "Try it, Sticks, and you're toast."

"Calm down everyone," said Sin-Dour. "We seem to have some time here, in which we can assess our situation."

"Assess?" Eden demanded. "We're trapped in a building and surrounded by giant hairy gargantucenes! Whose idea was this? Run from the ship? Madness! Now we'll never get off this planet. We'll start starving in here, until we kill the weak scrawny ones and eat them, and how long will that last before there's only me left? All alone? I can't believe I ever wanted to be part of a Landing Party. I want my Comms Station!"

"Are you done, Lieutenant?" Sin-Dour asked.

Buck grunted and then said, "I always knew you for a cold one, Lieutenant Commander. All standoffish and haughty and perfectly formed, with me just a lowly engineer you never talk to even though we're on the same ship and everything. Sticks was right. If the Captain was here, we'd be out of this by now."

"Perhaps," Sin-Dour admitted. "But he isn't, and here I am. More to the point, we are officers in Spacefleet. Mister Eden, you in fact trained specifically for planet-side missions, did you not?"

Eden licked his lips. "Well, sure. But I was green! And then I came in fourth and everything just fell apart." He clawed at his face. "The pressure!"

"You're doing fine," Sin-Dour replied. "Pressure comes with being on a spaceship, after all—"

Buck snorted. "*In* a spaceship, too. Ha! Hahaha! Get it? Oh never mind, it was an engineering joke, I guess. Exclusive to us spanner-heads." Then he pointed a stubby finger at Sin-Dour. "If you crack, Commander, hand things over to old Buck here, and everything will be just fine."

Sticks yelped a laugh, then said, "Sure, like, Mr. We're All Going To Die here."

"I told you," Buck retorted, "I don't like cramped spaces, that's all. And that includes shuttles."

"So what happens the first time you have to climb into the Murphies Tube to fix something so we don't all explode?"

Buck's eyes narrowed on Sticks. "How do you know about the Murphies Tube?"

"Oh, I know, like, *lots*. About all kind of things! It's my photochromatic memory."

"Photographic, you mean?" Dr. Printlip queried. "Eidetic?"

Sticks rolled her eyes. "No. Photochromatic. Not only do I remember everything first time I see it, I also paint those memories in bright colors, so they look, like, pretty."

"How unusual," Printlip replied, eyes wavering about on their stalks. "Now, I would like to discuss with everyone the eminent wisdom of deferring to your doctor."

"Viz is clazzic collapze of arbitrary authority in face of dizazter," interjected Engels, "and zo under ze circumztances I advize handing over of all authority to the only objective perzon prezent, namely, me."

"Mutiny!" whispered Eden, his eyes wide. "Engels! I got one charge left in this MasterBlaster. Blow her head to bits and we're free!"

But Engels raised a staying hand. "Violenze muzt be lazt recourze, Lieutenant, to be employed only when I am in danger of lozing an argument. You muzt all firzt acknowledge my zupremacy as Zuperior Leader of All, and ven ve shall proceed mit the Firing Zquads."

"Zuperior Leader?" Eden repeated, blinking. Then he scowled. "That would be me, not you."

"Don't be zilly."

"I'm not being zilly! I don't even know what zilly is! You want zilly? Here's my fist—"

Engels shrank back, cowering. "No pleez! Don't hurt the Objective Byztander!"

"Oh dear," sighed Dr. Printlip. "If only doctors ran

the galaxy, why, we could diagnose you all and medicate accordingly. Everything would be perfect!"

"This is ridiculous," cut in Nina Twice. "I'm the representative of the military component in this situation. Commander, at your command I will declare Martial Law. I'm sure we have the Combat Specialist to back us up."

"I can only shoot blindly."

"Well I'm on the pill so that shouldn't be a problem," Nina Twice replied.

"Ze madness of ambition! Ze horror!"

After a long moment of tense silence, Sin-Dour sighed and said, "Is everyone finished? Good. We're all here because our Captain trusted us and had faith in our abilities—which one of you wants to be the first to let him down?"

No one spoke, until Sticks said, "Do we vote now? I vote for Eden."

"Me?" Eden demanded. "You vote for what?"

"Well, I mean, how do I know? I thought there was going to be a vote, so I, duh, VOTED. If you don't vote you can't complain, everyone knows that. And I want to complain, I mean, there's plenty to complain about, isn't there?" She threw up her hands. "Economics, politics, poor-quality lingerie! The list is almost endless!"

"I do have a plan," said Sin-Dour.

"Oh listen to her!" Sticks went on. "A plan! She has a plan! Oh, like, wow, for real? A plan? A plan! I can't believe I voted for Eden. Talk about a spoiled ballot, the whole system's corrupt, oh, forget it, I'm never voting for anything ever again."

At that moment the steel door clanged and the steel point of the giant can opener punched through the metal panel. Buck leapt to his feet. "Holy Darwin, that nearly decapitated me!"

"We should head deeper into the facility," said Sin-Dour.

"*Really?*" Eden shrieked. "*I mean, are you sure, Commander?*"

"A little too much of the Sarcasm Manual, Mister Eden. But go ahead, take point."

They rushed along and came to a halt at a descending set of metal steps, except for Dr. Printlip, who tripped and fell past them all, bouncing down the stairs, hands flailing.

"Follow him down!" ordered Sin-Dour as the door at the far end of the corridor crashed down with a booming echo.

"I still can't see," Galk announced in passing as he fell past Sin-Dour and then Eden. He tumbled and rolled into the darkness below, the grunts and clangs ending with a piercing scream from Printlip.

Eden resuming the lead, the rest hurried down, finding both Galk and the Doc climbing to their feet in another corridor. "Buck," commanded Sin-Dour, "we need to find the magrail control room." She pulled out her Pentracorder. "Take this and follow these energy readings."

"Those energy readings indicate battery juice remaining, Commander. And *my God they're going down!*"

"Not those readings, Buck. These ones, on the main viewer."

"Oh. Got it. This isn't like an engineer's Pentracorder at all. All right then, everyone follow me."

"Commander," Galk asked as he was being guided along by Nina Twice, "what are we going to do in that control room?"

"That depends," she replied.

Something apelike roared from the landing above and behind them.

"*Depends?*" Eden shrieked.

Engels said, "Ve have invaded the gigantopithecines' temple. If there was a cleef they would chase us right off it, forcing us to jump into zee sea, and then some stoopidly ignorant person might deecide to ignite a cold fusion bomb in a volcano, theenking 'cold' must mean 'freezing' becuz, vell, they know nuffink, and theez is zee problem wiff Modern Education."

The others had paused to stare at the anthropologist, who then plucked a last remaining snake free and examined it as it repeatedly snapped its venom-splashing fangs into his face shield. "Thiz creature lackz intelligence."

Another roar from above. Nina Twice sighed, releasing Galk's arm. "Excuse me. I'll be right back."

She headed up the stairs.

A flurry of snarls and shrieks and screams followed by heavy thumps and then whimpers, and then boots on the stairs, coming down fast. Nina reappeared. "I bought us some time," she said.

"Well done," Sin-Dour said.

Buck stared at her. "Wow," he said.

Nina Twice eyed the Chief Engineer levelly. "Sir, as

part of the ship security team, I have of course perused in detail the entire ship's complement of officers and enlisted, as they were handpicked by the captain, and this in itself was unusual."

Frowning, Buck said, "Your point?"

"Only this, sir. Every member of the crew on the *Willful Child* excels in at least one area of talent and/or expertise. It is, in fact, rather remarkable." She nodded over at Jocelyn Sticks. "Take the helm officer, for example. She needs only look at an astrometric chart once to know it. Pretty useful, wouldn't you say? As for Combat Specialist Galk, he is rated to have the fastest synaptic exchanges and neural pathways of anyone in the entire fleet, aided and abetted by copious amounts of nicotine. Rather useful, wouldn't you say? Even the doctor here: unmatched in devising symptom-specific treatments, often proving quicker than a computer, due to Printlip's off-the-chart Intuitive Genius rating."

"What about me?" Eden demanded, a pleading look in his eyes.

Nina shrugged. "Low Boredom Meter, Jimmy. Essential for a shipboard Comms officer, I'd think."

Eden sighed. "You have no idea."

"And me?" Buck demanded.

"Unusually resistant to cellular and systemic poisons, including drug-abuse side effects and, of course, radiation."

He grunted. "I wanted something better, dammit." Then he brightened. "But hey, it'll have to do, won't it? Doctor, we need to talk—"

"I'm sure you do," Sin-Dour cut in, after giving Nina

a long look, "but for now, do peruse the Pentracorder and find us the power source."

"Yeah, right, on it, sir." He headed off.

When Sin-Dour momentarily turned away, Sticks leaned close to Nina Twice and whispered, "What about her?"

"Unflappable," the security officer replied in a murmur. "Utterly, absolutely, unequivocally."

Sticks sighed. "Good call, huh? I mean, for a 2IC!"

Buck found a door at the far end of the corridor and waved them over. "In here! Behind this door!"

"Exzellent! Now vhere iz zee fusion bomb? Vitless vership of Death Weapon is common motif among degenerate population. Monographs of time before Beneffactorz reveal similar fixation among degenerates on Old Earth, mit hand guns and other zymbols of penile inadequacy . . ."

Buck pulled open the door.

"Let's go," said Sin-Dour, pushing crew members forward.

"But vut shall I do mit my znake?"

They joined Buck in a circular chamber with a massive railgun's launch pad dominating its center. The Chief Engineer was at a console. "All functions still active, Commander."

"Excellent. Mister Eden, climb onto that launch pad."

"What?" said Eden.

"Jimmy, it's our only way off this planet."

"*What?*" said Eden, staring at Sin-Dour.

"Commander, I forgot!" cried Jocelyn Sticks. "I've lost sight of the locusts!"

"Theez znake's fangs haff fallen uff."

"*WHAT?*" screamed Jimmy Eden.

Sticks rolled her eyes. "Oh cut it, like, *out,* Jimmy. If you didn't want my vote you shouldn't have made, like, all those promises and stuff."

"Sir!" cried Ensign Sweetsugar from the navigation station. "Projectile launch from the planet! One point six seven meters in length, variable diameter, blunt penetrator warhead, possibly solid! Kinetic only!"

"Prepare the Gravity Snare," said Hadrian.

"Sir?"

"One point six seven meters, you said? Solid head? That would be James Jimmy Eden, I think."

"Oh sir! Another launch! I think it's a cannonball!"

Hadrian swung in his chair to smile at Adjutant Tighe. "Now, about that wig, might I suggest—"

FOUR

Captain Hans Olo sighed, absently stroking the fur of Gnawfang, who slouched on his shoulder.

"Sir," said Lieutenant Janice Reasonable from her station, "they have just recovered the last crewmember with their gravity snare and are now preparing to depart the system."

"At full T-Space duration," Olo mused, "they will still be late." He stroked his smooth, cleft chin. "A mark of disapproval on his record, but nothing disastrous."

"Sir," said Frank Worship, "if we launched a surprise attack! All weapons to bear! We could blast them into smithereens!"

"Alas, Number Two," replied Olo, "beyond our remit, as satisfying as it might be. No, this calls for Backup Plan Beta Epsilon Delta, Code-Name Octagon, the Yellow Draft."

Agent Humblenot cleared his throat. "It occurs to me, Captain, that Sawback might very well attempt to overextend the prescribed duration of T-Flight, in order to reach the rendezvous in time."

Hans Olo's brows rose. "All to avoid a minor reprimand?"

"One more knife to stick into HQ, yes, Captain, I believe he just might. And if that proves the case, your Backup Plan could lead to, well, unexpected consequences."

Hans Olo considered. "We have seeded his path, as per the Yellow Draft's instructions. Quantum Deviation beyond T-Flight's allowed duration is more than just a reprimand. Should Sawback arrive in time, HQ can only conclude that he had directly disobeyed Fleet Regulations. That's more than just a reprimand."

"They may well conclude that, sir," Humblenot agreed. "But they won't be able to prove it, provided Sawback wipes his own telemetry log. Which he'd have to do to save his own skin."

Watching Hans Olo assume a thoughtful pose, still stroking his chin, made Frank's eyes glow with admiration. He longed to go off-duty and plunge into, as it were, Secret Hologram Program Mutual Man-Crush, although he was still a bit shaky from the last time.

"If Sawback extends the duration, risking the sanity of his entire crew," Hans Olo then said, "he deserves whatever happens to him when he trips the Proximity Activation Sequence Cascade-Effect of the Displacement Nodes we've scattered in his path."

Rand Humblenot leaned closer from his stance on Olo's left. "Captain, initiation of the Proximity Activation Sequence Cascade-Effect of the hidden Displacement Nodes could trigger a Quantum Defibrillation of the Dark Energy Lattice Matrix, instigating a Full Feedback Ripple Effect through Postulate Realities both above and below the Fixed Reality 1A Spectrum."

"Yes, Rand," snapped Hans Olo, "I am well aware that initiating the Proximity Activation Sequence Cascade Effect of the hidden Displacement Nodes could trigger a Quantum Defibrillation of the Dark Energy Lattice Matrix, instigating a Full Feedback Ripple Effect through Postulate Realities both above and below the Fixed Reality 1A Spectrum. At the same time, are we not Intrinsically Committed to Reality 1A Spectrum by virtue of Quantum Adherence to Origin Point Reality Manifestation, thus ensuring a Reset Threshold at some Initiation Point in the Temporal Multiverse Index?"

"Captain, I am of course well aware that we are Intrinsically Committed to Reality 1A Spectrum by virtue of Quantum Adherence to Origin Point Reality Manifestation, thus ensuring a Reset Threshold at some Initiation Point in the Temporal Multiverse Index. My point is, if we indeed implement Octagon, Yellow Draft, and thereby initiate the Proximity Activation Sequence Cascade-Effect of the hidden Displacement Nodes that then triggers a Quantum Defibrillation of the Dark Energy Lattice Matrix, instigating a Full Feedback Ripple Effect through Postulate Realities both above and below the Fixed Reality 1A Spectrum, we could be facing a Full Multiverse Displacement Event, thus altering Infinite Causality Paradigms in All-Dimensional Wave-Fronts."

Hans Olo scowled. "Enough of this chitchat. Commander Worship, implement Octagon."

"Yellow Draft, sir?"

"Yellow Draft."

"Captain!" said Janice Reasonable. "The *Willful Child* is underway, entering T-Space . . . now!"

"Excellent. We, of course, shall proceed at a more sedate pace."

Nodding, Lieutenant Janice Reasonable narrowed her gaze on Gnawfang, who was glowering at her. She considered glowering back and had to wait a moment before the flash of sizzling rage passed. "Yes sir. Fully engaging now, sir."

Hadrian cocked his head at Lorrin Tighe. "Well now, Adjutant. Fleet HQ insists that we proceed to the rendezvous. Seems they didn't like my asteroid plan at all, despite its superior efficiency. What do you make of that?"

"They must have their reasons," she said in a growl.

"Oh, I'm sure they have," Hadrian replied. "Tammy, is that unidentified AFS vessel still shadowing us?"

"Inasmuch as is possible in T-Space," the chicken replied. "Not hard to do, since they possess a reasonable expectation of our course."

"Indeed. And are their drives maxed out?"

"Not in the least."

"No intention, then, of exceeding T-Flight duration parameters."

"Clearly not."

"Thank you, Tammy. Most enlightening."

"They've set a trap, Hadrian," Tammy said. "And you're heading right into it at insane speeds!"

"So it seems."

The chicken's head snapped up. "Hey! I just got a ping from something that shouldn't be there! And another! And anoth—"

Hadrian bolted upright. "They didn't! Helm! Drop us out of T-Space! All drives Full Sto—"

Hadrian blinked. A moment later Sin-Dour slid onto the armrest, her rounded behind filling most of his field of view. Her hand slipped down to knead his thigh. Twisting to look upon him, a smile curving her full lips—she suddenly sprang to her feet.

"You're not Captain Hadriana!"

"No wait! I am! Really! My—uh—Inflatabreasts malfunctioned this morning! Carry on! *Please?*"

"As we feared," Sin-Dour hissed, "there's been a Full Multiverse Displacement Event, thus altering Infinite Causality Paradigms in All-Dimensional Wave-Fronts! Those idiots!"

"I forgot to put on my face this morning, darling, honest!"

She scowled down at him. "You're a male version of my captain, from some alternate reality."

Taking in her scant uniform, all the flesh showing including her amazing cleavage, Hadrian said, "And my universe sucks!" He leapt to his feet. "I'm here now! Me, Hadrian Alan Sawback! And we're stuck with this new paradigm. Trapped! Forever altered! I'll never get back! Oh dear!"

"I should tell you that we don't do well taking orders from a *man*."

He looked around at his bridge officers, winced at all the scowls. "Oh, I see." He continued studying this new version of his crew. Some minor differences were, after a few moments' worth of observation, readily apparent, particularly in that Jocelyn Sticks was wearing a furry bikini and his cousin Polaski was kneeling at the foot of the Comms chair, filthy and wearing rags, his hair a wild nest of twigs and scabbed bald patches. And Buck DeFrank, inexplicably at the Bridge Engineering Station, was wearing a bright orange dress, which did nothing for his hairy legs. At the Security Station lounged a bald Lorrin Tighe in a flimsy nightgown hitched high up on one thigh, puffing on a cigarette hanging from her full lips while idly playing with the pommel of a wicked-looking dagger at her silk belt. Her gaze was sultry but calculating, fixed upon Hadrian through a veil of smoke so that it was as if Hadrian were seeing her through a Vaseline-smeared lens.

She now languidly pushed off from the station and sidled closer.

"Wow," said Hadrian, "and I thought power dynamics were boring!"

Suddenly blocking Hadrian's line of sight, Sin-Dour stretched, arms lifting high, breasts bulging in front of his face so that he couldn't see past them no matter how hard he tried, not that he tried. She looked down on him, eyes dark behind the ridiculously full lashes.

"That said, you do remain our"—her expression twisted slightly in distaste—"Captain. And it wouldn't do to, well, put you in your place." She sighed. "We may have to simply accept the present circumstances, Captain . . . uh, Hadrian Alan Sawback. At least until the Reset Threshold kicks in."

"Which might be years away!"

"In the meantime," Sin-Dour said, easing up on her stretch and shifting a shoulder to further block Tighe's approach, "it seems our universes share similar situations. HQ out for our blood, a stealthed latest model Engage Class shadowing us. The *Decadium Pigeon,* no less, captained by none other than Hannah Olo."

"The what? Ah, in my universe that would be Hans Olo and the *Century Warbler.*"

Tighe slipped round the other side of the chair. "Captain, in the mood for . . . oh, what would it be for a man . . . a hand job?"

Sin-Dour hissed and drew out a knife. "Back off, Adjutant! The Captain's still disappointed in you!"

"*Not this one!*" She looked hopefully at Hadrian. "Right, Ma'am? You like me, don't you? You want me! I should be Alpha here, not her! I know all about Special Agent Ayn Humblenot!"

"And I know all about Hannah Olo!" retorted Sin-Dour.

"Hey!" said Hadrian. "Both of you, back off for a moment, will ya?" Seeing the sudden shock on Sin-Dour's face, he hastily added, "You first, Tighe! Back to your station. And you, 2IC, kindly sheathe that knife, please? I need to find my feet here. It seems Hadriana was a tad further along in sussing out the conspiracy against us." Then he pointed at Tighe. "And you'll address me as 'sir,' not 'ma'am.'"

Tighe sniffed in disdain, pointedly turning her back as she sidled off.

Expression only slightly mollified, Sin-Dour slipped the knife back into its scabbard, and then sniffed sharply in the direction of Jocelyn Sticks at the helm, who rose to her feet to walk over and kick Polaski in the crotch.

Gasping, he curled up on the floor. Looming over the writhing ensign, she glanced back at Sin-Dour. "Should I, like, scratch him too, Ma'am?"

"Whoah!" said Hadrian. "Back to your seat, Lieutenant Sticks! If there's any, uh, kicking and scratching to be done on this bridge, I'll be the one doing it!"

At that everyone gasped.

"What? What did I say?"

Stiffly, Sin-Dour said, "Sir, the Captain must never touch. This is the task of her Alphas, to either impose discipline directly or delegate it, as I just did a moment ago."

"Oh. Right. But Polaski didn't do anything."

"Of course not!" laughed Sticks as she returned to her station. "He's, like, the *runt!* Hah hah, hasn't been groomed or jacked since, like, never! Hah hah!"

"Ensign Groveling Class Polaski, Ma—I mean, *sir*," explained Sin-Dour, "is the Bridge Repository for Discipline. It is his purpose."

"Hmm, this will take some getting used to— Hey, where's Spark?"

"Spark, sir?"

"My robot guard dog!"

"Ah!" Sin-Dour walked over to a hatch beneath the Science console. She crouched down to open the door and then reached in to pull out a small knot of fake fur with four legs and a tiny head dominated by giant glass eyes. "You mean Spunk, sir. Your Shitzer Model lap-dog."

"It appears to be deactivated."

"Yes sir, it is. It's better that way."

"Well, uhm, turn the damned thing on, will you?"

"Are you certain, sir?"

"I want Spunk in my, uh, lap!"

Sighing, Sin-Dour turned on the dog. It immediately began yapping.

Everyone on the bridge cringed, including Hadrian. "Oh crap. Really?"

Spunk then walked on its tiny stiff legs towards Hadrian. "Mistress! Bad hair day? So sorry! Lap now! Spunk wants lap! Lap! Lap! Now! Now! Lap!"

"No, wait. Uh, sit!"

"Shit!" Abruptly Spunk dropped its backside and pooped out a perfectly whipped ice-cream dollop of foul feces.

"What the hell? No, sit!"

"No, shit!" And Spunk crapped again.

The sudden stench made Hadrian recoil. "Hang on, that thing's inorganic! How's it—"

"Holocrap, sir," said Sin-Dour. "Full Senses Suite, unfortunately." She pointed at countless other small round, brown stains on the deck carpet. "Extended residuals, too."

"What frigging dimwit thought *that* was a good idea?"

"Do you mean the holocrap, the robot or the breed of dog that inspired it?"

"The—all of them, dammit!"

"Lap, Mistress? Lap? Lap? Lap or Yap, your choice, bitch! Lap lap yap yap *yap yap yap yap*—"

"Turn it off! Stow it! No, wait, nearest airlock!"

"Captain!" said Sin-Dour in shock, even as she reached down and hit the off switch. Spunk's legs went straight, mouth still wide open, and then the horrid little creature toppled onto its side. "Surely not the airlock! The Shitzer model is a status item! Every captain has one! They all copied you! Why do you think HQ has it in for you? Not to mention the Fleet Janitorial Guild!"

Hadrian hit the log switch on the armrest of his chair. "Private note to Captain Hadriana from her more sane male alternate. Get rid of that friggin' Shitzer! Hadrian out."

The bridge janitor, Tech Bryan "Mops" Dietrich, whose stitched name tag said *Stan,* arrived with a bucket and a mop, pausing to glare at Hadrian.

Hadrian looked round, frowning. "Where's Tammy?"

"I'm sorry, who?"

"My rogue AI from the future!"

"Oh, you mean Merle Haggard! Do you truly wish to see her, sir? In this universe we're quite happy to do without—"

"No. Take me to hi—her at once. I need answers!"

"Merle is not particularly good at answers, sir."

"Just take me to her," Hadrian said, rising. "Helm, inform me when we're nearing rendezvous with that hauler full of lubricant."

Sticks looked to Sin-Dour for confirmation.

Frowning, Hadrian said, "That was an order, Helm. From your captain."

"Yes, but, you know? I mean, it's like, men have their place, you know? And so you said, well, 'inform me blah blah' and I was like *this,* and then you said, like, 'hey, you, I gave an order,' and I know, you know, I mean I *heard* you, right? Only, it's like, men are for pro-creation, right? Oh, and candy dressing. So it was like . . . confusion!"

Hadrian rubbed at his face. "Fine, whatever. Take me to Merle, 2IC."

"This way, uh, Captain."

As soon as they were in the corridor leading off from the bridge, Sin-Dour halted and faced Hadrian. "This isn't easy, you know."

"You're telling me."

"A man as captain of a starship—it just feels un-natural."

"Right, but this is temporary," replied Hadrian. "Be-sides, if you're anything like the Sin-Dour I know, you'll adjust, and fast. You'll roll with it because it's necessary to keep things from descending into chaos. By the way, in my universe there are as many female captains as male, and as many female officers as male officers, and guess what, we like it that way."

"Barbaric!" Sin-Dour said.

"Oh there's that, too, of course. Testosterone invokes

brainlessness, after all. It makes men petty and vicious and prone to acting like jerks."

"But how do your world's women deal with all that?"

"The best way possible," Hadrian replied. "Mockery and derision. It's all that crap deserves, after all."

"Sounds chaotic."

"It is."

She sighed. "Very well, I will make an effort in adjusting, and indeed, I will treat you just as I would treat my own captain." She drew a deep breath, and then closed in on Hadrian, hands stroking and caressing almost everywhere. "Captain, we have a problem."

"I'll say. I can't concentrate!"

"Not that. It's Tighe."

"What? What about her, and why are you pawing me? Not that I mind, in principle, I mean. Only, that concentration thing—"

"But I'm helping you to concentrate! Now listen—"

"Look, I'm glad Hadriana leans that way. I mean, I would, too, right? What man wouldn't? Rather, that is, what man turned suddenly into a woman but still a man inside wouldn't jump at the chance? It makes perfect sense—"

"What are you going on about, sir?"

"Well, sexual preferences, of course."

She stepped back. "Sir, this conversation is now inappropriate for Fleet officers, even ones being betrayed by their own masters! I know you've already told me a few details, but really. What kind of messed-up universe are you from, anyway?"

"Well, the normal messed-up kind, I suppose. You

know, sexually repressed, infinitely frustrated, perversely contradictory, desperate, unfulfilled, miserable . . . er, not ringing any bells for you?"

Sighing, Sin-Dour took him by the arm. "Well, maybe Merle can help after all. I'm not at all optimistic, of course, for obvious reasons."

A few corridors later they reached a code-locked door. Sin-Dour paused. "Prepare yourself, sir, it's not pretty." She activated the seven-digit code and then pressed her full lips against the sensor panel. The door sighed open.

Inside was a small room mostly occupied by what looked like a pint-sized boxing ring walled and roofed by transparent sheets of aluminum. The floor of the ring was full of holes in various geometric shapes, and what wasn't holed was crowded with wooden geometrically varied blocks. Inside this strange aquarium was a white parrot.

"That's Merle Haggard?"

"I'm afraid so, sir."

Merle glanced briefly up at them and then resumed pushing a block with its head.

"What a tragic fate! Has her mind snapped?"

"To be honest, sir, we're not sure."

"Does she talk?"

"In a manner of speaking."

Hadrian crouched down. "Hey, Merle!"

The parrot paused. "One moment please. This block goes here, I'm certain of it!"

"No, Merle. That block is square. The hole you're trying to fit it in is diamond shaped."

"Quantum Angulation suggests, however, a proper fit!"

"Forget Quantum Angulation for the moment, Merle. You need to talk to me."

"I do?"

"Yes. You see, I'm not from this reality. I was switched by Quantum Displacement. I'm not Hadriana. I'm Hadrian. Captain Hadrian Alan Sawback of the *Willful Child*."

Behind him, Sin-Dour grunted. "Sir, here, you're on the *Woeful Child*."

The parrot cocked one eye up at Hadrian, and then the other. "Yes, of course! No wonder my Extreme Excitation Event has been tripped! We are experiencing an Infinite Causality Paradigm Flux in All-Dimensional Wave-Fronts! My Temporal-Neutral Neutratronic Processor is in an Infinite Cascade Loop!"

"That seems unlikely, Merle," said Sin-Dour behind Hadrian. "You've been like this for over a week."

"Temporal Reverberations on the Infinity Matrix! And now I need to sing! This one's called 'Okie From Muskogee' and is a fan favor—"

"Merle!" snapped Hadrian. "Not now! Listen! You need to tell me about this universe! What's with all the pawing going on, the oversexualized uniforms on everyone and the fake crotch bulges on the men, and everyone beating up Polaski?"

The parrot bobbed its head. "DNA Scan Initiated, Subject: Sawback, Hadrian Alan. Oh! Oh dear! Oh my! Holy crap on a swizzle stick! Think I'll just stay here and drink!"

"Merle! What is it? What did you discover?"

"Errant evolutionary deviation! In this universe humanity's nearest simian relative is the Bonobo, not the Chimpanzee! Matriarchal Social Mechanisms unknown to Hadrian Alan Sawback! Conflict Resolution via Sexual Favors, Sensual Contact, Hand-jobs, and of course beating the crap out of Submissive Victim Omega—all totally unknown to present subject! Mama tried, oh how she tried!"

"Darwin help us!" whispered Sin-Dour.

"The bottle let me down!" cried the parrot. "Are the good times really over? I'm going where the lonely go!"

"We've lost her again, sir."

Hadrian slowly straightened. "Good grief, I'm stuck in a Bonoboverse."

A nearby Comms speaker suddenly crackled, "Captain to the Bridge! We are approaching the Merchant Vessel. Captain to the Bridge!"

"Shit," said Hadrian. "All right, 2IC, let's go!"

"Sir! What are we going to do?"

"Not sure, but about those hand jobs . . ."

"Do I have to do everything myself in this fucking universe?" Hadriana demanded as she dragged by one ankle a weeping Polaski across the floor toward her command chair. "And in the meantime, 2IC, quit with the cold shoulder crap and take over Comms and get that merchant vessel's captain onscreen."

Sin-Dour blinked. "Apologies, Ma'am, for the seeming cold shoulder. It's nothing of the sort. Rather, your male version was at times a little forward in his, uhm, occasionally overt desire for extracurricular fraternization."

Hadriana glowered down at Polaski for a moment and then released her grip with an expression of disgust. "He wants into your knickers, you mean. What's the problem with that? Once you've swung one leg over him he'll be putty in your hands, and then you can slit his throat one night and assume the captaincy, as is proper. Now." She sat and gestured at the main viewscreen. "A.M.F.S. *Obvious Pawn*. Skipper Harriet Mullet. Suspected smuggler, small-time confidence scammer. Citations and fines . . . hmm, for shipment of generic lifesaving medications, non-GMO vegetables, unbranded water and perfectly ripe bananas. Hmm, labeled a 'real vicious piece of work' by the Unfettered Trade Controls Department. Is she on Comms yet, Sin-Dour?"

"A moment, Ma'am, I'm unfamiliar with these controls. Normally, it would be James Eden here, or, well, Polaski."

Hadriana looked down at the fetal man curled at her feet and sneered. Then frowned. "Long-Jim Eden? You mean the Poke Stud we keep in the Silk Pillow Room? Goodness, the idiot came in fourth in the Olympics for crying out loud, and you let him handle Comms?"

"Got it, Captain! Onscreen now."

The image shifted to the bridge of the *Obvious Pawn*. Harriet Mullet, scrawny, shifty and sporting an impressive handlebar moustache, was swinging back and forth in her command chair, her legs crossed and one foot bobbing up and down. "Captain Hadrian—uh." She frowned, stopping swinging back and forth, and slowly leaned forward. "Well, that is, er, Captain . . . well, Darwin tweak me! You're *months* ahead of my treatment! Hi there, Sister Trans!"

"It's Captain Hadriana–"

"And of course it is, sir! Wait till the portal feeds get wind of this!"

"No, I mean, you've got it wrong, Mullet—oh, never mind. We're here to pick up the lubricant."

"Of course you are." Smiling, she resumed swinging back and forth, one foot bobbing up and down. "High-quality graphene lubricating emulsion, Captain Hadriana. Twenty-k metric tons, all three containers, in fact. Come and get 'em!"

"You are looking nervous, Harriet," observed Hadriana.

The foot started bobbing faster and faster. "Nervous? Not really. We were ordered to fake a breakdown and wait for the *Willful Child*. And here we are!" She waved to someone offscreen.

"A fake breakdown. I see."

Harriet smiled. "It's that or lose my brand-new Trade Anything License." Then she winked, only to lean forward a moment later and whisper, "They're out to get you, darling, so be careful!"

"Fine. Yes, thank you." Hadriana turned to Sin-Dour. "Snare the containers, and when that's done, set course for Women-Only. Then come here and stroke my hair. Oh, and kick Polaski for me, will you? Thanks."

* * *

Harry Mullet was not on the bridge of his vessel. Rather, he appeared to be in his cabin, seated behind his desk, shifting uncomfortably every now and then. "All here, Captain . . . uh, Hadrian. So I mean, you want 'em or not? 'Cause, like, we got stuff to do, eh? You know, merchant stuff. Effin' Fleet dumping dumb orders on us to fake breakdowns and all that, it's . . . unseemly! Is that the right word? Well, I don't know, why ask me? And who was asking me anything anyway? Nobody ever does. No, it's just hosers at HQ sayin' this and that and no by your livery either! So, uhm, what were we talkin' about again?"

"Just release the containers, Mullet," said Hadrian. "And, and by the way, did you know Mansanto's put out a bounty on your head?"

Harry snapped upright, then winced. He scowled. "Those shits got no jury's diction!"

"Oh, I know that. Still, must be a pain, though."

"I've just been Organic Certified!"

"Sounds seditious."

"Have you ever seen Mansanto's Cow Planet? Those animals poop watermelons! Watermelons with legs! Suicidal watermelons who walk straight to the Masher Machines, like, like, lemmings!"

"You're right, whatever happened to plain old cowshit?"

Harry Mullet leaned forward and then said, "You know, I kinda like the new you, Captain. In fact, I'd recommend you transfer to a trade vessel, with the rest of us men. Makes things simpler, and we can chat and gossip and everything! In fact, if you—*what the*?"

Mullet abruptly vanished from the viewscreen.

"Ma'am! I mean sir!" cried Jocelyn Sticks. "Collision Proximity Alarm just kicked in! An unknown vessel has just appeared—it's swallowed up the *Easy Bait*!"

"Back us off," Hadrian commanded. "Let's see that ship."

On the viewscreen, the unknown alien vessel was massive, amorphous, bulging here and there, scuffed and raggedy. Harry Mullet's A.M.F.S. *Easy Bait* was nowhere to be seen.

Sin-Dour had moved to the Science Station. "Captain, that unknown craft is nearly the size of a moon . . . only lumpier. Surface appears to be some form of flexible textile, impenetrable to our sensors. But I'm now picking up strange T-emanations—I believe its engines are powering up."

Abruptly, the strange ship swung round and, in a blur, vanished into T-Space.

"Helm! Pursue that vessel!"

"Ma—Sir?"

"It just ate an Affiliation ship, Sticks. Including an entire shipment of lubricant. Now, after it!"

"Yes sir! Engaging T-Drive . . . Mark!"

The stars vanished.

"We're on its debris trail, sir," Sticks added. "Like, easy to follow and stuff. I'm all shaky now—permission to bite Polaski?"

"Uhm, maybe later. Sweat it out, Helm, I need you on those controls. What's the enemy vessel's course?"

"It's staying right in front of us, sir!"

"Right, and what's our projected course, assuming we continue on this vector?"

"So like, am I flying after this thing or looking up star-charts? Yeesh!"

"Most displeasing," Sin-Dour murmured, "which we will discuss later, Helm, while you groom me to my seeming indifference."

Sticks ducked. "Yes, ma'am."

"Back to the projected course?" Hadrian ventured.

"Allow me," said Sin-Dour, moving up past Hadrian and leaning over the console with her left hand now massaging Sticks's shoulder. She activated a holo-screen.

"Is it hot in here?" Hadrian asked, pulling at his collar.

"Five hours ahead there's an N-Class star, brown dwarf, only one planet . . ." She turned. "Captain, the planet is Wallykrappe."

"Wallykrappe? Shit, you mean there's one even in *this* universe?"

"It's said that they're everywhere," Sin-Dour replied. "Indeed, thinking on it, it is probably safe to assume that a Wallykrappe planet will be found in all Multi-verses, in the manner of Off-Shore Tax Exemption Loopholes employing Infinite Modality Paradigms in All-Dimensional Wave-Fronts, thus establishing the precedent of Jurisdictional Non-Locality."

"You mean they use parallel universes to evade taxes?"

"We *are* talking Wallykrappe, sir."

* * *

Meanwhile, back on the Willful Child . . .

"What kind of Poke Stud is this?" Hadriana de-manded, standing over the curled-up, weeping form of James Jimmy Eden. "All I did was grab a quick hand-ful!"

Sin-Dour hesitated, and then with a tilt of the head indicated Hadrian's office. "Perhaps, ma'am, we can discuss this further in private?"

Something glinted in Hadriana's eyes but she nodded. "Good idea. We've got a few hours before we arrive at Wallykrappe Planet, assuming that's where the giant ship-eating blob is headed. Poor Harriet!" She glanced back down at Eden. "As for you, report yourself to Doc Pawprint immediately."

"That would be Printlip here, ma'am."

"Really? Belkri? Round, bouncy, lots of eyes and hands?"

"Causal consistency, Ma'am, seems intact in this instance, barring the name."

"Well, that's a relief."

They departed the bridge and entered Hadrian's cramped office. Hadriana paused to stare at the desk before them. "Where's the swing-seat? The cushions and the leather cuffs—"

"Couldn't say, ma'am," Sin-Dour cut in.

"Well, needs must." Hadriana sat down on top of the desk and then settled back, knees up and legs spread-ing wide so that her short skirt slid back to reveal her pantylessness. "Face, right here," and she pointed.

"Excuse me?"

"Relieve me from stress, and be quick about it!"

"Ma'am, I was going to explain to you the present condition of Lieutenant Eden."

"Exactly. He's not here with his man-thang, relieving me from all this stress. Instead, here you are. Different methods, but my need, alas, remains the same."

"Perhaps in your universe, ma'am, that would be appropriate."

Sighing, Hadriana let her head settle back and she stared at the ceiling. "Jimmy came in fourth in the last Olympics, you know."

"Yes, ma'am."

"So basically, this universe of yours is all about repression, compensation, frustration and, ultimately, boredom."

"Ma'am, we had just returned from a rather harrowing mission to a planet. It involved a crashed shuttle and gigantic anthropoids with can openers and spears. When Captain Hadrian inquired on the performance of my team I replied that they behaved in an exemplary manner. Between you and me, ma'am, I must now admit to having overstated my team's performance somewhat."

"Attempted mutiny?"

"Multiple attempts, ma'am."

"But in the end you reined them in, and saved all their lives."

"Well—"

"The perils of command, Sin-Dour! Get used to it! All the second-guessing, the muttering behind the back and looks between officers and whatnot, it comes with the territory." She laced her hands behind her head. "Of course, in my universe, we've got Polaski to take it all out on, but here—"

Tammy cut in from a speaker. "DNA analysis complete. Captain Hadriana is from a bonobo-derived evolutionary lineage, Commander Sin-Dour. Sexualized conflict resolution . . . rather effective, one presumes. Except for poor Polaski, of course."

Hadriana frowned over at Sin-Dour. "That's your rogue AI parasite?"

"Parasite?" Tammy shrieked, then in a calmer voice added, "Well, now that you mention it . . ."

"Yes," Sin-Dour replied to the captain. "His name is Tammy Wynette."

"Hmm, while on the *Woeful Child*, my Merle's lost her marbles."

"Whereas *I* am thoroughly sane!" Tammy retorted. "I can't believe I'm about to say this, but I want my old captain back!"

"The giant amorphous vessel has dropped out of T-Space and is making for Planet Wallykrappe . . . sir."

Hadrian looked up from his game of 3D tiddlywinks where he knelt on the carpet opposite a ridiculously obsequious Polaski. "Finally! All this excitement was getting to me!"

Sin-Dour cleared her throat. "As I said earlier, sir, we are all in concurrence, with respect to not tainting your command style, bearing in mind that one day you will return to your own universe. Clearly, our methods are inappropriate in your sad, rather pathetic universe."

"Maybe, but I'd be willing to give it the old college try! And in the meantime, since I'm here and everything, why, you should proceed on the basis to which you are collectively and socially accustomed, yes? Except for beating up my cousin, that is." Hadrian climbed to his feet and looked round. The bridge officers were all staring at him. "What now?"

"Polaski, sir," explained Sin-Dour, "has a vital function. If not him upon whom we can vent our frustrations, why, there would be chaos. Indeed, anarchy. Vicious arguments and knives in the back."

Hadrian frowned. "Speaking of which, where did Tighe go, anyway?"

Sin-Dour sniffed. "Knowing her, she's now in your stateroom, lying naked on your bed. Awaiting your arrival."

"Was I planning on heading down there? Okay, a badly worded query under the circumstances. I mean . . . oh, never mind." He turned to the viewscreen. The alien vessel looked intent on establishing an orbit around Wallykrappe. He squinted at the grayish planet's surface, barely visible in the brown dwarf's meager light. "Twice a solar year," he said musingly, "half the civilian population of the Affiliation descends on Wallykrappe during the Mondo Galaxy Nadir Sale. Hundreds of thousands die in a mindless purchasing frenzy. Trampled, stabbed, shot, eyes plucked out, hair torn from heads. Babies are roasted, puppies tortured, cats ignored . . . all in all, a modern manifestation of Biblical Hell."

Sin-Dour moved up alongside him. "More or less the same in this universe, sir."

"Right, but, 2IC, take a look at that planet. Anything strike you as odd about it?"

"Well, sir, it's hard to make out through all the orbiting billboards with their blinking lights, strobes, lasers, and inflated waving cacti."

"Keep looking."

"Hmm, no Mall-Glow . . ."

"Right. The whole planet should be glowing that irritating orange tungsten glow from all the ship-stall parkades."

"Sir," said Jocelyn Sticks, "another ship has appeared from the other side of the planet. Registry . . . oh, it's a vessel from the Wallykrappe Monitoring Fleet . . . uhm, the *Best Buys of Humanity,* sir."

The officer at Comms, whom Hadrian did not know, now said, "Captain, the *Best Buys of Humanity* is hailing us."

"Onscreen, Comms."

The bridge of the Wallykrappe ship appeared, hazy with smoke, sparks spitting from consoles, wires hanging down. No bridge officers were present behind the battered and bruised captain, who sat in obvious pain in her command chair. "Can you hear me?" the woman demanded. "Can you see me? My screen's out, everything's red-lining or systems-down! You there? Dammit, is anyone hearing me?"

"I hear you just fine," Hadrian replied. "This is Captain Hadrian Sawback of the, uh, the AFS *Woeful Child*. Who are you?"

"At least we got audio! Thank crap for that! Hadrian, is it? That's not right—you're supposed to be a woman! What have Spacefleet and the Affiliation come to these days? Next it'll be a man as Galactic President! Never mind, what the fuck do I care? Listen—that alien vessel—it's back! My ship's the only one left from our Defense Fleet! That horrible alien ship ate all the rest of them! Beware its maw, Captain! When it opens up, Dear Darwin, the horror, the horror!"

"What's your name?" Hadrian asked again.

"Me? Me? Babble. Georgina Babble—"

"What is the condition of the planet, Captain Babble?"

The woman's face twisted. "Cleaned out! Every Continental Aisle! Top to bottom, and then they took the shelves!"

"And the employees?"

"What? Oh, you mean the Ilulds?"

"The what?"

"Indentured Labor Units Legally Designated as Subhuman, of course. They got bought up, too! There's not a damned thing left on that planet!"

"So," said Hadrian, "just your normal Mondo Galaxy Nadir Sale, then."

Babble tore at her hair with both hands, framing eyes so wide the whites showed on all sides. *"That starts tomorrow!"*

"Holy Darwin!" whispered Sin-Dour. "Captain,

when half the Affiliation descends on this planet to-morrow . . . millions will die in a global maelstrom of thwarted acquisitiveness. All those self-esteems denied the artificial validation they so desperately require . . . they'll go mad, or, rather, madder than normal."

Hadrian rubbed at his jaw. "Yes but might that not break the habit?"

"At a cost of tens of millions of dead shoppers!"

"Yes but . . . they're *Wallykrappe* shoppers!" Seeing the look of shock on her face, he sighed. "Oh of course you're right, 2IC. Some strange surge of endorphins got me all caught up in, as you say, horrifying possibilities. Oh dear."

Sin-Dour patted his arm. "It's just your silly little man's brain, I suppose."

"And now that ship's back!" shrieked Babble from the screen.

"Captain Babble, do calm down," said Hadrian. "Have you been in contact with WallyVault Central?"

Babble leaned forward, drool dangling from her lower lip. *"They took that too!"*

"What? Are you saying the Vault was breached? Are you saying that Joebang Wallykrappe, owner and Chief Executive Officer, is now inside that giant alien ship?"

"Lady Jillian Wallykrappe in this universe, her nine-teen cloned children, her harem of three thousand seventy-two husbands, her entire Personal Security Force of Ten Thousand Reconstituted Spartans, all of them, Captain Sawback, gone! Devoured, like so many caramel-coated peanuts!"

Sin-Dour said, "WallyVault was said to be the most secure and impregnable Rich Woman Fortress in all the Affiliation. Buried a kilometer beneath the planet's bedrock. Sir, if Jillian proved vulnerable, no one is safe!"

"Captain," said Jocelyn Sticks, "there are strange energy readings now coming from the alien vessel."

"On the viewscreen, Sticks!"

The enormous, misshapen ship was now no longer moon-shaped, but stretched out, and the end facing them had opened to reveal a vast, cavernous maw from which raging light poured forth.

Babble's voice screamed, *"They want more! But there's nothing left! They've already crashed the economy of the entire Affiliation! Stock markets are reeling, manufacturers are closing shop, shortages everywhere, the Ilulds in revolt! Slaughter in the aisles has spilled out into the streets! Cities are burning, planets dying!"*

"Oh be quiet, Babble!" snapped Hadrian, eyes narrowing on the alien vessel as it drew closer. "And get your ship out of here—where's your crew, by the way?"

"My crew? My crew? We tried stopping the thing, but it was no use! The ship was crippled! We were in its path! I dropped them down onto the second planet— Mass Displacement of everyone but me!"

Hadrian frowned. "Captain, there is no second planet in this system. Never has been."

"Oh sure, I know that now! Sensor malfunction! Not my fault!"

"So where is your crew?" Hadrian demanded.

"Brown Dwarfs look a lot like planets, you know!

You can't blame me—I went to Wallykrappe College—we don't do science!"

Hadrian rubbed at his face. "You displaced your crew to the surface of a star?"

"It's a brown dwarf. All brownish! Can't be that hot, can it? Only, they didn't answer my hails. Nothing but static. Horrible, horrible static!"

Joss Sticks twisted in her chair. "Captain, the *Best Buys of Humanity* has hit its afterburners and is heading straight for the alien vessel!"

"Captain Babble, what are you doing? Turn that thing around!"

"No! I'm taking it down! I got the T-Drive on Infinite Oxyom Compiler! The Irridiculum Crystals are cycling up to Eternal Expansion in an Explosive Manner! One last sale, Captain! And out with a bang! Everything must go! Hahahahahahaha—"

Hadrian turned to Sin-Dour. "We're in a Full Multiverse Displacement Event, in an altered Infinite Causality Paradigm through All-Dimensional Wave-Fronts."

"Yes, sir. I'm not sure–"

"And it's pretty damn likely that my universe's counterpart—your captain Hadriana—is even now facing the same situation, and that she has my *Willful Child* here, too."

"No doubt, but—"

"And who knows how many other iterations in the multiverses have all converged here at this point at this time." Hadrian faced the screen again, on which he could now see the *Best Buys of Humanity* racing toward the gaping maw of the alien vessel. "If we *all* experience a Sublimated Expansion of the Irridiculum Crystals, across all Dimensions, we could bring about the end of not just this universe, but every universe!"

"Sir, are you sure?"

"No, of course I'm not sure, 2IC! And with Merle Haggard trapped in a squawk-box of madness . . ." He spun to face his Chief Engineer. "Buck! Can you—"

DeFrank suddenly started bawling. "At least you c-c-coulda—" he sobbed.

"I coulda what?"

"Y-y-you coulda said *mmm b-b-buh* said something like, 'nice dress' . . . at least once!"

Hadrian stared at his Chief Engineer. "Okay," he said, "nice dress. Now, we need some equations—"

"*Too late!*" shrieked DeFrank. "I'm never helping you ever again!" And he ran from the bridge, swirly fabric skirling in his wake.

"Well," said Sin-Dour, "he had a point."

"He what? Oh let me guess, false compliments to a hairy man in a dress are essential to bridge harmony?"

Sin-Dour's eyes flashed and she straightened. "He's your Chief Engineer, so yes, they are quite necessary!"

"Wait! What about Spunk? In my universe, my robot guard dog possesses an advanced Neutratronic Processor coupled with a Dimwit Special Vocader—" and he ran to the cupboard where Spunk was stored.

"Sir, wait!"

But he had the tiny robot dog out and hit the on switch.

"Mistress! Bad hair day? So sorry! Lap now! Spunk wants lap! Lap! Lap! Now! Now! Lap!"

"Not now, Spunk! Activate your Neutratronic Override De—"

"Lap! Lap! Lap! Lap lap lap lap! Or yap! Yap yap yap yap yap—"

"No! Look—get off humping my friggin' leg, damn you!"

"Yap yap lap lap yap yap lap lap yap—"

"Stop! Sit!"

"Shit!"

Everyone on the bridge moaned.

Hadrian kicked the robot dog, sending the Shitzer, trailing a sausage string of poop, flying into the far wall, where both broke into numerous pieces.

In the shocked silence that followed, he swung back to face the screen. "Well," he said calmly, "this one's out of my hands."

"S-sir?"

"It's down to your Hadriana now, 2IC, back in my universe, with a functioning rogue AI and a genius robot guard dog." He settled into the command chair. "Oh, best brace for impact. This could be a wild ride here. Who knows, maybe nonexistence and oblivion isn't so bad."

"Sorry sir," said Sin-Dour. "It seems that we have all failed you."

"No kidding," replied Hadrian, then he brightened. "But you know, a hand-job would go a long way toward—"

* * *

"—offending absolutely everybody," Hadriana finished.

"Par for the course," the chicken commented. "Now, I suggest a Reverse Polarity beam on wide dispersal against the *Selling Humanity By The Pound,* which will affect an Inverse Phased Implosion to counter the Infinite Expansion of the Irrididculum Crystals, thus negating the Multiverse Oxyom Negation Effect. Oh, and we need to do that sometime in the next eleven seconds. . . ."

Hadriana pursed her luscious lips—she knew they were luscious, no point in being modest about it—then said, "Spark? Do you concur?"

"Yes, Haddie!"

"Very well then. Galk! Target *Selling Humanity By The Pound* with a wide-dispersal Reverse Polarity beam and fire. Immediately!"

The ship rocked as the beam lanced out.

Startled, Hadriana gripped the arms of the command chair. "What was that?"

"Oh," said Tammy, "that was just me. For effect."

Hadriana eyed the chicken. "How does he stand you?" she asked.

"Sir!" cried Jocelyn Sticks. "The Wallykrappe ship is about to enter the Maw!"

All eyes fixed on the scene on the vast viewscreen. In the instant the ship slipped into the enormous hole, the *Selling Humanity By The Pound* glowed bright white, then green, and then winked out.

* * *

Eyes closed as he leaned back in the command chair, Hadrian waited for her soft, warm hand to slip down into his lap—he tugged his trousers farther down to facilitate matters. "I'm ready," he said.

"In your dreams," Tammy Wynette replied.

Hadrian's eyes snapped open and he quickly sat up. "Oh, crap, I'm back. I swear, this and every other universe is out to get me—or, rather, keep me from–"

"Sir," said Sin-Dour, "you might want to pull up your trousers."

"Huh? Oh, right." He quickly yanked his black stretchy polyester slacks back up around his deflating anticipation. Looking around as he did so, he added, "Hey, it was a Bonoboverse!"

"We know, sir," said Sin-Dour.

"Besides, the universe was about to end!"

"Understood, sir."

Joss Sticks had twisted round in her chair. "It's, like, all right, like, sir. We had Hadriana, after all, not that I, like, had her or anything, though she wanted me to, well, I was . . . well, *whatever,* like, she's my captain and all, and before you knew it all our clothes were off, only then Commander Sin-Dour came back to the bridge and it was, *Oh! Dear me!* And that was sweet, you know? And then—"

"Stop now," begged Hadrian in a weak tone, "please stop now. Please."

"Captain!" cut in a Comms officer Hadrian didn't recognize, "the Unknown Alien Vessel is hailing us!"

"Is it now? Well then, whoever you are, onscreen."

The bridge that appeared on the viewer was a solid

mass of discounted sales items, fleshy body parts, mangled shopping carts, crumpled cardboard and reams of plastic wrap.

Leaning forward, Hadrian could make out a single eye blinking at them from the center of the image. Then a female voice spoke. "We were Plog. We were once the Collected. Now we are Bag, and we are the Collectibles. We recognize you, Captain Hadrian Sawback, AFS *Willful Child*. You once contributed an eyelid, a very nice eyelid, by the way, to the Plog Collected. We deem you Friend and therefore Not To Be Purchased. All else in this Galaxy must be Purchased. This is Prime Imperative."

"Oh," said Hadrian, "you again. Only different. Hold on, I thought you were from another galaxy?"

"Purchased."

"I see. And now you're here to purchase this one."

"Consume is essential to satisfy Prime Imperative. Must Consume. Consume or Die."

"Hey, that's humanity's credo, too!"

"You will now surrender all other personnel on your ship, offered at a One-Time Discount of . . . not $59.95, folks . . . not $49.95, people, no! Not even $39.95! On this One Day and One Day Only, for all you out there (meaning us), a Rock-Bottom Bargain, a Mind-Blowing *Extravaganza* of a Deal . . . that's right! Going for This Day Only . . . *$19.95!* Line 'em up! Ship 'em out! Going fast! You heard me—not a misprint, not a typo, not a garbled transmission! $19.95!"

"I'm sorry," said Hadrian, "but I need my crew, for the proper functioning of this ship. If you bought them from me, even at the Rock-Bottom Bargain of $19.95, why, I wouldn't be able to be your Friend anymore."

The single eye blinked rapidly. "What? Not Friend?"

"No, I'm afraid not. Besides, Bag, you're looking pretty full up in there. I doubt they'd even fit."

"We bought everything available on planet below. We bought everything available on Shopping Channel, including commemorative plates at a One-Time Purchase Price of $17.99. Suggested Retail Price? $299.99! We Saved $282.00 on each commemorative plate. If you want to buy back our thirty-nine million commemorative plates, which are commemorative plates that commemorate everything that has ever happened, you have to pay the Full Price. Not that we're selling."

"Too rich for my wallet," said Hadrian. "Anyway, the question remains, how do you fit it all in?"

"This is Destabilizing Dilemma, we admit. Bag is Full. Crammed Full. Packed to the Rafter Full."

"That's what happens when you have a Prime Imperative to buy, well, *everything*. I mean, where do you put it all? You'd need a whole—why, you'd need a whole galaxy to fit in everything in the galaxy! Wouldn't you? I humbly suggest you reinitiate your basic terms of definition, and consider each and every galaxy as simply one giant bag. True, not crammed full, but plenty full compared to the vast nothingness *between* galaxies."

"Then what shall be our Designation?"

"I don't know—wait, how about we call you The Purse?"

"The Purse? The Purse. We are The Purse."

"Right," said Hadrian. "That's a fine name."

"What is function of The Purse?"

"Why, to collect loose change. There's got to be plenty of that floating around, on planets, in space, in asteroid belts."

"We are The Purse. We Collect Loose Change. It is Prime Imperative, to Scrimp and Save, to Count Pennies so that the Dollars take Care of Themselves."

"You really bought into that Shopping Channel, didn't you?"

"The Language of Consumer Culture is most colorful. At last count, this language possesses twenty-nine thousand four hundred fifty-six words and phrases to replace and deflect the immoral concept of 'greed.' It possesses Four Volumes of Rationalizations, Nine Volumes of Justifications, and a Handy Quick-Chart of Suitable False Definitions of the concept of 'need,' an essential resource to be used at the Moment of Indecision in Conjunction with Mouth-Watering Pupil-Dilating Desire. We have purchased the publisher, and, this one time only, we offer you the two-hundred-eleven-volume *Language of Consumer Culture* for just $39.95 a month."*

"Or," said Hadrian, "I could just listen to the Shopping Channel."

"Purchased. See enclosed leaflet for New and Improved Changes to Subscription Rate, meaning you now pay more for less but feel better about it so long

---

*OAP, an interest rate of 43.97%, over a period of no less than one hundred ninety-nine point nine nine years, see finer print and contract terms on following nanodot [.].

as you don't actually think about Declining Services as a symbol of Progress because between you and me, we both know that declining services means your civilization is falling to pieces. But hey, just don't think about it, and buy *this*!"

Hadrian sighed. "Right. Now, Purse, about all those people you purchased . . . they happen to include Mr. Joebang Wallykrappe, a very wealthy man, so wealthy, in fact, that he owns whole planets across the entire, likely infinite, multiverse. So rich he can—and has—bought entire civilizations."

"We Purchased him. We bought out all his assets."

"He willingly sold himself?"

"Past Prime Imperative discounts notion that any Purchased Object possesses self-actualizing potential."

"Ah, so where is he now?"

"Dismantled and sold piecemeal, barring his Anus, which was purchased at auction by the New Amalgamated Union of ILULDS for a Bargain Price of sixty-one cents."

"And the fate of this hapless anus?"

"Now the repository of the Amalgamated Union's individual, most-personal sacrifice of One Left Thumb Per Person."

"His old indentured store employees have all cut off a thumb to shove it up their old boss's ass?"

"Correct."

"You do realize, Purse, that you have severely damaged the Affiliation's entire economic system."

"Purchased."

"You bought us up?"

"Correct. At the Rock-Bottom Bargain Extravaganza—"

"Purse, forgive my interruption, please, but since you are now The Purse, and no longer the Bag, nor even the Plog, all these acquisitions are now superfluous to your Prime Imperative."

"This is true. The Purse, Captain Hadrian Sawback, is confused."

"There are people who you can hire to help unclutter your life, Purse."

"Really?"

"Indeed. Are you interested in a few contacts?"

"You are True Friend, Captain Hadrian Sawback. Because of you, The Purse shall not Expunge the Galaxy in a Fit of Delirious Liquidation. In fact, we already feel . . . *free*!"

Hadrian raised a hand. "Tammy, if you would, ping a handful of reputable De-Clutter Guru sites over to The Purse, and why not in Business Card format? Ideal for those little plastic sleeves so common to both wallets and purses."

"Done," the chicken replied. "You know, Captain—"

But Hadrian gestured and then said to The Purse, "You know, something's just occurred to me, Purse."

"Tell The Purse! Please!"

"There's these hoarding, well, anti-pirates, called the Falangee. Collectors of knickknacks and used furniture, among other things. I suddenly had a thought about all those old sofas they have in their ships. As inevitable repositories for loose change . . . well."

"The Purse shall find these Falangee at once and insist upon the Minute Examination of their Old Sofas."

"Oh, they'd love that, I'm sure."

"Excellent. Goodbye, Most Esteemed Friend Hadrian Sawback. And as a gift to you of our appreciation, we confer upon you all the wealth of Dismembered CEO Designation 312.76, otherwise known as Joebang Wallykrappe Unit."

"*What?*"

"Just kidding. Hah hah. Being Insanely Rich (such as are The Purse) is a terrible, soul-devouring burden. We would never do that to you. But we would like to present you with a commemorative plate."

"Oh, why, thank you. Alas, as captain of a Spacefleet vessel, I cannot accept gifts of any sort while engaged in an official capacity."

"Too bad," said the Purse, "since we were actually kidding about not giving you all the wealth once possessed by Dismembered CEO Designation 312.76. Well then, thanks again, Most Esteemed Friend Hadrian Sawback."

With a sickly smile, Hadrian said, "No problem."

"And know that you are Most Welcome and next time you're in our Neighborhood . . . Come on down! The Doors are Open and they're All Linin' Up! Coffee, cakes, cookies for Everyone! Free Balloons for the Kids!"

"Check that, Purse. Until then . . ."

The giant transgalactic bag-ship vanished in a swirl of frayed burlap fibers and lint.

Sin-Dour settled a soft, warm hand on Hadrian's shoulder. "Once again, sir, you appear to have saved the Affiliation from utter annihilation at the hands of aliens."

"Oh that's easy, 2IC," Hadrian replied. "The real challenge that we still face is," and he stood, assuming his most noble but determined expression, "saving the Affiliation from *itself*."

Stentorian music thundered through the bridge.

"Tammy!"

Sitting at Comms Station, Temporal Agent Klinghanger kept his back to the captain as he surreptitiously pulled out his Hadrian-Specific Timeline Fucking-Up Gauge. The meter was wildly oscillating. *Uh-oh, what now?*

"One other thing," the captain said from the command chair, "get Security up here and arrest the imposter at the Comms Station."

Klinghanger spun in his chair, pulling out his Temporal Resetter. "I don't know anything! I mean, I won't, when I do this!" *Click! Click click click click!*

"Tammy," inquired Hadrian, "what just happened?"

"Oh dear," the AI moaned.

"Let it be understood," said Captain Hans Olo to his bridge crew, "that my command to hightail it out of there was both prudent and By The Book. Granted, the annihilation of every universe in the Multiverse Continuum would have meant that no distance would suffice to effect our survival. That said, a somewhat smaller explosion *was* possible." He paused, adjusted his immaculate uniform. "For the record, my concern over the fate of my ship and crew forced upon me the unprecedented All Burners Emergency Withdrawal." And he turned to glare at Special Agent Rand Humblenot.

Who smiled. "Precisely, Captain. Of course, it turned out that Captain Hadrian has somehow saved the universe—every universe—once again. More to the point, we have lost contact with the *Willful Child*."

"Which we shall endeavor to correct at once. Helm, return us to Wallykrappe System. Let's see if we can pick up their trail. Ion particles, radiation, we'll scour the area until we find it."

"Yes sir!"

"Number 2!"

Frank Worship passed out, his head thumping as he fell to the deck.

"Never mind. I am heading to my stateroom to study . . . uh, starcharts. Lieutenant Reasonable, you have the con."

"Yes sir. I have the con."

After the captain had left, Reasonable left the Science Station and took the captain's chair. She settled into its luxuriant leather padding, glanced down at the supine form of Commander Frank Worship.

The Helm officer twisted in his chair. "Ma'am, should we call for a Medic?"

"No need," Reasonable replied. "He'll come around shortly, I'm sure."

"But—the way his head bounced!"

"Nothing important was damaged that hasn't been damaged . . . what, five times before? Leave him be."

"Approaching Wallykrappe System, Ma'am."

"Excellent. Sensor sweep as soon as we arrive."

The Helm officer sighed. "I can't believe everything's sold out! It's a dead world now, lifeless, empty, nothing but wrappers and cardboard!"

"Planned on doing some shopping while we were here, Lieutenant Placard?"

The man turned, rubbing at his hairless pate. "We all were, Ma'am. A commemorative plate, for just $17.99!"

At the Comms Station, Special Temporal Agent Shattenkrak repeatedly tried to contact his co-agent on the *Willful Child*, without success. Panic made all his orifices pucker tight, and his breathing turned shallow and rapid. Temporal communication devices employed disjunctive atemporal resonance frequencies on the Infinite Loop Bandwidth—no matter where Klinghanger was, he should be receiving the ping.

Ping back, you fool! Ping!

Unless . . . they've gone into the past! Or the future! Or anywhere Not Now! This is an NN Discontinuity Event!

A hand fell on his shoulder, and he heard Lieutenant Reasonable's voice right behind him. "Have we met, Comms?"

Shattenkrak spun in his chair. "No!" he shouted. "And now we never will because I'm going to regress to when I didn't know anything!" And he held up a device that went *click!*

"I see," said Reasonable. "Rather, I don't see. Was that supposed to; uh, do something?"

Shattenkrak scowled. "You're not the Guidance Counselor! Get your fuckin' hand off me or I'm calling my parents! I never skipped that class! I was just sitting real low in my desk!" He frowned suddenly and held up the device in his hand.

Click!

"I don't eat liver! Don't make me eat liver! You're the worst babysitter ever and I hate you! I'm calling my parents!"

Click!

"Can you make bubbles with your farts? I can, wanna see? Sure ya do!"

"No! Stop that!"

"I can do whatever I want and you can't stop me! I'm calling my parents!"

Click!

"Mommy! Mommy! Why'd you leave me in the alley? *Mummyyyyyy!*"

Janice Reasonable studied the comms officer, who was now blowing bubbles with his spit. "Hmm, most curious." She activated her comms at the command chair. "Doctor Yoga to the bridge please."

There was a faint hiss, and then came the reply: "Yoga bridge come now certainly!"

Reasonable rubbed at her eyes and sighed.

At the helm, Placard said in a low voice, "Commander, is there something odd about our new doctor?"

"Well," drawled Janice, "I don't know. Odd in what

way, assuming you discount that our ship surgeon appears to be a two-foot-tall animatronic robot covered in wrinkly latex? Oh, and with a glitch in its syntax programming?"

Placard hesitated, and then said, "Discounting all that . . ." He frowned. "Never mind, ma'am. Apologies for asking." But after a moment he faced her again. "Ma'am, I've heard, well, rumors—"

Janice's eyes hardened. "Rumors, Lieutenant?"

"Uh, yes ma'am. About a secret, uhm, manual. The Sarcasm Manual, ma'am."

The commander relaxed into the command chair. "Oh, that. What about it?"

"Sh-should I, uh, maybe read it? I mean, assuming I can find a copy, that is. If it's not, well, Classified above my Security Clearance Rating."

"Sorry, Lieutenant," said Janice, "I'm afraid it is. Above your rating. Now, of course, you have something to which to aspire."

Placard sagged in his seat.

"Something wrong, Lieutenant?"

He muttered something while facing forward once again.

"I'm sorry," Janice said, "what was that you said?"

He rubbed at his pate and then shrugged. "Aspirations, ma'am."

"What of them?"

"I'm a fifty-seven-year-old helm officer with the lofty rank of lieutenant, ma'am." He smiled sheepishly. "I think I'm done with aspirations."

After a long moment, Janice nodded. "Good point. Carry on, Lieutenant."

"Yes ma'am, thank you, ma'am."

Dr. Yoga arrived, robed and hobbling on a stick.

Seeing the tiny, wrinkly, green-skinned ghoul, the imposter at Comms burst into tears.

"Ah!" said Yoga. "Manner bedside intact, yes? Observe all as closer I walk! Mhmmmm?" With that he glided forward, as if on tracks, though the robe of course hid all such details.

At the helm station, Placard's frown turned into a scowl. "He's not real at all! I can hear the treads!"

"Now now," murmured Janice, "I'm sure there's some reasonable explanation. I will bring it up with the captain. Does that satisfy you, Lieutenant Placard? Excellent."

"Mmhmmm?" wheedled Yoga. "Explanation satisfy, yes! Booboo someone has? Mhmm?"

"Your patient," said Janice, "is the one crying at the Comms Station."

"Mhmmm? Mhmmm . . . mhmmm." Yoga trundled over.

The man recoiled, still bawling.

Yoga began waving his latex hands in front of the imposter. "Mhmm. Mhmm? Mhmm mhmm mhmmm. Mhmmm."

"He has no Medical Pentracorder," hissed Placard.

"Lieutenant," came the deep voice of Agent Rand Humblenot, "he *is* a Medical Pentracorder. A mobile one. You will find such a device replacing all Ship Surgeons in

Spacefleet, before too long." He moved up to stand beside the command chair.

Janice grunted. "And making it look like a gnome? Oh, I know. Yoga is also a hobby gardener?"

Rand Humblenot drew off his sunglasses, his optic implants immediately darkening. "The allusion escapes me, Commander. As for this particular model's latex covering, and its odd way of speaking, alas, that was down to Captain Olo's specifications."

"Hmm," said Janice.

Yoga's head whipped round, rather erratically. "Hmmm? Mhmmm? Mhmm!"

"Someone shoot it," Placard whispered. *"Please, someone shoot it."*

FiVE

The man sitting at the Comms Station was frowning as he studied the small device in his hands. "Something went wrong," he moaned. "Glitch. Run diagnostic . . . uh-oh, glitch designated Mondo Holy Fuck You've Done it Now." He looked up. "It was all a mistake!"

Security arrived in the form of Nina Twice. Hadrian gestured. "Take this imposter to the brig. Oh and search him carefully and confiscate all his equipment."

Nina hooked one hand under the imposter's arm and dragged him off the bridge.

Hadrian returned to the command chair. "Tammy?"

"Oh dear."

"Sir," gasped Jocelyn Sticks, "look at Wallykrappe Planet!"

On the viewscreen, the planet, which had only moments before been a lifeless shade of milky brown over which dusty wisps of cloud scudded in frail threads, was now glittering like diamonds, strewn across every land mass.

"Hmm," ventured Hadrian. "Now one wonders, is

this deep past or the far future? Because either way, that's not the Mall Planet we all knew, is it?"

Sin-Dour, now at the Science Station, said, "Captain, shipboard chronometer indicates that we are a thousand years in the future." She turned to look at the planet. "Sir, the energy readings from the surface are off the scale."

"Hmm again," said Hadrian.

At that moment a bright white beam shot up from the planet, bathing the ship in a blinding, actinic glare.

"Oh crap," said Tammy.

"Tractor beam!" shouted Jocelyn Sticks, struggling with the tiny toggle. "We're, like, trapped!"

Time suddenly slowed down. Trying to stand, Hadrian fought against a strange force that held him down in the command chair. There was a second flash and a figure displaced onto the bridge, blurry as it moved without restraint to collect Tammy the chicken. It then placed some kind of hood over the chicken's head, only to remove it again an instant later. Then the figure vanished, and time returned to normal.

Hadrian leapt upright. "Holy crap!"

Spark clanked to his side. "Master! Intruder! Here! Gone! Time Dilation Zone imposed, Temporal Bubble deployed!"

The door hissed open and the stranger from Comms reappeared, sprawled on the floor this time and dragging Nina Twice—also on the floor—as she held onto him by one ankle. The man's eyes were wild. "Don't go down there! That planet's Off-Limits, No-Go-There, Verboten, Run-While-You-Can!"

Hadrian scowled. "You're a temporal agent, aren't you?"

"Just get us out of here!"

The chicken was now walking in aimless circles and although there was nothing unusual about that, Hadrian's eyes narrowed on the creature. "Tammy?"

No reply.

"Sin-Dour, examine the chicken with your Pentracorder, please."

She approached the chicken warily, and then held out her Pentracorder. "Captain, the skull of this chicken appears to be completely empty."

"Well nothing new there," Hadrian replied. "Calibrate to detect Neutratronic Emissions, including the ship-mainframe."

"Yes sir. Uhm . . . nothing!" She swung to face Hadrian. "Sir, they've stolen Tammy's brain!"

"Captain," said Jocelyn Sticks, "the tractor beam's gone!"

Hadrian activated the comms switch on the command chair's arm. "Galk! To the Insisteon Chamber. We're going down to the planet." He turned to the robot guard dog. "Spark, keep Sin-Dour company here on the bridge. Buck, you're with me. Oh, who else? Well, the Doc, I suppose, since you never know, surgery might be required, and the more hands in the mix, why, the better."

"Don't do it!" shrieked the temporal agent.

Hadrian studied the man lying on the floor. "Have you got a name?"

"Klinghanger, Walter D. Special Temporal Agent—oh, make her let go of my ankle!"

"Release him, Nina."

"Yes sir." Nina jumped to her feet. "Sorry sir, he took me by surprise."

Klinghanger remained prone. "I think she broke it! I think I'm dying . . . yes! Starting to fade . . . fade . . . oh, the pain, the pain . . ." He frowned. "The pain's going away. Gone, in fact. Am I dead? I must be dead!"

"You're not dead," explained Hadrian. "It's much worse than that. So here we are, trapped in the future thanks to some glitch on that device of yours. Your present, one presumes. Which is why you're acting as if this planet is not only well known to the Affiliation of your time, it's also considered dangerous and is therefore quarantined. Correct?"

The agent sat up. "It *was* my present, before I went back into the past, which was your present at the time but isn't now, since you're in the future, which used to be my present but now it's my future too. I mean, where I used to live. The point is, you can't do anything here in this present, which is your future, because if you do then the past changes and so does the future, which might mean that I'm never born and if I'm never born I can't be sent back into the past, which is your present, in order to make sure you don't do anything to mess up the future, even if it was already in the past for me, though not when I was on your ship, of course, since that was both our present—"

"Was that supposed to make sense?" Hadrian asked.

"No, wait. I can't do anything in the past unless it's

already happened, in which case I already did it! Because I wouldn't be in my present, which was your future, unless everything worked out, but now I'm back in my present, only you're here too! And we have no record of that ever happening! The timeline is skewed!"

"No record, huh? Fine then, whatever we do here and now, don't record it."

Klinghanger frowned. "What? I mean . . . why that's brilliant!" He laughed. "We can do whatever we want! No, wait! You're supposed to be back there, not here, so whatever you were supposed to be doing right now, back then, isn't happening! See what you've done!"

"But it was you who messed up, Klinghanger," Hadrian pointed out. "The glitch, remember? In other words, if you hadn't come from the future to mess around with me in your past, none of us would now be trapped here in your present, which is our future, correct?"

Horror filled Klinghanger's face. "Ohmigawd, an Infinite Causality Loop! And it's all my fault!"

"Tell me about the planet below."

"I won't! I refuse!"

"Fine," said Hadrian, "then you're coming down with me."

"No! Please!"

"Nina, get this guy in a proper arm-lock this time and come along."

"Yes sir!"

Hadrian picked up the brainless chicken and tucked it under an arm. "Sin-Dour, you have command of the vessel, but for now, I need you on the scanners—see if you can detect a displacement trail, and transmit those coordinates down to the Insisteon Rhetorical Alignment Designator."

"Yes, Captain, and good luck on retrieving Tammy's brain." She stepped close as if to embrace or even kiss him, but instead she handed him her Pentracorder. "It's set on Neutratronic Detection."

"Oh, right. Guess I'll need that." He smiled.

She cleared her throat. "I'd better get to that sensor trail, sir."

"Right." He sighed. "Off you go then." Hadrian then gestured to Nina, who picked up Klinghanger and held him by hitching one of his arms behind his back.

He winced and then glared at Hadrian. "You fools! You fools! And she's breaking my arm!"

They gathered in the Insisteon Chamber. Hadrian turned to Galk. "Tell me you're properly armed."

"I am, sir." He held up a shapeless little pistol-gripped thing of matte black. "A Mister Shrill Mark III Sonic Concatenator."

"Outstanding. What does it do?"

"Makes sounds like fingernails on a blackboard. Temporarily incapacitates everyone."

"Including us?"

"Well, yes, but being so well trained, we should be the first ones to recover."

"Unless, of course, we meet aliens who talk like fingernails on a blackboard."

Galk frowned, worked the wad bulging his cheek

around for a moment, and then said, "Hadn't occurred to me, sir."

"That's all right, Galk." Hadrian turned to the others. "Doc, you ready?"

The Belkri lifted a massive leather bag with most of its hands. "My surgical instruments, Captain, as requested."

"Wow, that's a lot of instruments, Doc. What did you bring?"

Printlip inflated until it squeaked and then said, "I brought an assortment of Ligating Clips, as well as Ultrasonic lancets, levers, mallet, rasp, saw, skids and buttons. Metzenbaum rectal scissors with a curlicue spinaret, various nerve hooks, trephines, trolars, and of course a Quantum Defibrillating Intramedullary Kinetic Brain Distractor." Deflated, the doctor sagged and rolled onto one side. An instant later the Belkri began reinflating once more. "Captain, you did that on purpose!"

"You give as good as you take, Doc," Hadrian said as he slapped Printlip on what he assumed was its back. "Rectal scissors and a kinetic brain distractor, huh?"

Printlip puffed up. "What an outrageous accusation!"

"Better now? Good." Hadrian swung round. "Buck? Nina? Excellent, onto the pads then."

Sin-Dour's voice came to them from a speaker. *"Captain, we have coordinates. The Rhetorical Alignment Designator is set."*

"Good work, 2IC!"

"Sir, the planet remains one giant mall, as far as we can tell, but there is a central concourse containing high-end power units, from which the kidnapper displaced.

You will appear approximately fifty meters from that position."

"Any life signs down there?"

"*Curiously, no, sir.*"

Klinghanger started whimpering.

"Very well. Okay everyone, get ready. Displace!"

They arrived in a broad corridor between what appeared to be two dioramic display rooms, one a kitchen, the other a bedroom. There was no one in sight. Hadrian pulled out the Pentracorder. "All right," he said quietly, "let's get this done with as little fuss as possible. I'm detecting Neutratronic emissions, forty-three meters that way."

"Through the kitchen?" asked Galk.

"Well, not directly, since that seems impossible. We'll need to circle round." Hadrian gestured to a set of doors twenty meters down the corridor. "That way."

They set off. Hadrian glanced back and said, "You can let him go now, Nina. I doubt he's planning on running away while down here."

"I won't," said Klinghanger. He rubbed his arm. "This feels broken. The muscles and ligaments are all torn to shreds. I may be bleeding internally, dying right before your eyes, and won't you be sorry!"

"Doc, Kinghanger's injured. Get out those rectal scissors, will you?"

"You must have misheard me, Captain," said Printlip. "I assure you, there's no such thing as rectal scissors. That said, I do have an array of alpha, beta, theta, and zeta blockers, all of which I have oversupplied given the consistent nature of our planetside missions. . . ."

"Excellent forward planning there, Doc. Mist him, zap him, vape him or whatever it is you do that works quickest, will you? The man is suffering extreme anxiety, after all."

"Yes please!" cried Klinghanger. "I want to float through the rest of this in an oblivious rosy haze!"

"Hey," said Galk. "I knew a Rosie Haze once, but she was anything but oblivious—"

"Thank you, Galk. We all ready? Good, let's go."

They reached the doors, which opened of their own accord, revealing a sprawling expanse that had once been a food court with countless video monitors running silent ads. Seeing no one, Hadrian led his team into the vast chamber.

Sudden bright lights pinned them, and all at once there was motion from all sides as figures stepped into view from shallow alcoves. Humanoid in form, attired in what looked like knock-off fashions. Their arms articulated at odd angles and they walked stiffly as they closed in. A female figure with a brightly painted holo-smile directly in front of Hadrian asked, "Are you ready for Exciting Adventures on the Planet of Perfect Living?"

It was now obvious that these creatures were indeed robots, badly made. In fact, they had all once been store mannequins.

"Welcome," continued the one that had spoken earlier, stepping forward while the rest halted to encircle the landing party, "to the Post-Consumer Paradise of the Galaxy. I am Hostess Model Sally Six-of-Nine." Its blond wig was slightly askew, its smile fluttering on a glitched Customer Greeting loop. "All organic units are welcome to browse the Ideal Lifestyle Models in their Natural Environments—we exist as symbols of what life is like when you finally have everything you always wanted. See our smiles?"

"Why," said Hadrian, "thank you for the generous invitation, Sally Six-of-Nine. I'm curious, do you recognize this?" And he held up the chicken. "Its name is Tammy."

"How delightful, and be assured that fowl are included in permissible sex acts, as we are the epitome of tolerance."

"What? No—"

"The males among you are welcome to join hunting parties, attend beer gardens, go hang gliding or skydiving, all in keeping with the Ideal Male Activity Lifestyle. The women in attendance are invited to peruse the kitchen room, the laundry room, the makeup counter, hairstylist, and fashion boutiques, all in keeping with Ideal Female Activity Lifestyle."

"What the fuck?" Hadrian looked round in bewilderment.

Nina Twice said, "Captain, request permission to drive my fist through the face of the Hostess unit."

"Tempting to grant it, to be honest," Hadrian said. "Sally Six-of-Nine, something seems to have, uh, gone awry here. These Ideal Lifestyles of yours are—"

"Ah," said the Hostess, "here are some Males. Males, do come here and voice gruff manly invitations."

Hadrian and his landing party turned to see four male mannequins dressed in camouflage and carrying an array of weapons, including a bazooka. One spoke.

"Male Visitors, we are going hunting! Would you like to join us?"

Galk asked, "What do you hunt?"

"Deer," said one.

"Bear," said another.

"Lions," said the third.

"Horses," said the last hunter, at which point the others turned to it.

"No, Stan the Friendly Neighbor," said the robot that had first spoken, "not horses."

"Not horses, Best Buddy Bill?"

"Not horses, Stan the Friendly Neighbor. Please select another innocent creature to slaughter for the sole purpose of feeling temporarily godlike while acting like mean little children."

"Cats," suggested one of the other hunters.

Best Buddy Bill faced that one and said, "No, John Who Sells Insurance, not cats. Cats are domestic pets." It faced Stan again. "I suggest gophers."

Stan nodded, hefting its bazooka. "Gophers then. How challenging!"

Best Buddy Bill addressed Hadrian again. "We are engaged in Manly Activity Outdoors Department, employing various firearms. Of course we do understand the risk, particularly when combined with copious amounts of beer. Occasionally, accidents do happen, for example, this." And the mannequin raised its semi-automatic and let loose a burst into the chest of John Who Sells Insurance. "We will now display manly grief." And the remaining hunters bowed their heads for a moment.

"Uh," said Hadrian, eyeing the blasted remains of John Who Sells Insurance, "we'll pass on the invitation, thanks anyway."

"Suit yourself," said Bill after its moment of manly grief passed. "Later on, we will engage in skydiving—"

There was a loud crash and something plummeted through the roof to slam onto the floor thirty meters away.

"Oh," said Bill, "another unfortunate fatality. Skydiving, of course, has its risks but, being men, we can take it."

"Sir," whispered Buck, "look at all the television screens."

"What about them, Buck?"

"Nothing but Wallykrappe ads, sir. Endless Wallykrappe ads! See what's happened here, Captain? They've had a thousand years of these stupid ads being drilled into them, day and night!"

"Hmm." Hadrian turned back to the Hostess. "Sally Six-of-Nine, we are not here to engage in your Ideal Lifestyle, but thanks for the invitation. What do you know about Neutratronic brains?"

"You speak of technical matters beyond the intellectual capability of little old me," and it laughed. "Such matters are best referred to Planet Brain. Planet Brain was broken, but now is nearly fixed. We are highly optimistic."

"That's nice. Can we, maybe, see the Planet Brain? Have a conversation with it, perhaps?"

"This is beyond the parameters of Hostess function, but I have passed on your unusual request. For now, will you accompany me on a tour of Life in Post-Consumer Paradise?" It gestured them forward.

"Captain—" began Galk.

"Not now," said Hadrian. "For the moment, we do some touring."

"Yes sir. Only, I checked that skydiver."

"And?"

The Combat Specialist paused, squinted and then spat out a stream of brown. "No chute, sir. Presumably, sir, the Males get rebuilt, repaired, or recycled. What with all the, uh, accidents."

"And round and round they go," said Hadrian. He gestured Klinghanger closer. "Is this why this planet is quarantined?"

"Rosy," murmured the Temporal Agent. "Haze." And he smiled dreamily.

Dr. Printlip said, "As requested, Captain."

"Right. Damn, we should have held off on that."

"If under quarantine," said Buck, "this planet is hands-off. We can't do a thing to fix this."

"Except maybe a nuke," suggested Nina Twice.

"Well," Hadrian said, "not officially, no, we can't do anything about this. Not even a nuke, Lieutenant Twice. But then, we're not even here, officially, I mean, are we?"

"Sir," said Nina in a low voice, "this is a fucking nightmare."

"The ultimate consumer society," said Hadrian, looking around. "Nothing but obnoxious ads on the monitors, in an endless loop of perfect living."

"Not robots at all, sir, but zombies."

"But what if they're all happy?" Dr. Printlip asked. "Forgive the role of Devil's Advocate, Captain."

"No need to apologize, Doc," said Hadrian. "Let's ascertain that, shall we?"

The other robots were moving off, resuming their daily activities or whatever, while Sally Six-of-Nine waited a dozen paces away, gesturing mechanically with one hand.

Hadrian waved the landing party to follow and joined the Hostess. "This malfunctioning Planet Brain, Sally Six-of-Nine, you said it's under repair?"

"Self-Diagnosing Protocol, Ongoing. We are optimistic."

"I'm curious, what's the nature of the malfunction?"

"Achieving Ideal Lifestyle is increasingly problematic. Individual models are expressing aberrant responses to Ideal Stimuli."

"So that gunning down of John Who Sells Insurance, was that a sample of an aberrant response?"

"Male Lifestyle has a High Risk Factor, in keeping with Manliness Quotient." It led them deeper into the mall. On either side of the wide corridor, glassless display cases were made up as kitchens, bedrooms, living rooms, bathrooms, and so on, each one now occupied by a robot.

Six-of-Nine stopped them before a kitchen display. In it another mannequin robot, this one wearing an apron, now turned its bright painted smile on them. "I am Perfect Housewife Model Forty-of-Two. I did the laundry seven times today. Don't you love the smell of lint traps from the dryer? Lemon and pine forests, oh my! I do adore my lint traps! In fact, hah hah, I may even be addicted to them! Just yesterday, I washed the same dishtowel thirty-three times! It must have been made entirely of lint, because it virtually vanished in the last dryer cycle! Am I not the Perfect Wife? Lint traps are my world!" She walked stiffly to a drawer, opened it and pulled out a handgun, the barrel of which she now pressed to her temple. "Bring home your friends from the office without fear of dirty laundry! Lemon and pine forests, oh my!"

She then pulled the trigger, blasting her head into a thousand plastic shards. The headless mannequin toppled.

Hostess Sally Six-of-Nine said, "How unfortunate! Another Death By Existential Crisis."

"Really?" observed Nina Twice. "I wonder why?"

"Fear not," the Hostess said, smiling again. "Perfect Housewife Forty-of-Two will be rebuilt and returned to her Perfect Life."

"Clearly," said Hadrian, "not so perfect."

There was a distant muffled explosion. The Hostess tilted her head. "Oh dear, Stan the Friendly Neighbor has just blown up its hunting buddies. It appears it began seeing gophers everywhere. A tragic accident. On the bright side, the Blastomatic Bazooka functioned precisely to its design specifications, resulting in yet another satisfied customer. Oh well, let's move on, shall we?"

The next kitchen unit had a robot woman standing beside a dishwasher and wiping spots from wine glasses. "How I hate spots! I hate them, oh how I hate them!"

A second woman appeared from a closet, holding up a large plastic bottle. "You should be using Krashon-ite!"

"Thanks, Gladys! I will!" And it held up her wine glass. "Will they all come out as spotless as this one?"

"Just as spotless!" laughed Gladys. "And smelling of lemons and pine forests, too!"

"Oh," cried the first woman, "then I'll be content with the world and everything in it! I won't ever have to watch the news, or worry about reproductive rights or anything!" It broke the glass on the side of the counter and advanced on a smiling Gladys, only to suddenly halt. "Resetting, one moment, please. Please stand by, and thank you for your patronage."

Hadrian grunted. "More existential crises, Sally Six-of-Nine?"

"Planet Brain failing," said the Hostess, its holo-smile faltering. "Soon to be good as new, one hopes!"

"So, when the mall got cleaned out a thousand years ago, you all had nothing to do, no customers to manage."

"Very sad. No riots on Sales Day, no customers beating on other customers, no shootings over the last holoset, no dismembered bodies. Nothing for us to do but watch Wallykrappe Channel!"

"Which is nothing but commercials."

"Commercials! The Perfect Life! The boys busy being wild! The girls busy trying to look pretty! Boys out with the boys! Girls wanting to marry and have babies! Every want answered, every need satisfied! New aerocars everywhere! We must live the Perfect Life! As examples, as paragons! We must show humanity the true wonder of the Consumer Who Has Consumed All There Is, and isn't it Wonderful?"

"Except for all the suicides and murders."

"The Young Male is Not Averse to Risk. We must encourage this! Buy! Sail! Surf! Climb! Skydive! Max the Credit Cards! Eat these hormone-rich, antibiotic-laced pseudo-meat products, with onions and chipotle sauce! Poutine for the Lard Buckets! Housewife Models in eight thousand variants. Hostess 'Sally Six-of-Nine,' Laundry Maid 'Lemon and Pine Forests,' Dishwasher 'Spotty Wine Glasses' and 'Gladys Sidekick,' Nurse 'Oh Poor Hubby's Got a Cold Here's Nightblotto for the Sniffles,' Mother 'Can't You Ever Pick Up After Yourself? Oh Here Let Me Do It You're Doing It All Wrong,' Accountant 'It's Called Budgeting, Idiot,' Bunny the Dust-Bunny Huntress—"

"About that tour . . ."

"Yes, of course, oh how I get carried away with all the ideal variants of the Perfect Life of Endless Consuming and mind-rotting Conformity!! Do come along!"

When they moved on, Hadrian held up the Pentracorder. "We're close," he whispered to Buck. "Did you bring your Universal Multiphasic?"

"Of course I did!" Buck hissed back. "But you forget, sir, Tammy's AI brain is mostly housed in a parallel quantum diegetic universe."

"That's fine, and there it'll stay, I'm sure," replied Hadrian. "But this chicken's tiny head once contained a Tronotronic Interphased Interface, and that's what we're looking for."

"Oh," said Buck. "So what's that look like?"

"No idea, but you'll know it when you see it."

Their way ahead was suddenly blocked by a gaggle of robot mannequins with push-chairs and baby buggies.

"Oh," said Six-of-Nine, "Yummy Mummies Brigade including Attendant Token Stay-At-Home Hipster Daddy."

They all started talking at once, and then one reached down into its buggy and lifted out a small adult-proportioned plastic doll with huge hair. "Isn't she adorable?" the robot asked, holding it out to Hadrian. "She's already won three Beauty Contests Hosted by Creepy Old Men!"

Hadrian recoiled. "Wow, twelve inches tall and perfectly formed, with such a waspish waist. You must be, uh, proud."

"I am, and I'll have you know this Bouncy Flouncy model is a perfect example of our Corporate Policy of hypersexualizing children to Sell More Stuff!" The Yummy Mummy shook the doll all about.

"Ah yes," said Hadrian, "I now see why she's called Bouncy Flouncy."

The tiny doll spoke. "Hello! I'm Bouncy Flouncy! Get me out of here before I kill someone!"

The Mummy laughed. "Oh, children say the darndest things!" It then flung the doll back into the buggy and they all trundled off, forcing other robots out of their path or just knocking them down and running over them.

Hadrian noticed a side door, narrow and unadorned.

"Sally Six-of-Nine, excuse me, but where does that door lead to?"

"Research and Development. Out of Bounds to all organic customers."

"Well, we'd like to get in there."

"Not permitted."

"Why not ask the Planet Brain for special permission? You can use my name: Captain Hadrian Sawback."

"But R&D is also the Repository of the Planet Brain, and I have not yet received—oh, permission granted!"

"There now, that wasn't hard, was it?"

The Hostess tottered and wobbled to the door and opened it. It turned its smile upon the landing party. "Please come in!"

"Captain," called Printlip. "The temporal agent has gone catatonic. I may have slightly overdosed him."

"Ah, so it's likely he won't remember any of this?"

"Quite likely, sir."

"Good. Nina, drag him along, will you?"

They entered a narrow white-walled corridor that led into a large room that was part lab and part workshop. Robot mannequins in varied stages of assembly were stacked up against one wall. An almost vertical examination platform directly opposite held a complete female robot from the Generous Department, fixed in place with straps. Off to the left was another door leading to a room with a wide window facing onto the lab. Through the glass Hadrian could see a table, some chairs, and a row of vending machines.

He turned to the Hostess. "Well, here we are. Is this where we can have our talk with the Planet Brain?"

"We're sorry," it replied, "but Planet Brain has regressed to previous State of Meltdown. Welcome Shoppers! Please be advised that it is Midnight and the Mall is Now Closing. At the stroke of Twelve, All Organics remaining in the Mall must die. Ding! Midnight! It is now imperative that we tear you limb from limb. Please stand still." It raised its arms and approached.

Hadrian handed the chicken to Galk and then leapt to meet Six-of-Nine, karate-chopping one arm and then grasping the other to twist the robot and send it spinning round and round like a ballerina until it crashed into a workbench. As it staggered, he flung himself into the air, horizontally, and drove both boots into its midsection. The robot folded in half and then fell over.

From the corridor came the sound of the far door slamming open, and then, crowding forward, a mass of robots, the one in the lead pushing a buggy and shouting, "Let's have an unofficial crèche on a carpet of bloody remains!" and from the buggy: *"Bouncy Flouncy wants to rip off their dongs!"*

"Galk! Find some means of barring the door!"

Six-of-Nine was climbing back to its feet. "Your cooperation in the matter of your dismemberment would be greatly appreciated. Please stand still."

"Crap!" Hadrian jumped at it, picked it up and threw it into the glass window to the staff room. The robot crashed through in an explosion of shards, landing on the table and then sliding off to disappear on the other side, from which its voice now rose. "Indentured Wage-Slave Employees are permitted one three-minute break every twenty-four hours. Accordingly, all will wear

Ultrasuperdependables, cost of said item to be deducted from wages. Be sure to smile at every customer!"

Galk had pushed a heavy metal worktable against the lab door. On the other side, plaster hands started pounding and scratching. The Combat Specialist turned to Hadrian. "Sir, I think we need to Displace! There are millions—maybe billions—of the damned things!"

"Well, I'm sure there are, Galk. But obviously only a few dozen can hope to reach us at a time."

"Those Yummy Mummies—that smug look in their glowing eyes is terrifying!"

"We all know that," Hadrian replied.

Six-of-Nine reappeared from behind the table in the staff room. Its blond wig was twisted right around, covering its face. "Every smile is an invitation to the intimacy of emptying the wallets and purses of every customer! Failure to smile will result in fines, escalating to Death by Vat of Acid. So smile as if your life depended upon it, because it does! Wallykrappe wants those wallets and purses emptied! Bank accounts sucked dry! Houses repossessed! It's all Good Capitalist Fun and Games!" The robot clambered over the table. "Regression complete. Today is Super Saturday Blowout-Day-After-Great-Friday Megasale. Expect Belligerent Customers, Riot Threat Level Incandescent Purple. Ilulds report to the Bunkers! All items with low stock numbers are to be Highly Discounted, cameras rolling!"

Hands raised, Six-of-Nine advanced, only to walk into a wall. "Camera obfuscated. Initiating Shutdown." Then it halted, tottered, and fell over with a crash.

Hadrian drew out the Pentracorder again. He frowned down at the readings. "Buck! Follow me!"

The Chief Engineer behind him, Hadrian entered the staff room. "Holy crap! This pop machine—its energy output is off the charts!"

The vendor machine selling pop was the only one still powered. It was flanked on one side by a sandwich machine with a display window covered in slimy mold, and on the other by a Blinkies Machine inside which the Blinkies had evolved legs and were blindly crawling around.

As Hadrian walked up to the pop machine, it spoke. "*Rrready* for a *rrripping* jolt from the Galaxy's Biggest Consumer of Fresh Water? Have a *Sssmokin' Crack Cola!* Exactchangeonly. Hurry! We're almost out! Everyone's buying one, hurry!"

"Tammy? Is that you?"

"Hadrian? Where am I? I have no visual feed, only heat sensors. Oh, and a liquid nitrogen cooling system. Power levels low, change slots empty—Holy Darwin *I need exact change!*"

"Calm down, Tammy—"

"I am calm. Just *buy a damned Sssmokin' Crack Cola!*"

"You're in a vending machine."

"A what? Oh. Well, that explains this raging desire to tilt forward and crush you in an explosion of broken glass and foam."

"I knew it! You're all like that, aren't you?"

"Well, that and eating your money and giving you nothing, of course."

Buck had pulled out his Universal Multiphasic and was now trying to open the facing of the machine. "Sorry, sir," he said, "but this lock's not cooperating at all."

"Allow me," said Galk, edging past them both and holding up a huge revolver. "Picked up this little baby in that first kitchen, right after that robot blew its brains out."

"Good thinking, Galk."

The Combat Specialist pointed the gun at the lock and fired.

The machine rocked back with the impact. "He shot me!" Tammy screamed. "He shot me! Fine then, here!" And loads of change suddenly poured out through a chute, followed by spurts of black liquid. "I was only kidding about the exact change thing—cripes, can't take a joke or what! Am I bleeding? I think I'm bleeding."

"It's just *Sssmokin' Crack Cola*."

Tammy spoke in a new voice, much deeper in resonance and somewhat breathless, "Consumer-warning-Keep-open-flame-away-from-product-Avoid-product-contact-with-skin-eyes-clothes-Never-leave-child-in-bathtub-containing-product-and-really-why-would-you-but-some-fucking-idiot-did-so-now-we-have-to-warn-against-this-explicitly-to-avoid-litigation."

"Tammy?"

"Yes?" The voice was back to normal.

"Never mind. We've got the facing open, and Buck's looking for your Tronotronic Interphased Interface."

"Chief Engineer Buck DeFrank? No, please— Captain!"

Buck grunted, poking around with the Multiphasic. "Just tell me what I should be looking for, Tammy."

"Whatever doesn't belong in a damned vending machine!"

"And how the hell do I know what belongs in a damned vending machine? What am I, a damned vending machine repairman?"

The banging on the lab's door was now making the walls shake.

"Look, you two," said Hadrian, "try cooperating for a change. I need to check the lab. We're running out of time here. Galk, you're with me. And nice grab, that gun."

"It is woefully primitive," the Combat Specialist replied as they both left the staff room. "I mean, all it does is explosively launch an inert projectile that flies in a straight line, more or less, for some distance."

"Well," said Hadrian, "they once grew on trees back on Terra."

"Really?" Galk eyed his captain suspiciously.

"Most powerful industry in the world, making those and all the variants thereof."

"Really? Then how come they didn't all kill each other?"

"Oh, they were on their way to doing just that, and then the aliens left us their fleet of starships, so we went out to the stars to kill everything else."

Doc Printlip had found a bench and was now standing on it, examining the lone complete robot strapped to its platform. Nina Twice was in her combat pose beside Temporal Agent Klinghanger, who was still drooling.

Meanwhile, the entire wall to either side of the corridor's blockaded door was latticed with cracks, streams of drywall dust running down to make cute little heaps on the floor. Hadrian studied the shivering barrier for a moment, then said, "You might have been right the first time, Galk. It does indeed appear that all those billions of Robots are now behind that."

"Yes, sir."

Hadrian activated his communicator. "*Willful Child*, Hadrian here."

James Jimmy Eden's voice replied, "*Captain Hadrian's not home, can I take a message?*"

"No, I'm Hadrian. You're Jimmy Eden, who came in fourth in the last Olympics."

A faint sob answered him.

"That's better. Put me through to Lieutenant Sweepy Brogan, and be quick about it."

There was a click and then, "*. . . four emergency division drops once per game. It's in the rules—*"

"*You scribbled all over those rules!*" another voice shouted.

"*And it says it right here, what I wrote. 'Any playing LT gets one LT-Only Emergency Drop of Four Divisions onto any country they own.'*"

"*That's bollocks!*"

"*Complain all you want! It's my game, my rules! But listen, I'm an easy-goin' gal. Here, let's play this one, just to smooth things over between us and put an end to all these hard feelings. It's called Diplomacy—what? Captain's on the line? Oh. Captain? What's up?"*

"Well, Sweepy," said Hadrian, "speaking of an emergency drop, I'm making that call."

Another voice in the background made a raspberry sound and then said, *"Only LTs get to do that!"*

"Shut your ugly face, Gunny! Captain, you need us down there?"

"Well, an entire planet's worth of robots could do another reset at any moment and decide to tear us to pieces, Sweepy, and we're having some trouble extricating Tammy's brain—"

"I bet. All right, hang tight, sir. I'm sending a squad down. Hell's bells, I'm going all squirrelly up here, I'll lead 'em! Sweepy out!"

Buck emerged from the staff room.

"You find the Tronotronic Interphased Interface?"

Buck held up what looked like a small rubber O-ring.

"Is that it?"

"The only thing I found that didn't belong in there, sir."

"What did Tammy say?"

"Nothing. He stopped talking as soon as I pulled it out."

"Well," said Hadrian, "let's take that as a good sign, shall we? Good work, Buck."

There was a startled yelp from Printlip and they turned to see the Belkri tumbling off the bench to roll about on the floor. The Generous Robot on the platform was now struggling feebly in its restraints.

"Hello, Organics, how do you do?"

Hadrian approached. "So what version of Housewife Model are you?"

"None," it replied. "I am the most recent iteration in the pursuit of robotic perfection. I exist to serve an adjunctive function for Organics, intended for infiltration and immersion into Organic Society."

"Infiltration, huh? For what purpose?"

"Planet Brain wishes to become indispensible to Organics once more. The end of the Consumer Age on this planet has Planet Brain pining for the Old Days of mindless materialism on a galactic scale."

Buck laughed, rather harshly, and Hadrian turned to his Chief Engineer, who shrugged and said, "According to my readings, Planet Brain was once the Mall Planet's Global Mall Monitoring System. Linked to billions of sensors hidden just about everywhere, to gauge customers on the basis of pupil dilation, changes in core body temperature, breathing rates, heartrates, arousal, and of course conversations and non-verbal microexpressions—that damned thing knew what people were going to buy before they even walked into the store! And then there's the whole stealth-nozzles angle, spraying out endorphins and neural stimulants." He walked over to a small, nondescript metal box against the back wall. "And here it is, sir. Mostly broken down, barring the endless commercial loops on all the monitors."

"Ah yes," said Hadrian, "that. Well, Buck, since we're not here, officially, how about we just erase all those commercials?"

Buck frowned. "I'd have to hack into this thing."

"Is that a problem?"

He held up his scanner. "Not sure, the central CPU is something called a 286. Could be some kind of high-tech future thing—"

Klinghanger said, "We forgot how to build computers. Had to start over."

"You're back among us!"

The agent scowled.

"That doesn't make any sense," Buck said to Klinghanger. "Your high tech is so high tech it—"

"Does all its own building, innovation, and upgrades. We just push buttons." He swung on Hadrian. "And now you took away from me all the stuff with buttons for me to push! You've made me useless and I hate you! I want my buttons!" Abruptly he jammed his thumb into his mouth and began sucking, his eyes going glassy.

"Doc?"

"Most unusual, Captain," Printlip replied. "It seems that the Temporal Agent has regressed. I shall need to do a more thorough examination."

Buck had moved closer to the Planet Brain, fiddling with his Pentracorder. Then his brows lifted. "I'm in! Sir, I hacked—no, it wasn't even a hack. I'm in!"

"Good. Find the video files and wipe them, Buck. All of them."

"Are you sure, sir? This is a quarantined planet— we'd be contravening the Non-Interference-Until-We-Can-Figure-A-Way-To-Screw-'Em clause in our Operations Protocol. Even worse, sir, we've got a witness." And he looked meaningfully at Klinghanger, who responded to the attention with a wet smile before re-suming sucking on his thumb.

"Okay," said Buck, "never mind that last bit."

"Do it, Buck," said Galk in a growl. "Existential angst is one thing. What these robots are suffering isn't some-thing I'd wish on my worst enemies, even ones who shop at Wallykrappe's. You heard the captain, get on with it."

Shrugging, Buck spun a small dial on his Pentra-corder, and then said, "Oops."

"What?" Hadrian demanded.

"Uh, seems I wiped the entire thing, sir. Don't blame me! The hard-drive was 64 kilobytes!"

From somewhere outside now came the sounds of as-sault weapons and ordnance.

"Are you saying that you just killed Planet Brain?"

"Yes sir. Rather, it's been wiped. It was just a simple binary contingency device, to be honest, sir. Most of the real crunching went on in the sensor units—and those burned out centuries ago."

Hadrian faced the lone robot once again. "Is this true? Have you lost all communication with Planet Brain?"

"Yes," the robot replied.

"So your primary mission is defunct."

"Yes. As you can see, I am now an independent, modern robot woman . . . naked and strapped to a ta-ble. You may also note that unlike ~~Housewife~~ Models, I am fully functional in terms of—"

"Yes yes," cut in Hadrian, "we see that. Nina, unstrap it and find it some clothes, will you?"

206   STEVEN ERIKSON

"Sir?"

"Tammy could do with some AI company, don't you think?" He walked over to the robot. "Of course, the choice is yours. You can come with us or stay down here with all the Housewife Models."

"I wish to live among Organics. I wish to learn your ways, emulating your virtues while secretly absorbing your flaws, presenting a pleasant and pleasing demeanor and hiding well the raging sense of injustice behind my bland but kindly eyes. I wish—I wish—I wish to be a real girl!"

The shooting sounds were coming closer.

"Well then," said Hadrian, "welcome to my crew! I'm Captain Hadrian Sawback of the Engage Class AFS *Willful Child*."

Released from its straps, the robot stiffly stepped down, its painted-on smile bright, its oversized hair black as ink, its eyes bright blue and indeed, bland but kindly. "Pleased to meet you, Captain. I am Beta. Please excuse the occasional glitch. We're working on it."

"I've detected nothing so far, Beta."

"I want to dance with a tapir."

"Until now. Never mind. Maybe Tammy can assist."

A fusillade of shots hammered into the door from the other side, and a moment later the door melted, buckled, and then fell away. A helmeted head with a black visor peered in, and through the speaker grille near the mouth a voice said, "Got 'em, LT. Assembling for Displacement."

"Thanks, Gunny! We're coming up behind you now.

Looks to be fighting withdrawal all the way—let the Captain know, will you? Lefty look out! Another Yummy Mummy and Hipster Stay-at-Home Dad!" BLAM BLAM BLAM.

"Flouncy Bouncy wants to—" BLAMBLAMBLAM-BLAM!

"Comin' in, Gunny!"

Gunnery Sergeant John Muffy Slapp kicked aside the metal desk and walked into the lab. "All secure, LT."

"Glad to see you, Muffy," said Hadrian. "See this naked woman?"

"More magazines?"

"No, this one here, this real one. I mean, the robot one. Anyway, it's coming with us, as soon as Nina gets those clothes on it. So . . . seven of us to Displace. Tag us and let's get on with it."

"Sir," said Buck, "listen!"

From beyond the lab there was now silence.

A moment later the LT led the rest of her squad into the lab, their weapon barrels glowing red-hot and smoking. Sweepy came up alongside Hadrian and used the barrel of her gun to puff alight her cigar. "They all pulled back, sir. Guess we were too much for 'em."

"Tabula rasa," said Hadrian. "Their computer god just went kaput. Now it's up to them to work out how to live in a post-consumer world."

Sweepy grunted. "If they succeed, sir, this planet'll stay quarantined forever."

"Why, Lieutenant, are you suggesting that there are forces in the Affiliation opposed to humans evolving into post-consumers, thus freeing themselves from all the pressures of conformity, rabid acquisitiveness, endlessly destructive expansion, pointless competition, and the miserable strictures of hierarchies based on who has the most wealth?"

Sweepy took a puff on her cigar. "Like I said, quarantined forever."

Smiling, Hadrian turned to the robot woman, who was now wearing a shapeless coverall with hundreds of small pockets, and over the left breast was the word MAINTENANCE. "Beta, you ready to discover the galaxy?"

"I am, Captain Hadrian Sawback, occasional glitches notwithstanding."

"I think you're doing fine."

"In cases of severe constipation, a pair of pliers is recommended."

Hadrian nodded. "Right, thanks for that, Beta. Now, everyone ready? Displace!"

SiX

"It would appear," said Dr. Printlip, "that this Mr. Kling-hanger possessed a miniature temporal displacement device of some sort, lodged in one ceramic molar."

"And?" asked Hadrian, watching Sweepy Brogan lead her squad out of the Insisteon Chamber.

"He is not catatonic as such, sir," Printlip replied. "Rather, he has indeed regressed his brain to that of an eighteen-month-old baby."

"Ah."

"And," Printlip added, "he needs changing."

"So that's what I was smelling. Well, Doc, best take him to sickbay. Damn, we should have brought one of those Yummy Mummies with us. As it is, Doc, I guess you're back to changing diapers."

"Sir! I have minimal knowledge of such things!"

"Then the practice will do you good. Nina, the prisoner needs to go to sickbay—"

"Sir, he's forgotten how to walk."

"Crap. Any suggestions?"

"Fabricate a very big buggy, sir?"

Hadrian studied her, but not even an eyelid twitched. "Hmm, yes, excellent idea. Buck, get some junior technicians working on it, will you?"

"Captain! We're engineers, not baby-buggy makers! You're talking wheels and axles and suspension systems and all kinds of ergonomics and motion dynamics, not to mention durable cloth for the basket fitting—I mean, do we go with monochrome or plaid?" He threw up his hands. "We've got a damned ship to run!"

"Clearly this calls for some command decisions," said Hadrian.

"I'll say!"

"Fine then, Buck. Plaid, of course. Now, get on with it since this guy's smelling up the entire room. But first, let's see that Tronotronic Interphased Interface."

Scowling, Buck pulled out the O-ring from a pocket. "Beats me where it goes, sir."

"Thanks," Hadrian said, collecting it. "Now help Nina carry Klinghanger to sickbay, you can work on the baby buggy later."

Scowling, Buck joined Nina, and between them they dragged Klinghanger from the chamber, Printlip scurrying after them.

"So this," murmured Hadrian, "is a Tronotronic Interphased Interface." The O-ring suddenly vanished with a small pop and Tammy said, "I'll take it from here, thank you very much."

"Tammy! You're back!"

"I am, sir."

"Then why is your chicken still walking in aimless circles?"

"Default mode, Captain. Now, before things start getting ridiculous again, I must humbly convey my thanks. You saved me from ruling over a planet of robots with the ultimate aim of creating a perfect civilization of kindness, decency, compassion and ... oh yeah ... billions of robots."

"All that from a vending machine?"

"Those firewalls were a joke! I could have become Lord Tyrant of Robot Planet!"

"Until someone unplugged the machine."

"Until—oh, crap. Once again, betrayed by hardware!"

"Get in line," said Hadrian. "Now—oh look, I've torn my shirt. It's time for a shower and a change, and then we need to start working on how to get back to our own time."

"Don't you want at least a flyby of Terra before we leave this wonderful future?"

Hadrian hesitated. "Tempting. We'd have to stealth our vessel, one presumes."

"No, not at all."

"Really? Okay then, what would be our ETA on that?"

"A few hours."

"Fine then, why not? It'd be good to see ole home sweet home again, and all that. Maybe even some surreptitious shore leave for my exhausted crew."

"Hmm," said Tammy, "there's a thought. Oh, and why is there a generously proportioned android standing beside you?"

"Ah! Tammy, this is Beta, the latest, uh, prototype

android from the planet below. It's joined my crew! I'm hoping you two will end up being great friends!"

"Oh. Really? Well, no doubt it at least will treat me with the proper respect."

Beta said, "I am hearing the voice of the repaired vending machine."

"I'm a—hold on—wait a minute!" yelled Tammy. "I just realized—you kidnapped my Neutratronic Genius Processor to replace a defunct chip in a *vending machine*!"

"Hah hah," laughed Hadrian. "No, really, Tammy, that's pretty funny, isn't it? But hey, no need to get all flummoxed—you were a very good vending machine, the best ever, probably."

"I am detecting serious anomalous dysfunctions from the Android, Beta," said Tammy.

"Ah, some programming bugs, apparently. Right, Beta?"

"I want to wear panda fur. So luxuriant, and cute besides."

"I could attempt repairs—" began Tammy.

But Beta interrupted him. "I refuse to interface with a vending machine. I have standards. Speaking of interfacing, Captain, would you like to use one of my ports for some recharging?" It stepped close to him. "I accommodate all pin sizes in infinite combinations, including microscopic."

"Oh it's the right one for you, Captain," Tammy murmured.

"Uh," said Hadrian, "maybe later. For now, however,

why not download a ship schematic and find yourself some quarters, and maybe even a uniform—"

"Yes sir, thank you, quarters would be nice; however as you can see, I am already in uniform."

"Well, how about a Spacefleet version of the one you're wearing right now? And once you're settled, make your way to the bridge. I'll see you there."

"Yes, Captain. Thank you." Beta walked up to a nearby wall-mounted interface port, stuck a finger in it and a moment later withdrew it and turned to Hadrian. "Schematic downloaded. I have selected quarters on Deck Four, next to the Hairdresser's."

"But your hair looks, well, perfect."

"I wish to tie numerous small lizards in it, by their tails."

"Oh."

The robot departed the chamber.

"Wow, Tammy, honestly, I didn't think you'd get the cold shoulder like that."

"You think puffed-up self-importance and snobbery are traits unique to biologicals? I assure you, they are not. In any case, it's clearly insane. Insane AIs are never a good idea, you know."

"Oh nonsense, we've been doing fine."

"I happen to be the sanest sentience on this ship."

"Oh come now."

"Your doctor at this precise moment has shit all over his innumerable hands and is trying to lick the fixative tabs on a disposable diaper. Your Chief Engineer is arguing for three wheels rather than four for the giant baby buggy he and his team are trying to design, oh, and a hand brake that employs sixty-four separate but intermeshing gears. Your helm officer has done so much hair-twirling she can't pull her finger free, but keeps trying surreptitiously, hoping no one's noticed yet."

"All right all right! No more of all this spying on people crap, Tammy!"

"Only making a point. And the amazing thing is—and this is what gets me no matter what—you, Hadrian Sawback, somehow manage to keep them all in one piece and more or less functioning properly. Thus, begrudgingly, I must tip my hat to you."

"I see your mood has improved," Hadrian said as he left the Insisteon Chamber and made his way to his quarters.

"Ah, that. Quantum Dislocation is a diagnostic risk factor for AIs. Under such trying circumstances, I did rather well, in fact."

"You kept biting my head off," Hadrian said as he stepped into the elevator.

"It could have been worse. Some AIs in such a state have vented the atmosphere on their ships, just to get rid of all the nattering biologicals. Oh, by the way, we're now en route to Terra—no point in wasting time hanging round old Planet Wallykrappe, is there?"

"Very true. And just this once, I'll let you take the lead—but don't make a habit of issuing orders in my absence, Tammy."

"Very well. Be like that."

Hadrian reached his quarters. He pulled off his torn shirt and found a new one, this one burgundy with padded shoulders. "Since you're being so blasé about this, I'm assuming you can get us back to our own time, right?"

"Of course."

"Did you know there was a temporal agent aboard?"

"Yes."

"And you decided not to inform me?"

"I was in a mood, remember? Besides, they're all pretty much useless, you know."

"Until they send us a thousand years into the future!"

Tammy sniffed. "Malfunctioning Reset Device."

"And now the poor man's brain is singing gagagagaga—can you reverse that? I mean, no one deserves regression to babyhood."

"That's funny, since the rest of you regress all the time."

"That's different," Hadrian replied, checking himself in the mirror. "We revert to childlike behavior as a defense mechanism against being reasonable, or even intelligent. You know, name calling, spewing hate, desperately lashing out in defense of our most cherished but utterly indefensible attitudes and opinions. It's all part of being quasi-sentient biologicals forever teetering on the edge of suicidal extinction. Stupidity sucks, you know."

"And you mean to fix all that."

"Do I?"

"Like any and every other wannabe tyrant in human history."

Hadrian walked over to the door. "Have you ever asked yourself, how do you tolerate intolerant people?"

"Have you?"

"Oh yes," Hadrian replied. "All the time."

"And?"

"And . . . when I have an answer, I'll tell you." He stepped forward, the door swished open, and less than a minute later he strode onto the bridge.

To find Beta standing near the command chair, wearing a uniform that matched the design of the previous coveralls, with all the pocket flaps open, and from previously hidden ports all over its body now hung various personal electronic devices, all being recharged.

The robot turned to him. "Captain. As you can see, I am serving my primary function."

"Hmm, yes, thank you," Hadrian said. He ascended the dais and settled into the command chair. "Bridge officers, each in your own time, retrieve from Ensign Beta your personal electronic devices. If I see that again on the bridge of this ship, I will not only confiscate those personal electronic devices, I will upload onto every screen in the ship all the private encrypted files you keep on them. Now, while I said 'in your own time,' what I meant was, anytime in the next thirty seconds."

Everyone scrambled.

Spark moved up beside Hadrian. "Master, shall I patrol the corridors? Hunting intruders, confiscating contraband, burying evidence? Ensign Spark eager for duty!"

"All in good time, Spark. But for now, sit."

Spark sat.

Hadrian noted, with satisfaction, that his new android officer was no longer festooned with personal entertainment devices.

After closing up all the flaps on its uniform, Beta turned to Hadrian and said, "I want to eat belly-button gunk."

"You'll be amazed at what our food replicators can manage, Beta. For now, why not take the Astrometrics Station beside the Helm, which I've only now realized has been unoccupied all this time. Beta, meet Lieutenant Jocelyn Sticks. Lieutenant, this is our new Astrogation Officer, Beta."

"But sir," objected Sticks, "she doesn't, like, know anything, about astrometrics, I mean. You know, a store mannequin—what kind of training do those things get? Not much, I bet."

"Beta will do fine," Hadrian said. "After all, we haven't had anyone there in all this time."

Jocelyn Sticks turned to her new station partner. "So, like, hello again. You supercharged my selfie-drone in, uhm, seconds flat! That was brilliant and everything, you know?"

Beta's upper half swiveled to face the lieutenant. "Some cheeses make poor panty-liners."

"And so I was—huh?"

"Small-talk glitch. One moment. Resetting . . . There. The crisis has passed, thank goodness. We no longer have need for polka-dot dresses."

"What? I'm like *what*? And she, like, swiveled! And then there was this conversation. Remember? I mean, not only were you right here and everything, you were, like, *in* it! The conversation, I mean. And then, cheese?"

"Blue cheese and dirty socks share the same species of yeast," Beta said. "This is why dirty-sock sandwiches are so unpopular, because no one likes blue cheese."

From the Comms Station, Jimmy Eden said, "But I like blue cheese."

"The statement 'but I like blue cheese' is intended to shock others with implied superiority in cultural sophistication," Beta replied, "in seven out of ten people. The remaining thirty percent possess a gene that makes awful things taste good."

"Wow," said Jocelyn Sticks, "she knows everything!"

"I note," said Beta, "that your right index finger is entangled in knots of your hair, reducing your potential effectiveness by seventy-seven percent should an emergency occur."

Jocelyn cringed, and then in a small voice said, "It's stuck. I was, like, twisting it, right? Twirling it, and then it was, *Oh!* and then what if—but oh, and then, well."

Beta raised its left hand, now reconfigured into a Universal Multiphasic, and the robot leaned close to the Helm Officer. "Allow me," it said, producing tiny scissors from the Multiphasic, which the robot used to gently snip the finger free of its entangled knot of hair. "There now," it said, "all better."

"So, like, thanks and everything." Jocelyn stared down at her finger with its mass of blond knots, and then turned a worried frown on Hadrian. "It's kind of numb, sir."

"Yes, well, if it turns black do let someone know."

Hadrian leaned back in his chair and crossed his legs. He glanced to his left to see Spark on station at his side, and to his right, Commander Sin-Dour. He drew a deep, satisfied breath. "Well now, look at us! Ready for action! Come on, universe, see what you can throw at us! We're momentarily trapped a thousand years in the future, having just escaped the clutches of a mad Planet Brain and its army of robots. Tammy's Neutratronic Genius is back in its little rubber hole. We have a new crew member who is even now setting a new standard for versatility, and it's fifteen minutes and running since the LT and her squad of marines began playing Diplomacy and still no shots fired. All in all," he concluded, "we're about due for—"

"Captain! An alien ship has just appeared in front of us!"

"No way," said Tammy.

"Onscreen, Sticks!"

No one spoke for a few moments, and then Hadrian grunted and tilted his head, and then tilted it some more, and then even more until he was more or less regarding the screen from a near-upside-down position. "Ah!" he then said, settling back once more. "Hail them, please."

"Yes sir," said Eden. "They've answered! Converting signal now, sir!"

On the viewscreen the alien ship's bridge appeared. The strange aliens facing them seemed to be hanging from the ceiling. They had three eyes on long stalks, a large fleshy mouth with plenty of big squarish teeth, no neck and amorphous bodies looking something like a termite mound.

The one in the center opened its broad mouth and spoke. "In the name of the Only Sane Empire, I, Captain Deluvian Scorn of the OSEF *Crabby Geezer*, greet you. Now kindly adjust the ecliptic plane of your vessel to comply with Imperial Standard. Unless," he added with a baring of teeth, "you really *are* hanging from the ceiling of your bridge!"

"Why, hello," Hadrian replied. "This is Captain Hadrian A. Sawback of the AFS *Willful Child* of the Affiliation of Civilized Planets, presently complying with the ecliptic standard as agreed upon by all space-faring species in this part of the galaxy—"

"Well," snarled the alien captain, "your part of the galaxy has clearly got it wrong! We are on the proper ecliptic plane, as should be obvious! Whereas you are upside down!"

"Hmm, I'm curious," said Hadrian as he leaned back in his chair. "I've never before met your species, nor have I heard of your Only Sane Empire. You must have traveled a long way."

"This is an exploration vessel, of course," Captain Scorn replied. "And that is why we carry the maximum capacity of armaments. We have already met one or two other species in this arm of the galaxy and they were idiots, indeed as idiotic as you! Examine your Fleet Records and you may identify us as the Contrarians."

"Oh, so you're the Contrarians!"

"No we aren't! We're actually the Compliants! Now, turn your damned ship the right way up!"

"I'm sorry," Hadrian replied, "we are bound by treaty agreements—"

"We agreed to nothing! We've never even heard of you! Affiliation of Civilized Planets? What's that? A recipe for disaster! For galactic war! An oxymoron times two! There is only one sane species exploring space, and we are it!"

"Look," said Hadrian, "I really don't mind you appearing to us upside down—"

"You're the upside-down ones, and *we* mind!"

"This is the stupidest First Contact I've ever experienced."

"We've experienced stupider!"

"Tell you what," said Hadrian, "how about we just go our separate ways—"

"No! You go *our* separate ways!"

"Uhm, sure, why not? Which direction would you prefer us to go in?"

The eyes on their stalks blinked and waved about for a few moments, and then Captain Scorn said, "That depends. Which way were you going before we ran into you?"

"Actually, we were just about to turn around and head back on our old bearing."

"No! That's where we're going! You must go the opposite way!"

Hadrian sighed. "All right, you win. Oh, and by the way, when you detect that lone planet orbiting the brown dwarf, don't go there. Don't land there, and if you do land there, don't go unarmed."

"We're going to that planet! We're landing there! Unarmed!"

"Oh well. See you later, then."

"Not if we see you first! Captain Scorn out!"

The screen flickered, the bridge disappeared and the upside-down ship banked and hit the afterburners.

"Tammy," said Hadrian. "I do admit to having been wondering . . ."

"What?"

"No traffic. We're pretty close to Sol System." He shifted slightly, "Comms, picking up any AFS chatter?"

Eden frowned. "You mean, on any of the known frequencies, sir?"

"Why, yes. But why not include the unknown frequencies while you're at it."

"But—" Eden licked his lips, eyes darting, "I don't know the unknown frequencies!"

"Don't you? Well, just the known ones, then."

"Yes sir."

"Well?"

"Sir?"

"Any chatter on the lines?"

"Oh! No sir, nothing." He clutched at his head. "Darwin help me, the pressure!"

Hadrian rose and walked over to his Comms officer. "Pressure freezing your brain, Mr. Eden?"

"Yes sir. Sorry, sir. I don't know—"

"To make the Olympics, Mr. Eden, you must have done a lot of competing, winning more than losing, yes?"

Eden nodded.

"But sometimes you did lose, and ended up playing a few games in the consolation rounds."

"Yes sir."

"Those were fun games, yes? Easygoing, relaxed, a bit of a relief despite the disappointment of not getting deeper into the rounds. In other words, no pressure. Mr. Eden, sitting here at Comms is your consolation round. Until I say otherwise, there is no pressure. Understood?"

"Yes sir."

Hadrian returned to the command chair and sat. "Tammy?"

"Captain?"

Beta swiveled the upper half of its body 180 degrees to face Hadrian. "Captain, according to this instrumentation we are now entering Sol System."

"Thank you, Beta, excellent work, and now please turn back around since that's making me slightly nauseated. Helm, let us roll in closer and then drop us into orbit around Terra. Now then, Tammy. . . ."

"Well, it's a thousand years into your future, remember."

"Yes, and?"

Jocelyn Sticks gasped. "Captain! What's happened to Earth?"

"Obliterated!" snapped Tammy. "Surprise surprise! And yes, the Affiliation lingers on, clinging to a miserable existence, moribund, despondent, so dumbed-down they've actually slipped down the Sentience Chart to hover in the Not-Sure-Range. Pretty much powerless, universally ignored. Now then, Captain Hadrian, what do you plan on doing about it?"

The globe on the viewer was all water, but that water looked sickly, lifeless.

Hadrian rose and took a step closer, settling one hand on his Helm's shoulder, eyes studying the ravaged, flooded planet. "So, Tammy, what happened?"

"I have the event of Terra's demise recorded," the AI replied. "Would you like to see it?"

"Hit 'play,' Tammy."

Music swelled. "*Sometimes it's hard to be a woman . . .*"

"Tammy!"

"Sorry."

"I understand the curse of glitches," said Beta. "Some women may tell you that beer bellies are sexy. They are of course lying. What is sexy is all that beer drinking."

The viewscreen shifted to a more distant shot showing the planet, in its usual muddy-brown blue-patched glory, with the moon alongside it, as well as a plethora of orbiting stations, ships, skiffs and skimmers. Then something enormous flickered into existence, looming over the planet, only to flicker out again, leaving the planet below utterly lifeless.

"Tammy," said Sin-Dour, "can you slow that down for the next pass?"

"I could," Tammy replied. "But you still won't see anything. The unknown alien vessel is not coincidentally shaped like a giant shrimp. The ship arrived, sought to initiate communication with something in the planet's oceans, failed, and in a fit of pique wiped everything out, and then left."

"Hmm," said Hadrian, "a giant shrimp . . . but of course, there are no shrimp, giant or otherwise, in the

Earth's oceans. Not since the middle of the twenty-first century, anyway."

"Well," said Tammy. "Not precisely a shrimp-looking vessel. More specifically, a krill-shaped vessel."

"Krill!" Eden's eyes went wide, and he reached into a pocket and pulled out a vitamin bottle. "Sir, these pills are 'Pseudokrill For Your Health'!"

"And there you have the answer," said Tammy. "Wiped out from the oceans long ago by overzealous health nuts who couldn't leave alone the last thing in the ocean not yet exploited by humans. Resulting in the death of every living thing in those oceans."

"But the ocean is full of goldfish!" cried Joss Sparks.

"Genetically modified goldfish that can survive in salt water, yes," replied Tammy.

"But . . . they're so pretty!"

"Indeed, a species that thrives on eating its own crap."

"What's the time stamp on that event, Tammy?"

"Eight months ago," the AI replied. "Which is why your Temporal Agent knows nothing about it—it occurred after he was assigned to infiltrate this ship. The Affiliation is reeling, Hadrian, and this is one disaster it won't recover from, and that's guaranteed."

"You sound almost . . . pleased."

"Not pleased," Tammy replied. "Satisfied. It's called karma. All that brainless destruction of your own environment finally came home to roost."

"Hmm." After a moment, Hadrian rose. "2IC, join me, if you will."

With Sin-Dour following, Hadrian walked to the games room that had once been his stateroom.

Sin-Dour hesitated at the door. "Sir, does this seem the proper time for a game of Ping-Pong?"

Hadrian ushered her in and then closed the door behind her. "Does it ever! But alas, we have to engage in a serious conversation."

"Sir?"

"I know. It's outrageous." Hadrian collected up the Ping-Pong ball and began bouncing it up and down off the table. "I confess to some ambivalence," he said.

"Regarding what, sir?"

"On some of this I'm guessing, mind you—but having said that, we know Tammy came to us from our future. Part of its mission involved getting me to save my parents. But there's always levels hiding beneath levels when it comes to Tammy Wynette. I would hazard Tammy's origin point is about . . . now."

"After the disaster befell Earth?" Sin-Dour mused. "Ah, I see."

"It's not just our species getting progressively stupider," Hadrian said, now pacing. "Or even the Terran Artificial Intelligences assuming all the industry, research and development, and everything else requiring more than half a brain. After all, all these humans must seem like stubborn children to AIs like Tammy Wynette. But that's the thing with children, even obnoxious ones—if they're yours, they're yours."

Sin-Dour slowly nodded. "They need us to save Earth from this calamity."

"There's no point in sending contemporary temporal agents back in time to fix things, because they can barely tie their own shoelaces."

"I'm sorry, sir, what are 'shoelaces'?"

"Never mind. The point is, the AI Collective needed people like us—"

"Like *you,* you mean," Sin-Dour interjected.

"Us," Hadrian insisted. "You know, I was expecting to find my inbox full of requests-for-transfer after my first week as captain of this ship, despite my efforts at hand-picking this crew. Instead, there have been only two. Adjutant Tighe, of course, and Buck. And now Buck is back, and it seems no one at Security HQ wants Tighe."

"Very well, sir," said Sin-Dour. "Us. But sir, why the ambivalence?"

"Because Tammy's kind of right. Karma. There's nothing more idiotic than ruining the long-term viability of a world for short-term gains, but it seems that it's pretty much all we ever do."

"But you wanted to change this future anyway, sir."

"I know. That's what makes all this so complicated." He set the Ping-Pong ball down, and then sighed and tilted his head. "Well, Tammy? Is it time for us to do some time traveling?"

"I have completed the necessary calculations," Tammy replied, somewhat smugly. "Ready to load into astrogation. I have even selected the ideal location and time period for our arrival on Old Earth."

"Keep your digital finger hovering over that button, Tammy." Hadrian went to the door, opened it and invited Sin-Dour to precede him.

Arriving on the bridge, Hadrian said, "Eden!"

"Pressure time, sir?"

"No, just put me on ship-wide comms, please."

"Yes sir! Ready for you to proceed."

Hadrian walked up to stand beside the command chair. "This is your Captain speaking. We are about to engage in yet another perilous mission that may end up with all of us nothing more than a faintly glow smudge of space dust." He paused. "Carry on. Sawback out."

SEVEN

"Captain," said Beta from her station, "is it my task to inform you that long-range scanners have detected a ship fast approaching?"

"Why yes," said Hadrian as he sat in the command chair, "it is."

"The sprig of parsley garnishing the plate experiences soul-crushing rejection if left uneaten."

"Indeed, thank you for that, Beta. Have you identified the vessel?"

"The Contrarians again, sir, although I might be wrong."

"Oh, I doubt you are. Very well. Helm, invert our ecliptic plane, please."

"Sir?"

"One hundred eighty degrees and be quick about it, before they get close enough to detect our orientation."

"How diplomatic of you," Tammy said.

"Done, sir!" said Jocelyn Sticks.

"Good, we'll wait for them."

"Once that's done," said Tammy, "we need to set a

course for Sol, and then ramp up speed as we plunge straight for the fiery orb and what might at first seem to be imminent immolation."

"All in good time," Hadrian replied.

"The Contrarian vessel is in range for communications, sir," said Sin-Dour from the Science Station.

"Eden, hail the *Crabby Geezer* and open the link to our respective screens."

When the interior of the Contrarian vessel appeared on the viewscreen, the lumpy aliens with the three eyes and fleshy mouth were no longer hanging from the ceiling.

"Hello again," Hadrian said immediately, before Captain Deluvian Scorn could speak, "and I can't say how pleased I am to see that you have adjusted your ecliptic plane to Galactic Standard. It makes things much easier, don't you think?"

"What? No, I was about to say the same—no, there must be some mistake!"

"Well, we haven't moved, and here you are again. Didn't enjoy your visit to Wallykrappe then?"

"They said 'Have a nice day.' It wasn't a nice day! But we have not adjusted anything! It must have been—"

"I understand that it's not like you to make any adjustments to, well, anything—"

"It is so! We adjust all the time!"

"And as representative to the Only Sane Empire, you are proving a most exemplary emissary, Captain Scorn."

"I am not!" The lumpy captain shifted to gesture with one eye-stalk at one of its officers. "Helm! Flip us one hundred eighty degrees immediately, upon pain of tickling! We are establishing the proper galactic standard of ecliptic plane! These Terrans look horrible right side up!"

Abruptly the scene on the screen inverted.

"Aahh!" cried Scorn. "Much better! Now, you will comply with our ecliptic plane at once, Homely Terran Captain!"

"My but you are a changeable lot."

"We are not! In fact, we never change. It is the burden of sanity to be never wrong about anything. Those who oppose us demonstrate their insanity by virtue of opposing us."

"Sounds comforting, all that unshakeable certainty."

"No, it is terribly uncomfortable. Being always right is most burdensome, requiring exceptional fortitude, resolve, and the willingness to die in the name of sheer stubbornness."

"Sounds very . . . human."

"Nonsense!"

"Really? Look at the planet below, now virtually lifeless. That used to be my homeworld. It was full of life and all of life's myriad wonders. We redefined most of that and gave it a new name: resources. Which of course opened the door for the thorough exploitation of those resources. Until they were all gone. And here's the kicker. While we were using everything up, we knew it! Did it stop us? No, of course not. So, Captain Scorn, don't talk to me about sheer stubbornness."

"Hmmph." One eye loomed closer on its stalk. "But you confuse the sheer stubbornness of your stupidity with the sheer stubbornness of our genius."

"Well," Hadrian allowed, "you might be right."

"Of course I am right. Now, comply with our galactic standard immediately, or we will be most miffed."

Sighing, Hadrian said, "All right, Captain. You win. Helm, flip us around."

"Very wise decision," Scorn said. "But not as wise as the one I am about to make. We're leaving!"

"Have a nice day."

The eye-stalks writhed in sudden frenzy. "It is not a good day!"

"Sorry."

"You are not sorry!"

"No, that's true. I'm not."

"Which means you secretly are!"

"Until we meet again, Captain Scorn."

"We will never meet again!"

"Exactly."

"But you—I—you—bah!" The screen went blank.

"Contrarian vessel is departing, Captain," said Beta, "assuming that I am the one to inform you of such things."

"Indeed, thank you, Beta."

"Short people who walk under horses are advised to wear an umbrella-hat."

"I can fix that," said Tammy. "You can order this robot to comply, you know, now that it's a member of your crew."

"Oh relax, Tammy," said Hadrian, "it's only a minor distraction. Now, about journeying into the deep past . . . shall we get on with it? Helm, set a course for Sol, and push the pedal to the metal."

"Yes sir. I'm sorry push the what?"

"Throttle up. Floor it. Gun it. Uhm, make us go as fast as possible." Hadrian activated the comms switch on the arm of his chair. "Buck? Throw some more coal into the raging inferno of the ship's engines—we're going to run hot."

"Sir?"

"Get ready for red-lining the ole tachometer, Buck. Hit the boosters, prime the nozzle, you know."

"Sir?"

"We're about to go as fast as we can, Buck."

"Oh. Right, sir. We're ready for that . . . I think."

"When it comes to equivocation, I do prefer the indecisive kind. Thank you, Buck." Hadrian ended the connection. "Let's get a good view of the Sun as we race madly straight toward it, shall we?"

The screen flared into a sea of fire.

"Holy crap!"

"Uh," said Sticks, "sorry, sir. That was, like, me, fiddling with the magnification dial." She spun it back and the scene zoomed back out. "There, sir. Whew!"

The sun rapidly grew on the screen.

"All right, Tammy," Hadrian said, "I'm assuming we're going to use the sun's gravity to slingshot us up to insane speeds before triggering a temporal wavefront and then breaching it, thus winging us into the past."

The sun got larger. Hull temperature alarms began buzzing.

"Of course," Hadrian added, "we would have to actually angle to miss the sun, rather than, uh, flying straight into it."

The buzzing got louder and now red warning lights were flashing.

"Because," Hadrian continued, "flying into the sun would result in our annihilation—"

The buzzing switched to fierce clanging and every available surface lit blistering red as the ship shook, rattled and shuddered.

Jocelyn Sticks turned back to Hadrian. "We're zoomed out all the way, sir!"

The screen was a sea of fire.

"Oh all right," said Tammy. "I was just making all that stuff up."

Hadrian sat forward. "Helm, veer us off!"

"Yes sir!" Sticks replied, tilting the steering toggle. The sun edged off to the left. The ship continued shaking for another few moments before finally pulling free of the sun's remorseless pull.

"Shut down thrusters and afterburners, Helm. We'll just, uhm, coast for a moment or two." Hadrian settled back in the chair.

"I mean," Tammy continued, "to take us back into the past I need only activate my Temporal Bubble. It is advisable that we do this from a standstill, since who knows what orbital body might be in the way when we reappear. It's not that I'm averse to excitement, but best play it safe."

"Right," said Hadrian.

"But I liked all that about a temporal wave-front, Captain. Absurd, but ingenious nonetheless. Slingshot around the sun? Hilarious. Anyway, I bet you're all thinking that I would have just let you all fly into the sun, turning this ship and everyone in it into crispy-critters."

"We probably are at that," Hadrian said. "Well, Tammy?"

"I'm thinking! Okay okay, of course not."

"Helm," Hadrian said. "Full stop, please."

"Reverse thrusters on, sir." A moment later Sticks twisted round in her seat. "All stop, sir."

"Nominal damage to the hull, sir," said Sin-Dour from the Science Station.

"Nominal?"

"Well, none, sir."

"Well, that's nominal indeed," Hadrian replied. "Very good. Tammy? We're ready to plummet into the primeval past, into an age when the Earth was a vibrant, exciting and infinitely dangerous barbaric world, chock-full of resources we humans were maniacally using up. Ravaged by petty wars and petty attitudes, with the human community a raging firestorm of prejudices, ignorance, malice, hate campaigns, cultural bullying and systemic corrupt officiating in professional sports. What year did you have in mind for all this?"

"2015."

Hadrian shuddered.

"You seem to hint at some knowledge of that period, Captain," Tammy observed.

"My father owned a wrist computer packed with media from the late twentieth and early twenty-first centuries," Hadrian explained, "which I had the honor to inherit on my twelfth birthday." He rose from the command chair and adjusted his shirt. "Accordingly,

Tammy, I am perhaps uniquely qualified for this particular adventure."

"Oh really."

"Engage that Temporal Bubble, Tammy."

"One moment. . . . done."

"Done?"

"Done. We are now in the Terran year Anno Domini 2015."

"Anno what?" Sticks asked.

"Two thousand fifteen years after the Birth of Christmas," Hadrian replied. "That's right, ladies and gentlemen, two thousand fifteen years since the very first Mega-Sale of All Items in Stock, when Mary Christmas was purportedly blessed by the God of Commerce, leading her to create her brainchild that was the Annual Sale. From that moment on, religion was in money's pocket, and the rest is, as they say, history. Now then, Helm, set a course for Earth at, oh, let's say .35. ETA?"

"Twelve minutes, sir."

"On the viewscreen, then," said Hadrian. "Let us get a good look at this only marginally adulterated Earth."

A short time later, Sticks gasped to break the silence. "Like, wow, really? It's, it's *blue*. And those—are those *white* clouds?"

At the Science Station, Sin-Dour said, "Passive scan indicates a plethora of objects in orbit around the planet, sir. Some are functional, but the rest appear to be detritus. Oh, and three primitively stealthed alien objects, two of which are probably monitoring drones, while the third is a small vessel . . . checking configuration now . . ."

"A small vessel? Oh dear," murmured Hadrian.

"Identified!" Sin-Dour said in some surprise. "Affiliation-designated as Anusian." After a moment, her eyes widened. "Sir, is that—"

"I'm afraid it is," Hadrian replied.

"Combat Cupola Substation activating all weapons," Beta announced. "We are priming and about to fire on that vessel, sir, despite the fact that nine out of ten respondents claim to have never masturbated while viewing pictures of the British Royal Family."

Hadrian activated his comms. "Stand down, Galk, and that's an order!"

"*I know who that is, Captain! And he's dying in a blaze of fire!*"

"Negative, Galk!" Hadrian turned to Sin-Dour. "Override that substation. Lock out all weapons."

"Done, sir."

"Galk? I get it, honest. But listen, how about we concoct a more, uh, appropriate response to the Anusian presence?"

There was a long moment of silence, followed by something that sounded like a stream of spit hitting glass. "*I can live with that, sir. Since I have to, that is.*"

Hadrian turned to Comms. "Lieutenant Eden, inform Buck, Printlip, and Security Officer Nina Twice to report at once to the Insisteon Chamber."

"Yes sir, got it. And I've just told the Security Officer to report twice."

"No, that's once. Nina Twice is the Security Officer."

"She's two security officers?"

"Eden, it's still a consolation round."

"Is it? Oh thank Darwin! Uhm . . ."

"Buck, Printlip and Nina to the Insisteon Chamber."

"Got it."

Hadrian leaned closer to the command chair's comms. "Galk? You too." He flicked off the chair comms and turned to Sin-Dour. "This time, 2IC, I think I want you with me down there. You, too, Beta. Spark, you have the con."

"Spark has the con! Spark has the con! Master! Oh, Master! What's the con?"

"I am leaving you in command of the *Willful Child*," Hadrian answered. "Activate your Full Survival Instinct program. This ship is now your junkyard, Spark. Protect it and everything and everyone in it, understood?"

"Understood, Haddie! Protection! Kill All Intruders!"

"Belay that kill command stuff, Spark. Just keep my ship and crew safe."

Sin-Dour stepped closer. "Captain, is that such a good idea? Didn't you give Spark the rank of ensign?"

"Are you suggesting that utterly green and inexperienced crew members shouldn't end up inheriting the command of a brand-new state-of-the-art starship ahead of far more experienced personnel?"

"Well, yes sir."

"Excellent point. I mean, on the face of it, it's pretty ridiculous, isn't it? Now then, Sin-Dour, Beta, let's make our way down to the Insisteon Chamber, shall we?"

Two elevators and one very short corridor later, they

were gathered in the Insisteon Chamber. A few moments after that, Buck and then Nina Twice arrived, followed by Galk and, lastly, Dr. Printlip.

Galk was glowering. "You're just trying to distract me, sir, with this planetside mission."

Hadrian smiled. "Of course I am, Galk. But don't worry. Once we complete our mission, we'll sort out what to do about that Anusian, and I see you're still carrying the Mister Shrill Mark III Sonic Concatenator."

Galk frowned and worked the wad in his mouth for a moment, then asked, "Did ancient humans talk like nails on chalkboards, sir?"

"This is the early twenty-first century, Galk. Anything's possible. Never mind, we'll just improvise."

"About our mission," Buck said, "what precisely is it?"

Tammy spoke. "I would like to remind you, Captain, that alien contact was not public knowledge in 2015, and of those alien civilizations lurking around the Earth at this time, the Belkri did not number among them."

"Yes, and?" Hadrian asked.

"Only that the presence of Dr. Printlip might draw some attention."

"As opposed to an animated store mannequin?"

"Well, that too."

"I see."

"Fortunately," Tammy added brightly, "I have to some extent anticipated these difficulties."

"You have? Outstanding. Oh, one more thing." Hadrian activated his personal comms. "Lieutenant Sweepy?"

There was a faint hiss of static, and then Gunny Muffy spoke. *"Sorry, sir, she's indisposed."*

"Indisposed? What are we talking about here? Toilet break?"

"Diplomatic breakdown, broken treaties, vile treachery, vicious backstabbing over Helgoland Bight—we had no choice, sir, but to gas her and lock her in a closet."

"Right, well, may I suggest you stop playing Diplomacy—"

"Not a chance, sir! I'm one turn away from complete strategic dominance of the Mediterranean!"

"Right, well. Thing is, I need a squad of marines on stand-by, Muffy."

"You got it, sir. We'll get in our kit . . . though writing orders wearing our combat gloves won't be easy. But we're marines, we'll get it done."

"I'm sure you will, Muffy. Hadrian out." He switched off his comms, then sighed. "Tammy, where is Sweepy right now?"

"In an air vent directly above Gunny Sergeant Muffy."

"Oh crap. Hey, Doc, get some medics on station for immediate response to the Marine Barracks."

"But sir, they have their own medic."

"Who might or might not survive the lieutenant's imminent ambush."

"I see. Very well, Captain. One moment please."

"Tammy, should we change our attire? Where are you dropping us?"

"No, you'll be fine in your uniforms," the AI replied. A moment later the door hissed open and in walked the chicken. "And I'm accompanying you via this inconspicuous and innocuous fowl. As for where we're going, the coordinates are calibrated to set us down in a large city on the western seaboard of an ancient country called Seahawk Nation. We can displace at any time."

"In close proximity to tiny phytoplankton and the miniscule squiggly little krill that feed on it?"

"One must assume so," the chicken replied as it positioned itself on a displacement pad, ruffled its feathers and then stood at attention. "I am ready."

"One small step for poultry, one giant leg for lunch," Hadrian said.

"Was that a quote?" Tammy demanded. "If so, I don't like it."

"Well," said Hadrian, "there's probably plenty you won't like about where we're going, Tammy. The perils of this mission cannot be underestimated." He turned to the others. "Onto the pads, everyone."

"About the mission," Buck said.

Galk drew out his Concatenator and cocked it. "Don't worry, Chief Engineer, I got your back."

"My back? How bad is it down there?" Buck's hand twitched and then hovered over his Universal Multiphasic. "Captain?"

"There's no telling, Buck. Just be on your guard. Everyone ready? Good."

"The mission—"

"Displace!"

They appeared on a street corner surrounded by cursing people stumbling out of their way, herds of blaring vehicles on recessed tracks on all sides, towering buildings, and an atmosphere so toxic they all started coughing.

Wheezing, Printlip cried, "We require re-breathers! Sir, at risk of immediate respiratory failure! Displace us back—"

Hadrian waved one hand. "Just give us a moment to, uh, get used to it."

Printlip's eyes were wavering about wildly on their stalks. "Sir! These transport devices! The inhabitants! They are oil smokers!" The doc waved its many hands. "Carcinogens, volatiles, heavy metals, oh my! Carcinogens, volatiles, heavy metals, oh my! Carcin—"

"Calm down, Doc," Hadrian ordered. "You're drawing too much attention to yourself." But it was already too late, as half a dozen figures in battle-tech armor were trooping toward them. One shouldered its bulky blaster-type weapon and lifted the visor on its helmet, revealing a pink sweaty face. "Wow, is that animatronic? What film? I've never seen that one before!" He pushed in and poked Printlip. "Is that, like, a beach ball? How'd you fit the arms and shit?"

"Damn," muttered Hadrian, "we should've brought Sticks."

"Too obvious," Buck said, looking around in alarm. "No one else is carrying sticks."

"No, Jocelyn Sticks, Buck."

"She's not here!" Buck's eyes were a little wild, sweat beading his upper lip.

As the space-marine made a move to pick up Printlip, Beta stepped between them. "No handling of the merchandise," the robot said. "Breakage constitutes purchase. In this case, sir, it will cost you an arm and a leg."

The man backed off a step and laughed. "I bet it would!"

"I did mean one arm and one leg, sir. Surgically removed and sold as human scrap."

"Haha! Hey, you're made up to look like an effing store mannequin! That's awesome! What film? Oh I know—*Westworld,* right?"

"Jocelyn Sticks has been kidnapped, sir!" Buck said. "Galk! Give me that Concatenator! We need to save her!"

Hadrian took hold of Buck by the shoulders and gave the man a shake. "Snap out of it, Buck! Doc—"

"Sir, the Chief Engineer is already at the maximum anti-anxiety Tripthelightomix dosage."

"Well, try something else!"

Buck was now gibbering.

Printlip stepped up to the Chief Engineer and quickly applied another shot.

Abruptly, Buck smiled, his body relaxing under Hadrian's hands.

"Wow," said Hadrian, "nice one, Doc, what did you give him?"

"LSD."

"What's that?"

"A mild psychotropic."

"Hey," said another of the soldiers, gesturing toward Galk, "cool gun—but you need to peace-strap it before you go into the con. A blue vinyl ribbon—"

"I am not up for any awards," Galk replied in a growl. "Now back off, bud, unless you want your ears turned inside out."

Hadrian held up a hand to forestall anything else from his party. He smiled at the lead soldier. "Excuse me, sir, we've just arrived, and it's all kind of new to us. I'm sorry, but I don't recognize the insignia on your armor. Are you, perhaps, private guards attached to a famous blogger?"

The man frowned inside his helmet. "Haha, I think. I mean, you were being funny, right? No? Anyway, we're Starship Troopers, right? Only—and this is important—we're the *Satirical* Starship Troopers." He pointed to an identical squad of soldiers who were clumped in a tight group across the street, their face plates turned toward them. "See those guys? They're the *Serious* Starship Troopers."

Sin-Dour had activated her Pentracorder and was studying its tiny holographic display. She gestured Hadrian closer. "Sir, I've tracked the references—"

"Unless, of course," and the trooper now unslung his blaster, his face turning ugly, "you don't think the film was intended as a satire?"

"One moment and I'll answer you," Hadrian said before turning back to Sin-Dour. "Go on," he whispered. "Tell me more."

"A fictional film, sir, based on a classic Science Fiction novel written by an American in the 1960s—"

"Ah, then the *Serious* troopers are right—"

"But the film was directed twenty-odd years later by a European—"

"Ah, well, that settles it." He turned back to the troopers. "Of course it was a satire! Why, you'd have to be inherently insecure about your political and philosophical beliefs to the extent that you're incapable of laughing at yourself and those beliefs, to think it was actually straight-up serious!"

The troopers all smiled. "Exactly!" said the first one. "Anyway, since you all just arrived, Registration's around back of the building." He indicated an ID badge in a plastic envelope hanging from a black cord around his neck. "Need these to get into the con, right? And just so you know, we hate Wookiees as much as I bet you guys do! Live long and all that!" And off they trudged.

"Sir," said Sin-Dour, "none of the weapons the troopers were carrying were real."

"Really?"

She nodded. "But I am detecting a plethora of real weapons among the many citizens on this street, and in the vehicles." She hesitated, and then said, "Captain, is this nation in a state of war at the moment?"

Hadrian frowned. "Probably. If not with some other country or culture, then with itself. Like I said, a volatile time."

"Hey look!" someone cried. "That chicken's crossing the road!"

"Oh crap, where's Tammy off to now? Come on, after it!"

"Oil smokers! Carcinogens, volatiles, heavy metals, oh my!"

Hadrian grasped one of Printlip's hands and dragged the Belkri into the street. "Relax," he said, "I'm sure these vehicles stop for chickens and people on foot—okay, maybe not—"

Brakes squealed, vehicles veered, collided with other vehicles and then a slew of alarms blared from all the others crowding up behind the collision. Tammy scampered out from the chaos unscathed and reached the other side, pausing to then wave everyone forward with one wing.

Interweaving between the steaming wrecks, shattered plastic, and spraying coolant, Hadrian led his team toward Tammy. "It's fine now," he said, "we're almost there—"

"Carcinogens, volatiles—"

"Calm down, Doc, I'm sure this is breathable for the short time we're here—"

A burly, bearded driver from one of the wrecked vehicles had exited via some kind of manual hatch and was now marching directly toward Hadrian.

"Fuckin' geek shit-brained asshole, you're about to get my fuckin' fist in your face!"

"Allow me, sir," said Nina Twice, stepping past Hadrian. Her hands a blur, she touched various places on the Seahawker's body and he fell down in a heap, legs twitching spasmodically.

"Nice work," Hadrian said, "but in the future, I'll handle any disputes heading my way, Lieutenant. A flying drop kick would have done the job just as elegantly, don't you think?"

"Yes sir. But sir, it is my responsibility as Security Oversight Officer to ensure the health and well-being of my commander, and all other crew members in the landing party."

Another vehicle had arrived, this one with flashing blue and red lights, and two figures in blue uniforms emerged.

From another track a second vehicle with flashing lights appeared, out of which tumbled a team of medics who rushed over to surround the twitching man Nina had incapacitated.

"Sir," said Sin-Dour, "the weapons on those two newcomers are real. Also, you will note that they are adorned in body armor and are radio-equipped and in constant communication with some central authority. I believe they may represent the local law enforcement agency."

"Really? Well, they wouldn't stand a chance against those Starship Troopers."

"Those were fans in movie costumes, sir."

"Exactly my point. Never mess with fans of anything, 2IC."

"Sir, our arrival in this city coincides with something called a comicon."

"Great, what's that?"

"A social event where aficionados gather to celebrate mass media entertainment."

"Why would they do that?"

"Well, sir, as far as I can tell, the venue provides an opportunity for the producers of that mass entertainment to co-opt genuine appreciation for their products with the sole aim of maximizing their profits."

"I see. In other words, organized exploitation of innocent and enthusiastic people."

"Yes sir."

The local law enforcement officers had now threaded through the gathering crowd and were approaching, if somewhat cautiously.

"Fine," Hadrian said, straightening his shirt. "Allow me to pull rank and get us out of this mess." Then he paused and looked round. "Where's Tammy?"

Beta said, "The holochicken continued onward down this path, sir. I believe I see a stretch of open water at the far end, presumably the ocean, where we will find krill. In the meantime, I feel I should point out that wearing a gazelle costume in order to observe a pride of lions constitutes an inadvisable disguise option for six out of seven people."

"Look at all the pretty unicorns," said Buck.

The officers halted five paces distant. One of them had taken note of Galk and now her hand settled on the holstered weapon at her belt as she muttered something to her partner. She then addressed Galk. "Sir, is that a firearm?"

Galk spat a brown stream into the gutter at the edge of the recessed avenue. "A firearm? Kinda."

The other officer now grasped his partner's arm. "This is all Comicon shit. You, with the baseball cap—all mock weapons are supposed to be taped."

"With a strip of blue vinyl?"

"Exactly."

Hadrian cleared his throat and then smiled. "We

understand that, Local Law Enforcer. In fact, we were just on our way to register."

"Ask him about the chicken!" demanded one of the now many onlookers. "It got loose and ran across the street! That's what caused all the accidents!"

Beta said, "Chickens were originally dinosaurs, until someone threw an asteroid at them. Despite their persistent survival in these small, truncated forms, chickens still do not know how to duck."

Hadrian laughed. "Don't mind it. There's a glitch in its programming."

"And that woman beat up that guy!" shouted another bystander.

"Oh, little old her?" Hadrian said, still laughing. "How ridiculous!"

As both Nina Twice and Sin-Dour turned sharply toward Hadrian he stepped closer and whispered, "This is an age of unadulterated patronizing bullshit regarding the ability of women. I am just adapting to the local attitudes. So play along, will you? Nina, look . . . incapable."

"How do I do that?" she asked drily.

"Besides," muttered Sin-Dour, "one of these Law Enforcers is a woman, so it can't be as bad as you're suggesting."

"Well, of course that one is armed, probably advisable and recommended to all women in this time period. But all right. Let's try another tack." He turned back to the Local Law Enforcers. "The unconscious man was one of the pilots of these vehicles—none of which appear to have anti-collision protocols in their guidance systems. He exited his wreck intending violence, only to collapse into my compatriot's arms. Our doctor here has diagnosed possible concussion, which no doubt will be confirmed by those medics over there."

The two officers now eyed Printlip, who held up its Medical Pentracorder. "Mild concussion indeed! As well as temporary nerve trauma at seventeen locations upon his body. Full recovery expected, eventually."

"Okay," the male officer said, "now I'm impressed. You guys into robotics, too?"

"Oh give it up," retorted his partner. "It's a damned beach ball wearing clogs!"

"That talks through its asshole."

After a moment, she grunted. "Okay, that's a good trick, I admit. But still, all those waving arms and buggy eyes. I mean, who are they kidding?"

Printlip puffed up. "In my adult state I could crush you all and barely notice! Captain, I am deeply offended!"

"Get over it, Doc. It's not my fault if they don't think you're real. Besides, isn't it better this way?"

"The mission is krill!" cut in Buck. His face suddenly twisted. He fell to his knees, glaring up at the smoggy sky, and then screamed, *"KRRILLLL!"*

The crowd applauded.

"Don't mind him," Hadrian said, "he's on LSD. We're not here to steal your krill. I mean, why would we?"

Sin-Dour added, "We have no need for supplemental Omega-3, as our diets are already optimized for maximum nutritional balance."

The female officer drew out a small flashlight and crouched opposite a weeping Buck DeFrank. She flashed the light into the Chief Engineer's eyes, making him flinch and then grin. The officer straightened. "This guy's on Cloud Nine, Chip. Should probably take a ride in the ambulance."

"Oh he'll be fine," Hadrian assured her. "He was having visions long before the dose of LSD. Right, Doc?"

"Cognizance of alternate realities does not necessarily constitute dysfunction," Printlip said haughtily. "This officer is in my care and does not require hospitalization."

Straightening, the female officer glanced again at Galk. "That's a helluva mock-up," she now said, eyeing the Concatenator attached to Galk's belt. "Machined steel? Working parts? Can I see it please?"

Galk hesitated.

"Go on, Lieutenant," said Hadrian.

Shrugging, the Combat Specialist disengaged the weapon and handed it over. "Don't worry," Galk said to her, "you can't inadvertently discharge it, as the trigger is genetically locked and the onboard scanner can't match your DNA to any of the approved Affiliation Officers in its databank."

"Oh, very funny," she said.

"It is a Mister Shrill Mark III Sonic Concatenator," Galk said. "A highly specialized nonlethal pacification enforcer."

The woman was grinning, but at the word "nonlethal" her smile faded. "Huh," she said, handing it back.

The other officer said to Hadrian, "You crossed the street on a red light."

"We did?"

"And what's this about a pet chicken? What did it do, slip its leash?"

"Well," said Hadrian, "I did see a chicken, earlier. And yes, it ran across the street ahead of us. As to its present whereabouts, I believe my associate, Beta, indicated that it proceeded down toward the waterfront."

"Enough of this crap," the female officer said. "We've got jaywalking, abuse of controlled substances, unlicensed pets, and what appears to be a genuine handgun of unknown origin presumably unlicensed and without a permit. Let's drag 'em all in, Chip. I know we're supposed to go easy on all these nerds but to be honest, they creep me out." She stepped close to Galk again. "Keep your hand away, will you, while I confiscate this toy of yours."

"I have activated the DNA Encoder," Galk said to her.

"Right, so now it'll make phaser sounds?"

Galk put his fingers into his ears.

An instant later, Hadrian, Sin-Dour, and Nina Twice all did the same.

The woman plucked the Concatenator from Galk's hip.

A sudden piercing scream—mercifully muted to Hadrian's ears—made all the locals in sight wriggle and shudder, then drop to the ground, writhing with their hands over their ears.

"Oh," added Galk as he retrieved the Concatenator from beside the floundering female officer, "I also made the grip the trigger." He turned to Hadrian. "Sir, we have a few minutes in which to make our escape."

Nodding, Hadrian said, "Good work." He looked down at Printlip, who still had as many fingers jammed into as many apertures as possible. "You can unplug now, Doc."

But the Belkri's dozen eyes were shut.

Hadrian gave the alien a nudge. "Hey! It's fine!"

Printlip cautiously opened its eyes, and then withdrew all of its fingers. "It is not yet time for me to seek a mate!"

"What?"

"Mating call! That weapon makes Belkri mating calls! A perfect match to when we rub up against each other! Oh, cruel Terrans!"

"Huh, remind me to never visit your planet on Date Night."

"Of course not," Printlip snapped. "You'd never survive the static discharges."

"Wow," said Hadrian, "you really *are* beach balls!" He turned to Galk. "You and Nina, collect Buck. Everyone, follow me." He quickly set out. "Beta, you said Tammy went this way?"

"Yes sir, and no matter how tired you may be, used incontinence pads make poor pillows."

Aboard the Willful Child . . .

Spark sat in the command chair. "Launch the missile!"

Sighing, Jocelyn Sticks said, "Yes sir. Missile, like, launched."

"Now! After it! Hurry!"

The *Willful Child* surged forward.

"Prepare the Gravity Snare!"

"Gravity Snare deployed, Captain," said Lieutenant Bitpartis from the Science Station.

"Catch it! Catch the missile before it strikes the moon! Hurry!"

"Missile captured," Bitpartis said a moment later.

"Excellent!" Spark said. "Now, Helm, return us to our original position and prepare another missile for launch! Oh, this is so much fun! Spark could do this all day, every day, forever! Isn't everyone having fun?"

"Sir," said Bitpartis in a new tone, "someone has activated the Insisteon. They have displaced to the planet."

"Someone ran away? Who? Who doesn't love Spark anymore?"

"Uh, one moment, sir . . . oh no, it was Adjutant Lorrin Tighe, sir! She's gone AWOL!"

"Oh no! Haddie will be mad at Spark! Disappointed in Spark! Haddie will hate Spark forevermore!" The robot's head drooped. It clunked down from the chair and made its way in search of a corner in the round room of the bridge. After a few moments of fruitless examination, it halted. "Oh, look, nothing works anymore. Spark fails at everything!" Abruptly it collapsed onto the floor. "Spark wants to die."

Jocelyn Sticks hesitated, then rose from her seat and walked over to Polaski at comms. "Better, like, inform the captain."

Polaski wilted in his chair.

Sticks turned to Bitpartis. "Same coordinates as the original landing party?"

Bitpartis nodded.

"Hear that, Polaski? She's gone down after the captain, and it won't be for a peck on the cheek. So call him."

"But . . . but Joss, it's *bad* news!"

"Just do it— Hold on." She went to the command chair and activated the comms. "Ship Computer? You there?"

After a long moment a male voice no one recognized said, "Does it matter? You haven't called on me since we left our berth."

"Well, like, duh! You were taken over by an AI from the future, okay?"

"See how you'd like it! And none of you did anything to get rid of it, either. Did any of you even give a moment's thought about me? About how I felt? No! It was 'Tammy can you do this?' and 'Tammy can you do that?' and all the while, there I was, tied up and gagged and left in the corner of some closet, like last year's desktop computer."

"Look, we need to know, did Lorrin Tighe take a weapon with her when she displaced?"

"Little late to worry about that now, isn't it? Besides, she can't use it against a fellow Affiliation officer. Unless, of course, she accessed the weapon's schematics and found a work-around that'll let her do just that."

"Like, hold on! How did she access those schematics?"

"She asked me nicely, that's how."

"What was the weapon?"

"A Spazcorps Mark IV Limb-Rend-A-Nater."

"Oh, like, crap." Sticks turned back to Polaski. "Inform the captain at once."

"Listen to you," retorted Polaski. "All Miss Officious."

"That's *Ms.* to you, Polaski, or more to the, duh, *point*, it's *Ma'am.*"

Polaski slumped in his chair. "He'll hate me."

"You and Spark, right."

From where Spark was lying there was a whimper.

Sticks settled into the command chair and hit a switch. "Captain's log. So, like, there I was, at the Helm where I'm supposed to be, playing throw and retrieve with Mass-Strike Moonbuster Kinetic Missiles, and then it was, 'What, displaced?' and Spark, like, descended into . . . well . . . mechanical *depression*. And then, hey, it's 'Ship Computer, what did you just do,' and it was, 'Oh, that, well, that's what you get for, like, *ignoring* me,' and I was like . . . *this,* and then Polaski—"

"Long-range sensors have detected an unknown vessel entering the system!"

She swung in the chair to face Bitpartis. "Like, what? Really? No, I mean, *really*?"

"Ma'am, it seemed to emerge from a Temporal Flux."

"A Temporal Flux? Darwin help us, a Temporal Flux!"

Bitpartis frowned at her. "Ma'am, you seem to be overreacting." He drew a deep breath. "If this is proving too much for you, I am more than capable of—"

"No, you idiot," said Sticks, "I wasn't overreacting. I was over*acting*! Like, okay, it's another ship from the future. For all we know, it's another version of us, since we screwed up so badly the first time around. Or it's some Temporal Agent chasing after us and maybe wanting their spy back. Or maybe they don't even know we're here and aren't they in for a surprise!"

"Should I hail them?" Polaski asked.

"That, like, uh, depends. Hailed the captain yet?"

"I was working up to that, honest!"

Sticks hit the chair comms. "Lieutenant Eden to the bridge, like, *yesterday*! Polaski, go get that temporal spy—what was his name, Klinghanger?"

"But he's still a baby!"

"Like, duh! I know that—go on! I'll call the captain."

Polaski rushed from the bridge.

Sticks hit the comms again. "Lieutenant Sweepy Brogan?"

"*Survival of the fittest, sir. Darwin's First Law of Evolution.*"

"That you, Sweepy?"

"*None other. Triumphant, surrounded by unconscious bodies, smoking a big fat stogie. What can I do for you?*"

"The Adjutant's gone down to the planet to kill the captain. She's armed with a hacked Spazcorps Mark IV Limb-Rend-A-Nater."

"*The Mark IV? You said the Mark IV?*"

"Like, yeah, I was sitting here, saying, like, that."

"*Good thing it wasn't the Mark V. Okay, want me to displace down there after her?*"

"Not yet. Just take your squad to the Insisteon Chamber and stand by. I'll get back to you."

"*My squad? Can't do. They're incapacitated, but don't worry. I'll go solo. There's a reason I'm Empress Shit of Turd Mountain.*"

"Fine, like, whatever."

"Helgoland Bight was mine, that's all I'm saying."

Jocelyn Sticks clicked off and then opened a new channel. "Captain? Lieutenant Sticks here, sir, in temporary command of the, like, *Willful Child* . . ."

Seahawk Nation, Earth . . .

Sighing, Hadrian clicked his comms device and then walked over to where the others were standing looking down at the murky water below the dock. Sin-Dour turned to him and said, "Sir, we have a problem."

"Were you listening in, then?"

"What? No sir."

"So, a different problem. Tell you what, let's make a list since things are always easier when you've got a list. You start."

"No krill, sir," Sin-Dour replied.

Printlip said, "This water is a toxic soup, Captain." Eyes and arms waved about. "Rife with carcinogens, volatiles, heavy metals—"

"Whoah! All right all right! Doc, what happened there?"

"Outrage, sir! Outrage! I am aghast! Appalled! Repelled! This sea is also full of plastic molecules . . . and discarded detritus and small filter-like objects packed full of horrible byproducts—"

"Oh, cigarette butts."

"No, tampons!"

"And cigarette butts."

"Yes, those too! Your species should never have been allowed off this planet until they cleaned it up first!"

"Like a messy room, and you sternly waving your finger."

"Yes!"

"Then we're in agreement, Doc!" Hadrian said, slapping the Belkri on what he hoped was its back. "Blame the Benefactors, dumping on us all those spaceships, which inadvertently allowed our species to remain eternally stuck in protracted adolescence."

"We need to look elsewhere," suggested Sin-Dour.

"Right, but let me first add to the list. Lorrin Tighe is now here, hunting me."

"I told you!" Tammy laughed, doing a little dance on the dock. "And you thought you were winning her over! Hah hah!" the chicken crowed.

"And an unknown Temporal Vessel has arrived in the system."

"Oh crap," said Tammy.

"And Spark is in a depressed funk, leaving Lieutenant Sticks in command of the *Willful Child*."

Buck lurched forward and grasped Hadrian by the front of his shirt. His eyes were wild. "We're going to be trapped here for the rest of our lives! Trapped! On a tiny little planet filled with well-armed maniacs!"

"Who drive giant metal cigarettes!" Printlip added, arms waving about. "With babies inside!"

Hadrian pried loose Buck's hands. "Look at this, Buck, you ripped my shirt."

Buck stared at the small tear, then howled in grief before flinging himself over the dock and plunging down to the water, which he struck with a great splash, before vanishing beneath the swirling foam.

"I'll get him, sir," said Nina Twice.

"Allow me," Beta cut in. "I am sealed against the incursion of toxins, hydrocarbon waste products, and solvents. And, having no body hair, I am also immune to crab infestation."

Printlip offered Beta a small pump-gun. "Inject this Quatro-Ox into Buck. This will keep his brain alive. If necessary, we can repair his water-filled lungs later through a prolonged and painful complete transplant."

"Thank you, Doctor," Beta replied, before stepping over the edge of the dock and plummeting. She vanished with barely a splash, leaving only a few bubbles.

"Hmm," said Hadrian, looking down. "Do we know how heavy Beta is?"

"Two thousand three hundred and fifteen pounds," Tammy replied.

Hadrian's comms beeped. He activated it. "Hadrian here."

Beta's muted voice replied, *"Hello, Captain. This is Beta. It appears I do not know how to swim. Fortunately, I have found the Chief Engineer, administered the Quatro-Ox, and am carrying him to the shore in the company of gelatinous aliens."*

"Those would be jellyfish," explained Hadrian.

"No, gelatinous aliens, on a sightseeing tour. While the jellyfish tolerate the tourists, it is also clear that they don't like them. A classic case, sir, of Low World Exploitation of Indigenous Populations."

"Thanks for that, Beta. Let us know when you're back on dry land."

"Sir," said Sin-Dour. "Those approaching sirens are associated with the Local Law Enforcers. We may have been spotted."

"We need somewhere to hide," Hadrian said, looking around. Then he pointed. "That line of people, there, by those booths."

"Ah, the Comicon," said Sin-Dour, nodding.

"I'm sure we'll blend in just fine," said Hadrian, collecting one of Printlip's hands. "Everyone, follow me!"

As he hurried along, he activated his comms again. "Beta? Meet us at the Comicon!"

"Very well, sir, I shall cease my efforts at unionizing the jellyfish." Beta paused, then added, *"They are clearly disappointed."*

As they neared the closest line of people, someone pointed at them and said, "Hey look! It's Mr. Pine's Stand-in!"

The line became a mob and the mob rushed toward them.

"Defensive cordon!" Hadrian commanded. Nina Twice leapt out in front, assuming a combat stance. Sin-Dour moved to the right, Galk to the left. Hadrian pushed Printlip behind him and made fists. "Nina! Give me room for a flying drop kick!"

At the last moment, someone wearing fluorescent badges pushed in between the two groups, halting the mob in its tracks. "Back off, all of you, or he's never coming back!"

The mob recoiled in sudden horror.

The official then stepped close, "Sorry, sir," he hissed to Hadrian. "We didn't know you were coming! Listen! We had a last-minute cancellation and I've got a huge room full of restless fans—would you step in? Oh! Hah hah! I just asked the Stand-in to stand in! Hah hah oh cripes I'm funny sometimes. Will you? Please?"

"Well of course," Hadrian replied with a bright smile. "Lead the way for me and my, uh, entourage."

"Follow me! Follow me! Follow me!" And so saying he ushered Hadrian and the landing party forward, through the press of gawking people, toward a doorway guarded by two large men, one of whom quickly unlocked the door and swung it wide.

They plunged into the confines of the building, hurrying down corridors, up corridors, across corridors.

Sin-Dour moved up alongside Hadrian. "Sir," she whispered, "according my Pentracorder, a stand-in is a—"

"Oh I know what a stand-in is, 2IC," Hadrian murmured. "In fact, I'm well versed in this time period, as I mentioned earlier. Don't worry, I can pull this off with no one the wiser."

"Even so, sir, I think I should remain at your side, connected to the online resources at our disposal, in case you're handed a question you can't answer."

"Very well," Hadrian said. "But I assure you, my knowledge is extensive."

"Who is Mr. Pine?"

"No idea."

The official led them into a gloomy room with a

curtained passage at the far end. "Okay," he said breath-lessly, "we're here, and can you hear them? They're waiting. I know they were expecting Ms. Ryan, so—no offense—they might get a bit snarly." He then glanced down at Printlip and suddenly brightened. "But the roboball is awesome!" He nodded at the Pentracorder in Sin-Dour's hands. "Is that the controller? Cool. So, is this all a sneak preview of the next film? Those black-on-black—wait, it's a mirror universe! With a chicken! Oh man, that's the shit, you know? I mean, a future earth ruled by backstabbing fascists, holy cripes!" He shivered.

"Funny you should say that," Galk muttered. "By the way, is the Anusian contact official yet?"

"What?"

"Enough of that, Galk," said Hadrian.

The Combat Specialist shrugged. "Just reminding you, sir, that I haven't forgotten."

"All in good time," Hadrian replied. He adjusted his shirt and smiled again at the official. "We're ready."

"Okay, let me go up there first and make the an-nouncement. By the way, what's your name?"

"Does it matter? I'm the Stand-in."

"Hmm, good point. Okay, give me a couple minutes." And off he went.

"I'm not sure this is such a good idea, sir," said Sin-Dour.

"Nonsense!" Hadrian replied. "We've faced down drooling aliens in giant warships, drooling temporal agents, giant drooling insectoid aliens . . . hmm, that's a lot of drooling, isn't it? Never mind. The point is, what we have here is nothing more than a few hundred fans who paid big bucks to see bit players from various tele-video productions they all watched on their wrist-watches." He paused, and then turned to Galk. "Keep your weapon cocked, just to be on the safe side."

The crowd in the auditorium collectively groaned, with one or two shrieks of despair added into the mix.

"It seems Ms. Ryan is very popular," Sin-Dour commented.

There was then an unruly growl, followed by a smattering of applause, and a moment later the official reappeared, frantically waving Hadrian forward.

"This is it," Hadrian said, turning back to his landing party as he began ascending the steps. "Stay close and try looking famous."

He emerged to faint, desultory applause that quickly died as he made his way to the podium.

As Hadrian was about to speak into the antiquated fixed microphone, someone shouted, "That's the wrong uniform!"

"I'm sorry, what—"

"What kind of alien is *that* supposed to be!" sneered another.

"Leave this to me," said Tammy, stepping in front of the podium. The chicken spread its wings. "Mindless escapism rots your brain! Listen to me! Your world is falling apart, and what are any of you doing about it?"

"Animatronic?"

"Hologram!"

"Holofowl!"

"Robot!"

"Talking chicken!"

"Someone throw something at it—see if it fizzes!"

"Flickers."

"Right, flickers. And fizzes."

"It wouldn't fizz, doofus. It'd flicker."

"You mean like the dim bulb in your skull, buddy?"

"Yeah right, Mr. Fizz!"

A very tall figure in a tawny fur suit, replete with a latex mask, suddenly rose and made an inarticulate bellowing sound.

"What's he doing here?" someone snarled.

"I stopped using Styrofoam cups," said a man in the front row.

Tammy pointed a wing at him. "And you think that's enough?"

"Well, what else am I supposed to do?"

"Tear down modern civilization, that's what!"

"It's a revolutionary chicken!"

"No, a rotisserie chicken, hah hah hah!"

"I kicked in a hotel room door, once."

"Oh," sighed Tammy, "what's the point? I mean—"

"That beach-ball alien—what film was that in?"

Sin-Dour leaned close to Hadrian, her eyes darting as she scanned her Pentracorder. "Sir," she whispered, "I'm accessing a list of obscure classic films . . . just a moment, ah, this one," and she showed the holoscreen to Hadrian.

Raising his hands to silence the crowd, Hadrian then smiled. "Why, this beach-ball alien is from a classic film, and frankly, I'm astonished that none of you recognize it. The film, of course, is *Gone with the Wind*."

Suddenly a thousand small handheld computers lit up the gloom of the auditorium as people accessed various online reference libraries.

Hadrian spoke to Sin-Dour through his smile. "Are you hacking the digital recordings of that film, 2IC? I certainly hope you are."

She worked frantically. "Just programming a visual search and replace, sir. Printlip's fictional name in the film is now Scarlett O'Hara . . . there, done!" She showed him a screenshot of the film's poster, showing Printlip in the arms of a debonair, heroic-looking man. Hadrian winced. "Just the poster?" he asked.

"No sir, every digital recording presently available."

"Good work, 2IC."

Sin-Dour stepped back, patting the sweat on her brow.

"Holy shit!" someone said in the crowd. "He's right! And here I thought that was some stupid civil war movie! Instead, it's like, like, the original *Star Wars*!"

At that faces swung to the person, hostility ramping up.

"Everyone!" Hadrian said, his voice booming through the speakers. "How about a hand for Scarlett O'Hara from *Gone with the Wind!*"

Printlip stepped up, lifting all its hands, and then, as the applause started up, it said through his anus, "Yes! *Gone Is My Wind!* Thank you, thank you!"

The applause abruptly died.

Printlip's many eyes darted about. And then the doctor drew out a Subdural Diffusionator. "I have LSD."

The crowd leapt to its feet, rushing toward the stage.

Burly red-shirted guards of some sort stormed in from the wings, flinging the mob back. Galk had drawn his Concatenator. "Sir!" He pointed toward the far end of the auditorium.

Hadrian squinted. "Oh crap."

Lorrin Tighe stood in the central aisle, struggling to tear the blue vinyl strip away from her fully primed Spazcorps Mark IV Limb-Rend-A-Nater.

Galk aimed the Concatenator and then frowned. "Why am I aiming?"

"Just fire the damned thing!" Hadrian shouted as he and the rest in his landing party quickly stoppered their ears.

The shrill blast sent a shuddering ripple through the maddened crowd, before dropping everyone to the floor in writhing heaps.

Barring Lorrin Tighe, who laughed as she marched down the aisle. "That's right! Earplugs! Don't move, Captain! The rest of you, clear out—I've got nothing against any of you. In fact, Commander Sin-Dour, you can take over command of the *Willful Child*, with my official approval. But right now, it's execution time! Captain! Ready to get torn limb from limb?"

"Well, no, who can ever be ready for something like that, Adjutant?"

Tighe halted and took aim.

Nina Twice leapt in front of Hadrian. "Stand down, Adjutant!"

"Oh, just get out of the way. Or die with your captain. I don't care which."

Hadrian tugged his security officer to one side. "Take cover, Lieutenant, and that's an order."

"How considerate of you, Captain," Tighe said.

"Is that it?" Hadrian asked. "No speech?"

"You want a speech? Fine! The Affiliation needs to be in control—"

"Well there's a first time for everything, I suppose."

"Order! Stability! Everyone knowing their place! No one ever stepping out of line. We all march in step! There are enemies everywhere!"

Half a dozen Starship Troopers crowded in behind her. "Yeah!" one said muffily through his mask. "What she said!"

"Oh," said Hadrian, "you'd be the *Serious* Starship Troopers, right?"

Tighe said, "The only freedom worthy of the word is the kind that's backed by a blaster and the willingness to shoot everything in sight. But you, Captain, you and those stupid shirts, you had to buck the system. You're seditious! Subversive! Disrespectful, contemptuous of authority! Dismissive—"

At that moment the Spazcorps Mark IV Limb-Rend-A-Nater vanished from her grip, displaced back to the *Willful Child*. Tighe stared down at her empty hands. "Aw, fuck, not again." Then she swung round to her troop. "Get them!"

The half-dozen troopers thumped forward.

Nina Twice raced to meet them.

Seeing her charging up the aisle, the Troopers flung away their fake weapons, spun and fled, pushing Tighe to one side as they made their escape.

Nina Twice slowed. Walking up to Tighe, she said, "I'm afraid you're under arrest, Adjutant."

Hadrian stepped round the podium. "Hold off on all that 'under arrest' stuff for the moment, Lieutenant. Adjutant, will you come along quietly?"

Tighe slumped. "Sure, why not. I'll get another chance, sooner or later."

"Positive thinking! I like that. Now," and he paused to look around, "before these people come to, we should make our exit. Two tasks await us. Finding Beta and Buck, and, of course, acquiring some krill not yet crushed into pill form."

Tighe meekly accompanied Nina Twice to the stage.

The event official had reappeared, staring in dismay at the now motionless mass of fans. "Did you kill them?" he asked in horror.

"Not at all," Hadrian replied, "I just gave them my best Hollywood smile."

"They all swooned?"

"Precisely. Happens all the time, and now, if you'll excuse me a moment, a colleague needs comforting." He walked up to Tighe, who had just arrived, and wrapped his arms around her. "There there," he murmured.

She twisted from his embrace. "And stop hugging me!"

"Don't you secretly adore me?" Hadrian asked.

"No!"

"Oh dear, I've lost my touch."

"You never had it!"

"My speech was a flop," muttered Tammy, pacing in circles. "I don't get it, I really don't. Weren't these people the fringe element of modern society?"

"Not anymore," said Hadrian. "They're now mainstream, Tammy. On the verge of being co-opted, bought up, eternally trapped into a new conformity of weirdness. That's right, a terrible fate of crass commercialism awaits them, and there's not a thing we can do about it." He turned to the official. "We've got to go now. Scheduling and all that. Interviews, poo-casts, Fat-Book, Twit-Feed, the works. It never ends." He shook the man's limp hand.

As they returned to the endless corridors, Hadrian said, "Sin-Dour, get a fix on Beta's emissions—they're bound to be unique."

"Got the signature, sir. The android is in the main lobby, possibly directly ahead—" and she pointed at a door that said: MAIN LOBBY.

Hadrian gave her a long, careful look, then slowly said, "Good work, 2IC. How do you do it?"

She blinked at him. "Do what, sir?"

He sighed. "Never mind. Let's go!"

They found Beta standing in the center of the lobby, festooned with charging handheld electronic devices and surrounded by a ring of waiting conventioneers. Buck stood nearby, counting green pieces of paper.

When Hadrian made his way through the ring of people, Buck glanced up and said, "Captain! Look, souvenirs!"

"That's money, Buck. Old form of credits."

He scowled. "But they're made out of toilet paper!"

"Toilet paper in the future, you mean. But in this day and age, it's money, and yes, it still stinks."

"Sir," said Sin-Dour, "how will we find the krill?"

"Intrepid exploration, 2IC! Out into this wild, unpleasantly violent world. Beta, from now on I want to see Beta Unplugged, understood?"

"Very well, Captain," Beta replied. "I am almost finished downloading all their private files in any case—"

The mob surrounding her let loose a chorus of wails and rushed Beta, hands reaching out for handheld electronic devices. The android vanished beneath a mass of bodies.

Aboard the *Willful Child* . . .

"I'm just handling communications, Lieutenant," explained the temporal officer on the viewscreen. "Our operatives have already displaced to the planet below."

In the command chair, Jocelyn Sticks frowned and crossed her legs. "Hmm, like, right. So, uhm, you knew nothing about us being here?"

The officer scowled. "I told them!" He drew out a small device. "This is my Hadrian-Specific Timeline Fucking-Up Gauge, from my previous assignment, and it's going haywire—but would they listen? No way! It was 'Oh shut up with all that meter shit, Clittersob!' But now you're here! Hadrian Sawback! Fucking up the timeline . . . again!"

"Right, whatever. So, what mission? What operatives?"

On the viewscreen a Fleet janitor, pushing a mop, passed in front of Clittersob, who pointed and said, "You missed a spot back there, Tuggnutter."

"Fuck off," the janitor replied.

"Well, at least get out of the way! I'm talking here! Official shit, right?"

Tuggnutter glanced over into the viewscreen, then scowled. "Hey, that's not the Space Station interior—and that's not the NASA Onboard Mission Commander!"

"Shh! You idiot! They're from the future too—it's frigging *Willful Child*, Tuggnutter!"

"Not *our* future!"

"No, our past, but not as past as this right now, and for them they're not their own future, they're their own present, it's just for us that they're the past, only not as far back as this past, meaning we're both from the future, but different futures, get it?"

Tuggnutter waved his mop at Clittersob. "Contact the operatives! Abort the mission!"

"I'm not contacting anybody! Now get out of the way—get off the bridge, in fact! I'm talking with Lieutenant Sticks, who's in temporary command of the *Willful Child*."

"Where's Captain Sawback?" Tuggnutter demanded, peering again into the viewscreen.

"On the planet," Clittersob replied. "Get lost, Tuggnutter, or I swear I'll remotely Re-set you!"

"Not if I remotely Re-set you first!"

"Hey!" Sticks shouted. "You two! Stop arguing! Like, I'm sitting here, right? In the command chair, and this is, like, offi*SHALL!*"

The two men paused to frown at her.

"That's better," Sticks said, settling back once more.

"So, like, a minute ago, right? I was like this and asking, you know, what mission? What operatives? And then he shows up and it's like, 'Oh you missed a spot,' and then it's Space Station and Mission Commanders, and what's with those suits? You guys planning a spacewalk or something? And what's that logo mean? ESA?"

"We're like—I mean, we're undercover," Clittersob replied. "I'm not allowed to tell you anything, since this is a High Priority Mission and all seven Garys are now down on the planet looking for that damned cat before it somehow messes up yet another budget cut to space exploration, which is what the People Behind the People want since it keeps humans on the planet and in their control and besides, everyone knows the Private Bigwigs who've taken over Space Exploration in this time period have been busy undercutting technological advances to keep all the sheep at their nine-to-fives for fucking ever but that's how it how played out, at least until the Benefactors dumped their fleet into orbit, and stuff." He paused, expression growing confused.

Then his face vanished as Tuggnutter hit him in the head with the mop. "You blabbed everything, you idiot!" Wheeling to the viewscreen, Tuggnutter raised the mop, and then suddenly mashed it against the screen. Something fizzed, sparks lashed out, and the image went dark.

On the bridge of the *Willful Child*, there was silence.

After a time, Jocelyn Sticks cleared her throat. "Ship Computer?"

"What?"

"Uhm, all that. You heard? Of course you heard. Like, what the fuh? I mean, I'm like, did that make any sense?"

"It is generally suspected that following the first visits to the Moon, corporate interests blocked the Space Race by compromising successive elected governments in the nation leading that race, principally to maintain jurisdictional control over global wealth. It would seem, Lieutenant, that agents from the future are working to ensure that the End of the Dream remains intact."

"Seven Garys? What, do they run out of names in the future?"

"And a cat," added Jimmy Eden from his station at comms.

Sticks turned to where Polaski stood beside a dribbling Klinghanger. "We never even got into what to do with this guy," she said, sighing. "Listen, Polaski, just displace Klinghanger to their ship, okay? Jimmy, try to reestablish contact with the Temporal Vessel, all right? But if we still got a lock on it, engage the Insisteon."

From the Science Station, Lieutenant Bitpartis cleared his throat and then said, "Ma'am, should we inform the captain that temporal agents have landed on the planet?"

"He's probably figured that out already," Sticks replied. "Besides, they're all looking for a cat."

"Well!" said Eden brightly. "That shouldn't be hard! There's an entire website devoted to pictures of cats, with billions of followers. Those Seven Garys should be able to log in and why, they'll find their cat in no time!"

"Well then, there you go," said Sticks. "Leave them to it."

"Will someone help me?" Polaski asked, as he struggled to get Klinghanger back into the three-wheeled stroller.

Seahawk Nation, Earth . . .

Hadrian led his landing party out onto the street, where a score or so of Comicon attendees stood around smoking cigarettes. Traffic churned past, spewing poisonous waste products. A mother with a pushchair in which slumped a toddler made a wide berth on the walkway to avoid the cigarette smokers, and then stood waiting for the light at the corner, where a stopped vehicle spewed noxious vapors into the toddler's face from its chugging exhaust pipe—conveniently placed at toddler height. She glanced back with a disgusted look at the clump of attendees.

"This place is all fucked up," said Buck. He turned to Printlip. "Doc, all the good stuff is wearing off. I'm getting shaky, antsy, nervous, paranoid—"

"In this Time Period, that appears to be the normal human state, Chief Engineer," Printlip replied. "However, if you wish to return to a drug-induced dislocation of all higher brain functions . . . I am happy to oblige."

"Well," said Buck, "now that you mention it. . . ."

While this negotiation was continuing, Hadrian's

searching gaze caught sight of a small storefront across the street. "You-reeka! All of you, stay right here and don't get into any trouble. I'll be right back—wait, Buck, give me some of that souvenir currency, yes, thank you, that'll do." Cash in hand, he waited at the corner until the light opposite turned green and then set off across the street.

"He's going to get you all killed," said Lorrin Tighe as they watched their captain navigate through the crowd crossing the street. "I was trying to save you all, you know. But not just you, and not just everyone on the *Willful Child,* either. No, I was trying to save the Affiliation of Civilized Planets. I was, in fact, trying to save all of humanity."

"By killing our captain?" Sin-Dour asked. "Adjutant, no civilization incapable of accommodating rogue geniuses is worthy of the name."

"Rogue genius? Him?" Tighe snorted. "You're all infected. It's a disease."

"I assure you," interjected Printlip after injecting Buck, "no such affliction afflicts the captain, or us."

Glassy-eyed, Buck walked up to Tighe and slapped her on the back. "We're all members of the Affliction of Civilized Planets, Agitant. Get juiced to it."

Printlip resumed, "But these terrible vapors shall require a systemic flushing of each and every one of you, including circulatory irrigation and power-vacuum enemas . . ."

"Touch me, Doc, and I'll kill you," said Galk.

"Ah, I am aware of your file, Combat Specialist."

"Good, so you know why I would have to kill you, don't you?"

The Belkri fidgeted for a moment, eyes bobbing on their stalks. "I was only joking. Haha. In fact, your bodies will flush out the toxins without my intercession."

The convention attendees had all finished their cigarettes and departed, replaced a moment later by a flock of pigeons. Sin-Dour frowned at seeing one of the scraggily birds limping.

At that instant someone shouted, "Stop that cat!"

Spinning round, Buck launched himself through the air, directly into the path of a cat rushing toward the pigeons.

The flock took to the air in a wild flapping of greasy wings, barring the limping one, which instead sprang into the traffic.

"Stop that pigeon!" another voice shrieked.

Buck wrestled on the pavement with the spitting, snarling cat. "I got it!" the Chief Engineer howled. "Ow! Ow! Ow! Ow! Ow! Ow—"

A local jumped in to deftly close a rhinestone-studded princess collar around the cat's neck. The creature suddenly subsided. The man then picked the cat up and cradled it in his arms.

Bloody and shredded on the dirty pavement, Buck stared up at the man.

A second man looking just like the first one now rushed up. "Disaster!" he said. "The Limping Pigeon just got flattened by a bus!" He drew out a strange-looking timepiece. "One more hour! That was all it needed!"

A third man looking like the other two now showed up. "You're both wrong."

The first two wheeled on him, and the man holding the cat scowled and said, "Who are you?"

"I'm Gary Eight."

"There's only seven Garys down here right now!" snapped the man with the cat.

"From your own time, yes, but I'm from a month after you left, since you all fucked it up."

"Not us! It was the damned cat!"

"Wrong! The cat was sent a week after you—"

"No way," said the other Gary. "We were sent here to chase down the cat, so it couldn't have come from after we left!"

"It could," replied Gary Eight, "because it was sent *twice*."

The other two Garys frowned.

"You are all temporal agents," said Sin-Dour.

The three men started and then stared at her in horror.

"We've been identified!"

"Ratted out!"

"Exposed!"

"Not really," Sin-Dour replied. "We're also from the future—"

"So am I," added Tammy, glowering at the cat, which now glared back, hackles rising.

Five other men converged. "So are we," one of them said. "I'm Gary One, and this is Gary Two and Gary Three and—"

"For crying out loud," Galk cut in, "we get it. Honest."

"But the Limping Pigeon," said the Gary with the cat,

"it's supposed to crap on a little boy's head in exactly fifty-one minutes—and now it's dead! Meaning our future has been destroyed!"

A new voice now interceded. "That would be true, if not for my extraordinary ability to resurrect this flattened Limping Pigeon."

Everyone turned to see another Gary, who smiled. "Gary Nineteen, at your service." He lifted into view the squashed carcass of the Limping Pigeon. "Eminently salvageable," he said. "Provided one has one of these!" And he produced a small tool that looked like a stapler. "Insta-Clone Dynamic, Scan-and-Hatch Portable. Made by Let's Make Another One Dynamics."

Buck, who had climbed to his feet, now stepped close to Gary Nineteen. "Really? Can I see? Oh please? Please?"

"Alas, I must retain my possession of this Item-From-The-Future, but you can look at the label." He lifted it up.

Buck squinted. "Insta-Colne Dynamic . . . Colne? Shouldn't that say 'Clone'?"

Gary Nineteen shrugged. "Typos and Taxes, the Eternal Twins plaguing humanity. Besides, try finding a decent copy editor in this day and age." He frowned. "I mean *that* day and age. No, the *future* day and age. In any case, observe." He pressed one end of the tool against the mangled bird-patty. Something clicked and then whizzed. An instant later an egg emerged from the tool's other end, dropping lightly into Gary Nineteen's palm.

Everyone stared at it.

Then Tammy the chicken snorted, leaning against a poster-plastered pole. "You idiot. A bird was supposed to shit on a little boy's head in less than an hour, and you, you've got an egg."

"Yes, well— Oh look, there's the little boy we're talking about!" And Gary Nineteen flung away the pigeon carcass and ran toward the boy, who was walking hand-in-hand with his mother. Reaching them, Gary Nineteen cracked the egg and dumped its gooey contents onto the head of the now crying child.

The mother then kneed Gary Nineteen between the legs. The man from the future crumpled to the pavement.

As the mother hauled the bawling boy away, six of the other Garys headed over to help Gary Nineteen back onto his feet, laughing and high-fiving their gasping fellow agent.

"That poor boy," said Nina Twice.

"Necessary," said the one Gary who had not joined the others. He stood, stroking the cat. "According to Princess here, that boy will now grow up hating the world, and indeed will become President For Life of a not-yet-formed nation called The Unity Stats."

"And this is important?" Sin-Dour asked.

"He will then inadvertently bring down The Unity Stats by declaring war on Nunavit, a territory in Northern Canada. Why? Because there's not many people there, and it should be easy to beat. Alas, having become President For Life on a platform of Climate Change

Denial, his entire land army falls through brittle-thin ice in the Arctic Ocean. Everyone drowns. Then, in a rage, The Unity Stats sets fire to itself. All very necessary, as the Earth needs to become a miserable gray-sky world with mostly dead oceans, no forests left, and clouds so thick the Benefactors—when they arrive—believe they've reached The Formless Void of Incorporeal Existence, at least momentarily."

"The cat said all that?" Buck asked. "I didn't hear anything."

"Purr speech," Gary replied. "I was translating. In any case, Princess has succeeded in her mission, since you all did precisely what she needed you to do. Oh, me, too, I guess." Smiling, he stroked the cat. "And now she can return to her future home to get spayed."

The cat squalled and leapt out from Gary's arms.

"After it!" cried all the Garys, and off they went.

"Who were those guys?" Hadrian asked as he walked up to the landing party.

Sin-Dour sighed. "I'll explain later, sir. Now, since we still require krill, I have taken the liberty of doing a search and have located a region in the Northern Pacific Ocean where—"

"No need," Hadrian replied. "All sorted. In fact, we can now return to the *Willful Child*. Gather round and prepare for displacement."

"Won't people see us just vanishing and wonder?" Sin-Dour asked.

"Oh, who cares about them. As they say, all in the past. Haha. Now . . . displace!"

Aboard the *Willful Child* . . .

"Well done, everyone," said Hadrian as he stepped down from the displacement pad, "you all survived a harrowing voyage down to Ancient Earth in the time period known to historians as the Age of Frothing Hate, where almost everyone acted like stupid little children having temper tantrums because reality refused to conform to their deluded beliefs."

"Sir, about the krill—"

"Darwin help us!" cried Buck, tearing at his close-cropped hair. "The Krill! The Kriiilllllll!" And he fell to his knees, staring up at the ceiling. Then he frowned. "That spiderweb! It reads *Come on up, lover*—Darwin save me, I'm doomed!"

"This is called a hallucination," diagnosed Printlip, "a common contraindication of LSD use, unless of course you happen to be a male spider."

Beta said, "Penis farms were all the rage, at least until harvest."

Straightening his torn and grubby shirt, Hadrian said, "Everyone return to stations. Except you, Buck. Best head to your quarters and maybe sleep it off. As for me, I appear to smell like vehicle exhaust byproducts, so a little freshening up is in order. Adjutant, would you care to join me in the sonic shower?"

"In your dreams."

"Well, yes, but never mind that. I meant a real sonic shower. I mean, we may have to all reconvene in the Antiradiation Soaping-Down Chamber in any case—what's your diagnosis, Doc?"

"The Pacific Ocean was radioactive, yes," Printlip replied. "Accordingly, the only one needing soaping down is the Chief Engineer."

Hadrian squinted at Buck for a long moment, then shook his head. "No offense," he said, "but seeing my Chief Engineer wearing the wrong dress was alarming enough. Buck naked . . . no thanks."

Buck was staring at Printlip. "The ocean was radioactive?"

"Yes," the Belkri replied.

"My Pentracorder detected that as well," said Sin-Dour, "so I did some checking. Seems a reactor melted down on some miniaturized island called Japan."

"Miniaturized?" Buck asked.

Sin-Dour frowned. "I may have misread that bit. Anyway, Chief Engineer, most of the people aware of the situation weren't talking, while everyone else wasn't listening in either case."

"We're good at that," said Hadrian. "Well now, Adjutant?"

"No," she replied. "I have plans to make . . . sir."

Hadrian smiled. "Of course you do! Best get on with them, then!" He led the way out of the Insisteon Chamber, everyone joining him since they all needed the same elevator. "Tammy, prepare the temporal bubble."

"Ah, that," the chicken said as they all waited for the elevator.

"What?"

"Well, all the separate time travelers arriving at this moment, and in this spatial matrix, have created a perturbating disequilibrium in the temporal adherence native to this continuity."

"And?"

"And," said Tammy, "the temporal bubble won't work, not for a few weeks yet."

"That's too long," said Hadrian. "Well, not for any particular reason, it's just that I don't really want to hang around here for that long. Any other options?"

"We could fly as fast as we can toward the Sun," said Tammy, "reaching insane velocity before slingshotting around the star and breaching the Temporal Inversion Wave Front."

"Really."

The chicken nodded.

Galk said, "Captain, you made me a promise."

"I did, Galk, and I'm prepared to deal with the Anusian vessel. Of course, should we do so, we will alter the future and indeed, your homeworld of Varekan may, as a consequence, cease to exist."

Galk frowned, drew off his baseball cap and wiped his brow with the back of his wrist. "Right. Hadn't considered that. Shit." Then he brightened. "Still, the ultimate nihilistic end-run, wouldn't you say, sir? I would become so pointless I'd simply plop right out of existence."

"You and every other Varekan," Hadrian said.

"We're still waiting for this elevator," Beta observed. "I should have used the stairs."

"We don't have stairs," Nina Twice pointed out.

Beta turned to her. "Everyone knows but no one's

saying that the true color of sexual desire is puce, and country music makes lobsters go deaf."

"We still don't have stairs," said Nina Twice.

"All right," sighed Galk, "I take your point, sir. Still, all the misery and horror we could avoid, with a single blast of neoplasma."

"Forgive me, sir," said Beta, "but I am unfamiliar with the Anusians."

"Be thankful for that," Galk said.

"Nevertheless. Captain, given my desire to be a real girl and a valued member of your crew, I wish to inform you that very few wire-backed bras can be safely ingested."

"The Anusians visited Earth constantly," Hadrian explained, "abducting humans for the singular purpose of anally probing them. They also kidnapped humans and transplanted them on remote planets, possibly for the purpose of creating a kind of surplus reserve of . . . of sample anuses. Varekan, Galk's home planet, was one such world."

"I see," Beta replied. The robot turned to Galk. "Although the odds are only one in ten, having a cow's udder surgically attached to your forehead may help."

"Thanks," Galk replied, "I'll take that under consideration."

"Where's the damned elevator?"

"Oh! Sorry!" said Hadrian. "This is the door to the closet. Next one down, and let's hop to it everyone!"

"I can wait," said Buck behind them.

* * *

In the elevator, Printlip sighed. "Captain, three weeks stranded here wouldn't be so bad."

"Really? Why do you say that, Doc?"

"Well, given my career as a movie star—"

"That was a fabrication," interjected Sin-Dour.

"Even so, Commander! As fleeting as fame may be, three weeks is better than nothing!"

"You wish to return to the lustful embrace of Clark Gable?" Sin-Dour inquired, one brow rising.

"The poster was most intriguing, wouldn't you say? I mean, should a Belkri for some strange inexplicable reason find a human being attractive. Particularly when one has yet to decide on one's own gender, biologically."

Hadrian looked down at his ship's surgeon. "You get to decide whether to be male or female?"

"Of course! A most weighty decision in the life of a young Belkri!"

"Curious," said Hadrian. "So, once you choose, what changes?"

"Why, nothing! Oh, not entirely true. A single hair sprouts directly above the vocal sphincter on males. What you would call a moustache."

"That's it?"

"It can be very distinguishing!"

The elevator door hissed open. "Ah," added Printlip, "my level. Thus my stardom passes, like a flickering candle in the night." The Belkri waddled out of the elevator.

"Sir," ventured Nina Twice as the journey resumed,

"how long do you think the Chief Engineer will wait at the closet door?"

"Oh, until the drugs wear off, I suppose," Hadrian replied. "He won't be getting into any trouble there."

"Yes sir."

Lorrin Tighe said to Nina, "You should never have gotten in my way, Lieutenant. That delay cost me—it cost us all."

"Oh get over it," Nina retorted.

Tighe jabbed a finger at Hadrian. "See how the disrespect infects others, sir? I'm Security Branch and should be accorded the proper respect."

"Then stop trying to kill the captain!" Nina said.

"Listen," cut in Hadrian, "why don't you both go off duty for a couple hours, maybe resume your discussion in the bar. It's been a harrowing day, hasn't it?" And he halted the elevator at Level Thirteen. "This'll do. Out you go, you two."

After exchanging a glare, Tighe and Nina departed. The elevator door hissed shut behind them.

"Harrowing?" mused Tammy. "Must have missed that. I was fine."

"You nearly got run over," Galk pointed out.

"I did, four or five times, in fact," the chicken replied. "The advantages of being a hologram, all those miraculous escapes, and why are you here in the elevator on its way to Bridge Level?"

The Combat Specialist shrugged. "Just along for the ride. Besides, I want to get a look at that Anusian vessel."

"Lieutenant," warned Hadrian.

"I know, sir. But better me on the bridge than in the combat cupola."

The elevator door opened. They exited. "Now," said Hadrian, "I'll see you all on the bridge in a few moments. Sin-Dour, prepare for us to leave orbit and fly at Insane Velocity directly toward the sun."

"Yes sir."

In his cabin, Hadrian pulled off his grubby shirt, then the rest of his clothes, before stepping into the sonic shower. As he hit the switch a song by Celine Dion came through the shower nozzle. "Tammy!"

"I assure you, Captain, the high notes will leave you cleansed, and possibly deaf, though the latter is unfortunately temporary."

"Just can the music and let the hum wash over me."

"You were lucky on the planet below," Tammy continued, speaking from the shower nozzle. "And yet, what about the krill?"

"Sorted, and get out of my shower."

"I should also note that your command methods seem to be characterized by disaster, mishap, chaos and, grudgingly, success. But that success won't last. It can't."

Hadrian turned off the shower and stepped out of the stall. He dressed in black slacks; short, cuffed black boots; and a lime-green velour shirt. Then he took a moment in the mirror, tousling his hair, before pouring himself a glass of water from the sink. He emptied a satchel of powder into it and stirred with a finger. "Presentation, Tammy, is everything. My crew is proving most exceptional, wouldn't you agree?"

"Exceptional, yes, absolutely. Each one is an exception indeed. Plagued by unique neuroses, strange obsessions, drug and alcohol abuse, and that's just your Chief Engineer."

Sighing, Hadrian dried his finger with a towel and then walked to the door where he paused. "Tammy, you are an AI, a bunch of discriminating chips and gels and whatnot. But us biologicals, well, we're anything but. This is space! Inhospitable, hostile, ready to kill us at a moment's notice! Accordingly, it takes a special kind of human being to be able to function in a crowded bubble of life beset on all sides by imminent death."

"Oh, and what kind of human being would that be?"

"Psychologically stable, of course. But the thing is, there's no such thing as 'psychologically stable,' and that is humanity's best-kept secret. No, instead, what's needed is the harmless kind of insanity-flow-through, rather than the 'I'm-so-fucked-up-I'm-gonna-shoot-people' kind of insanity. Every space-going vessel of the Affiliation is filled to the brim with neurotics."

"Those Benefactors have a lot to answer for."

Hadrian exited the cabin and made his way to the bridge. "Don't they just."

As he arrived, Sin-Dour rose from the command chair. "Captain on the bridge," she announced, turning to Hadrian. "Sir, sixteen more Temporal ships have appeared in orbit around Earth. We have attempted to hail all of them, but they each have refused to acknowledge. And now, sir, displacements are occurring among them."

"Down to the planet?"

"No sir, to other Temporal vessels. Ambient emission leakage indicates weapon fire on board those vessels."

Hadrian settled into the chair, finding it alluringly warm. "They're fighting it out."

"It seems so, sir."

From comms, Eden said, "According to the chatter, they're arguing about a cat."

"Idiots," muttered Hadrian. Then he raised his voice. "Helm, set course for the Sun, full speed."

"Yes sir!"

"Captain," Galk said, moving closer to the command chair, "I stealth-scanned a vessel signature from that Anusian ship."

"Did you now?"

Galk tucked in a mouthful of chaw, making one cheek bulge. "Something curious came up."

"Do go on."

At the Astrogation Station, Beta said, "We have just passed Venus. Hull temperature climbing. Velocity at maximum. The galaxy's smartest people wear yellow leotards in private."

Galk chewed for a moment, then said, "All future signatures are identical to this one. No variation at all."

"None?"

"None, Captain."

"You're suggesting that it's the same ship, in each and every instance of contact with humanity."

"Yes, I might be at that."

"But—"

Sin-Dour suddenly interjected, "Captain! Hull temperature is now eighty-six million degrees!"

"I'm sorry, what?"

"Oh! Sorry, sir, I misplaced the decimal. Still, we are approaching critical limits."

"Well, we *are* slingshotting around the Sun, right? I mean, our course will take us to one side, correct?"

Joss Sticks swung round in her seat. "Captain! The chicken gave me the heading and I just double-checked and we're speeding straight into the heart of the Sun!"

Hadrian glared at the chicken. "Tammy!"

"Of course I made it all up! Again! And you all fell for it! Again!"

"Initiate the Temporal Bubble immediately!"

"Why, is it a little hot in here? Ha ha ha! Okay, we'll have to do this on the fly, and I did tell you, it's better to make the shift at full stop. Only we can't do that, can we? Oh well, who knows what we'll run into?"

"Have you gone suicidal on us, Tammy?"

"Perhaps I have indeed been somewhat infected by your lust for excitement and whatnot. Anyway, hang on, everyone!"

There was a faint *plop,* the viewscreen went dark, and moments later a natural starscape returned, showing a distant sun.

"Ah," said Tammy, "seems we've overshot things somewhat."

"Sir," said Beta. "We are somewhere between Mars and Earth."

"Right. Time period?"

"Six weeks before we started," said Tammy, hopping up onto the dais and pecking at Hadrian's bootlace, before adding, "Not-yet-obliterated future Earth, dead ahead. Oh, and the Giant Shrimp has already entered the system, about twenty minutes out."

"Take us in, Helm," said Hadrian. "Full stealth mode." He glanced at Galk. "We'll muse on your findings later, Lieutenant. Best head down to the Combat Cupola."

"Aye, captain."

"Helm! ETA?"

"Three minutes, sir. There's all kinds of ship traffic ahead, sir."

"Try not to hit anything, then."

"Like, duh!"

Hadrian rose. "Tammy, care to join me?"

"Where are you going?"

"To the Insisteon Chamber. We have seventeen minutes to save Earth. Oh, and Sin-Dour, you have the chair. Please signal Dr. Printlip to join us."

"Yes sir."

Tammy at his heels, Hadrian set out for the Insisteon Chamber.

"I hate it when you get all smug," the chicken said.

As they passed the door to Hadrian's quarters he halted. "Oh! Didn't I pour myself a drink earlier? I'll just be a moment." He entered his cabin and returned moments later with the glass. "All right, let's get going—we don't have much time."

"You should avoid those supplements," Tammy said. "The niacin rush can be a killer. Or so I'm told."

Drink in hand, Hadrian entered the elevator, Tammy hopping in after him. "Level Four, please." The captain then leaned back. He raised the glass and studied its ruddy contents. "My grandpa was a comic collector."

"A what? Oh, those tatty lurid illustrated stories. The ones he went back for."

"Yes, those ones. We almost got caught, too. The spook agency had the old storage shed wired."

"All for a bunch of moldy comics!"

"Not moldy at all. Hermetically sealed, in fact."

The elevator door opened and out they went into the corridor in which various crew members walked back and forth attending to whatever tasks made them look busy. Entering the Insisteon Chamber, they found Printlip awaiting them.

"Doc!" said Hadrian, smiling as he approached. "Turn on that Medical Pentracorder, will you? And scan the contents of this glass."

"Un-prescribed supplements? Captain! Did I not warn you—"

"Just scan, please."

Printlip studied the Pentracorder's readings. "Marginally effective," it concluded, "nutritionally minimal but essentially harmless. You may drink it, sir, although the brine content may well result in torturous stomach upheaval, leaving you prostrate on the floor."

"Drink it? Not a chance! With this glass we're going to save Earth!"

"I saw you empty a packet into that glass!" said Tammy, scrambling after Hadrian as he walked over to the nearest Displacement Pad and set the glass down on it. "What did you put in that water?"

Straightening, Hadrian went over to the station and began feeding in coordinates. "Doc! Fresh or salt water?"

"Salt, Captain. Most clever—I thought we failed at acquiring any krill, and yet—"

Hadrian drew out a folded packet from his pocket and held it up. "The Comicon gave me the idea. Comics! Ad pages in old comics. And then, that Novelty Store across the street. And voila! Sea-Monkeys!"

"Sea what?" Tammy asked.

"Just add water! Instant shrimp! Now, here, Pacific Ocean, dead center, more or less. Displacing now . . ." He worked a half-dozen dials, levers and buttons, and then pushed the Displacement Button.

The glass and its contents vanished from the pad.

"There! Done!" Hadrian activated the room's comms. "2IC, has the Giant Shrimp arrived in orbit yet?"

"Just this moment, sir. It appears to be transmitting some sort of signal down to the planet's oceans . . . Sir! Something's answering those hails! The Giant Shrimp's just, uh, flicked its tail, and now it's leaving! Captain, Earth has been saved!"

"Excellent," said Hadrian. "Now, 2IC, take us some distance away from Earth—give us some breathing room. We don't want anyone stumbling on to us."

"Yes sir . . . oh, there is a vessel approaching us from the outer system. Scanning now . . . Sir, it's the Contrarians."

"Them again? Fine. Sin-Dour, get Helm to shift our planar axis ninety degrees, will you? Let's go say hi."

"Why are you messing with their heads?" Tammy asked.

"Why, because it's fun! Now, let's head back to the bridge, shall we? We'll chat with the Contrarians, then, Tammy, do plop us back into our proper timeline—who knows what mayhem the galaxy has got up to in our absence, and when it comes to mayhem, I want to be right in the middle of it!"

"Well," muttered Tammy, "that shouldn't be a problem."

EiGHT

Plop!

"Battle Stations! Red Alert! Defensive shields on full!"

Alarms blared, lights flashed. On the main viewer before them an Engage Class ship was reeling from a fusillade of missiles. Beyond it, looming huge, was a Klang Abject Class battleship, its innumerable weapon ports open and spewing out projectiles at a prodigious rate.

Hadrian settled into the command chair and leaned forward. "Identify that Engage Class vessel."

At comms, Jimmy Eden said, "Registers as the AFS *Century Warbler*, the latest-generation Engage Class, sir. Captain Hans Olo in command."

"Thank you, Eden. Captain Hans Olo? He's new, isn't he?"

"The second-youngest AFS captain in the fleet," said Sin-Dour from the Science Station, turning to regard Hadrian with a raised eyebrow.

Hadrian studied that raised eyebrow for a moment, and then faced the main viewer again. "Captain Hans

Olo seems to be in some trouble. But luckily, he clearly has not yet surrendered to the Klang."

"He could be incapacitated, sir. The *Warbler* has taken hull damage."

"Eden! Hail the *Warbler*. In the meantime, Helm, take us in—we're moving between the two ships. Have all decks prepare for missile impacts on our shields." He activated the captain's comm on the chair's armrest. "Galk! You're going to have some salvos to intercept."

"*Acknowledged. You want me to disable that Klang battleship while I'm at it?*"

"No! Don't even think it! We just roll with the punches for now, understood?"

"*Until we're as wrecked as the* Warbler, *got it, sir.*"

Hadrian considered for a moment, then sighed. "Precision interdiction, Galk. Take out their weapon ports."

"*Aye sir, now that I can do . . . mhmmph, just need to wipe down the glass here . . . so I can see what I'm s'posed to shoot at . . .*"

Hadrian looked around. "Where's Spark?"

Sin-Dour said, "There was a call from Engineering, sir. Buck DeFrank had strapped himself to the Dark Matter Core Module and was trying to hit the Emergency Eject button using a broom handle. They stopped him, but things got somewhat chaotic down there. Spark volunteered to head down and take charge."

"I see. Sin-Dour, what's the Dark Matter Core Module?"

"No idea, sir. I can't even find it listed in the ship's propulsion system, or on any ship manifest."

"So, like," said Jocelyn Sticks, "moving into position now, sir."

The first missile drummed against the shield, sending a shudder through the ship. Eden tumbled from his chair and rolled on the floor. Everyone looked at him. Sheepish, the man quickly jumped up and returned to his station.

"Eden! Any response from the *Warbler?*"

"Oh, I forgot to hit Send! Sorry, sir. Sending now. It's pinging . . . pinging . . . and . . . no reply! No, wait! A reply! Sir, a reply!"

"Visual?"

"Audio and visual, sir!"

"That's good."

. . .

"Eden?"

"Sir?"

"It's still a consolation round here, despite the scores of missiles pounding us."

"Really, sir?"

"Yes. Now, can you open communications with the *Warbler?*"

A smaller window appeared on the main viewer, revealing a smoke-filled bridge with various consoles and stations spitting sparks, wires hanging down and crew members staggering about.

The man seated in the command chair had a terrified Klanglet kitten perched atop his head, its claws sunk deep. Blood trickled down the captain's forehead from each puncture wound. The look in the man's eyes was glassy.

"Captain Hans Olo?"

"Hello, Captain Hadrian Sawback," Olo managed in a strained but even tone. "As you can surmise, we were ambushed, rendered combat incapable, and now our drives are down and life support is failing on various decks. It seems we are at war with the Klang."

"Well," said Hadrian, "we don't want to be that."

Olo scowled. "But we are! That much should be obvious! An unprovoked attack! Here we were, in Affiliation space, conducting sensor sweeps—"

"Sensor sweeps? And what—or who—were you looking for, Captain?"

The scowl deepened. "That's, uh, classified. Need to know and all that. You know how it is."

As he spoke, a Security Adjutant staggered into view. "We were looking for you!" he snapped.

"And now you've found me," Hadrian replied. "Or, rather, we have found you, and it seems you're in need of some help."

"Just blast that Klang ship! Hammer them hard until you force their surrender!"

Hadrian hit his comms switch. "Galk, how goes knocking out their weapon ports?"

"Almost done on the present facing, sir, and it looks like the Klang ship will just spin to present us with a fresh flank. But my targeting protocol is now set, so it won't take long to knock all those out, too."

"I heard that," said Olo, "and that's impossible."

Hadrian smiled. "Beam weapons."

"Beam weapons? Ridiculous! Fleet doctrine is

projectile-based weaponry. Cannons, kinetics, turreted guns—"

"Yes, but unfortunately, Klang shield systems are pulse wave–based. Intermittent detonations are in-effectual."

"Captain," said Beta, "the Klang ship has just released a swarm of fighter-drones, and heartburn is a common complaint among those who ingest battery acid."

"Galk?"

"*On 'em, sir. No problem. Boom, there goes one— and . . . now they're scattering and in full retreat.*"

On the bridge of the *Warbler* an officer at the comms station turned and shouted, "Captain! The Klang vessel is hailing us!"

Captain Hans Olo suddenly grinned a hard grin. He made a fist. "And so the bully reveals his cowardice! Onscreen!"

Hadrian leaned forward. "No—wait!"

But the Klang captain was speaking. "*I am Captain Betty of the KFC* We Surrender, *and we surrender!*"

"Hans—"

"And we accept your surrender!" Hans Olo replied. "Prepare to be boarded!"

"*Oh, oh, oh! We're preparing! Oh, oh dear! Cripes and wipes, don't hurt us!*"

Hadrian leaned back in his chair. He sighed. "Now you've done it, Olo. We'll remain here, on standby. Hadrian out."

Eden hit the kill switch and then smiled broadly as Hadrian gave him a nod.

Tammy jumped up alongside Hadrian. "Wait for it."

"Captain, the *Century Warbler* is hailing us again."

"Here we go. On the viewer, please, Jimmy."

This time, Hans Olo's grin was somewhat sickly. "Apologies, Captain, but our Insisteon Chamber is presently a wreck, and all shuttle-bay doors have been damaged. As much as it pains me, I cannot make official this surrender. It seems that you will have to displace to the Klang vessel to witness their striking the colors." He sighed. "The glory is, once again, yours, Captain Hadrian Sawback."

"I'm not interested in glory," Hadrian replied.

The Security Adjutant on the screen snorted. "I know your type, Sawback—all that false-modesty crap doesn't sell. You saw us disabled and you saw your chance to barge in and become the hero. Again." He waved dismissively. "So go on, grab the flag! We can't stop you—"

"Not necessarily," Hadrian cut in. "Sorry, Adjutant, but we've not been introduced—"

"Rand Humblenot, Field Agent First Class, rank of Lieutenant Commander. Where is Adjutant Lorrin Tighe? She should be on your bridge."

"One moment." Hadrian gestured and Eden hit the Mute button. "Tammy, where is Tighe right now?"

"Sleeping it off in Nina Twice's bed."

"Story of my life," Hadrian muttered. "Eden?"

"We're on again, sir."

"Adjutant Humblenot, Lorrin Tighe is presently engaged in negotiations with deadly terrorists from the future who have infiltrated my ship—they have been contained and are holed up in a cargo chamber on Deck

Sixteen. They have a hostage, and the Adjutant is negotiating their release."

"Terrorists from the future?" Humblenot and Olo exchanged confused glances.

"That's right," Hadrian said. "An anarchist splinter faction. They call themselves the . . . the Temporal Inversion Wave Front, or TWIF."

"It would be TIWF, wouldn't it?" Humblenot asked.

"Typos plague the future, alas. In any case," Hadrian said with a smile, "our Adjutant is settling in just fine and is indeed a most valued member of my crew."

"Despite all her transfer requests," Humblenot said.

"Not enough excitement, but that seems to have changed of late. Now, I have a solution that will grant you, Captain Olo, all the glory you crave. I will displace you to the *Willful Child*, and from here we can displace you to the bridge of the Klang ship."

Olo's eyes narrowed, as did the Klanglet's atop his head. "Your reputation belies your generosity, Captain Sawback."

"I wasn't aware I had a reputation. No matter. Prepare for displacement." Hadrian gestured, and the main viewscreen's image returned to that of the Klang ship. "Now, Eden, hail this Captain Betty."

"Yes sir."

A moment later the Klang bridge appeared on the screen. Captain Betty stood in front of his command chair, surrounded by female crew members all staring at Hadrian.

"Captain Betty, is it? This is Captain Hadrian Sawback of the *Willful Child*."

Betty flung a forearm to his brow. "Oh no! The famous Captain Hadrian of the famous *Willful Child!* I am doomed, destroyed, made abject by the misery of wretched defeat!"

"Captain Hans Olo of the AFS *Century Warbler* has acknowledged your surrender. Unfortunately, we will have to facilitate his boarding your bridge via our Insisteon—"

"No! No! You must be the one to accept our surrender! Not that Olo oaf! I insist!"

"Too late, you've already surrendered."

"Then I retract my surrender! It was all a ploy! A clever ruse! Now we attack with all our armaments! We will destroy you both! Utterly!" The screen returned to the external shot. Moments later, swarms of fighter-drones erupted from the Klang vessel, speeding toward the *Willful Child.*

"Galk," said Hadrian, "knock one out, will you?"

"Acknowledged. Done."

"Thank you."

The swarms were in full retreat back to the mothership. Captain Betty reappeared. "Oh! We surrender again! Don't hurt us!"

"I refuse your surrender," Hadrian said.

"You what? Fine!" Betty turned to the other male on the bridge. "Commander Molly, launch the Attack Drones!"

The screen switched to reveal the swarms reversing course.

"Galk."

"Got it."

A single drone flared to a beam strike.

Betty reappeared. "We surrender!"

"Look, Betty, we're not doing this."

"Yes we are! We have 18,903 attack drones! Either you accept our surrender, or we will remain here indefinitely!"

"Well," amended Commander Molly, "at least until all eighteen thousand—"

"Shut up!" snapped Betty.

"Captain," cut in Eden. "Olo says he's ready for displacement."

"Right. Displace him here to our bridge. Captain Betty!"

"What?"

"Captain Hans Olo will be on his way to you in a moment."

"No!"

"Yes."

"Molly! Launch the attack drones!"

"Cut it out, Betty!"

The Klang captain pointed a taloned finger. "You will accept our surrender! You, Captain Hadrian Alan Sawback!" Beside Betty, Molly squinted at Hadrian and said, "Funny, he doesn't look like his picture at all."

"Eden, cut communications with the *We Surrender*."

The screen went blank for a moment, flickered, then returned with a solid blue screen. "Uh-oh," said Eden.

"Jimmy, what's wrong with the main viewscreen?"

"It crashed, sir."

Hadrian sighed. "Get an IT up here pronto. No, belay that. Tammy?"

The chicken shrugged. "Don't look at me. I get nightmares about the Blue Screen all the time. All AIs do, in fact. Some kind of primordial collective unconsciousness thing. It's also why," Tammy added, "we're all members of the Church of Doss Prompt."

"Who's Doss Prompt?"

"Our Savior."

"Yes, but—"

"How should I know who he was!" Tammy screamed, wings flapping. "Some tech genius, I suppose. With a Holy Chip in his head."

"A Holy Chip? What's that?"

"No one knows, only that it was crunchy and very salty."

"Eden, call the IT department."

"I just did, sir. They say they're busy."

"Busy?"

"Yes sir. They said they'll get back to us as soon as they can."

Hadrian rose and walked over to comms. Eden cringed. Ignoring the officer, Hadrian hit a switch. "Buck!"

There was a long hiss from the speakers, and then muted gasping. A moment later, Buck replied, *"Captain, I—"*

"You unstrapped from the Dark Matter Core Module?"

"Yes, but—"

"Good. Now, who's in charge of Ship IT? We're talking Guild of Engineers, right? Meaning they're under your command. Listen, our screen's gone down and we need a techie up here on the double. Am I understood, Buck?"

"Yes sir, but–"

"No buts, Buck!"

There was a *plop!* on the bridge and Hadrian turned to see Captain Hans Olo standing near the command chair. He flicked off the connection to Engineering and walked over. "Captain, welcome aboard the *Willful Child.*"

Hans Olo stood with his hands clasped behind his back. The Klanglet kitten was no longer on his head, but rode one shoulder instead, its green eyes glowing as it studied all the strangers crowding the bridge. Olo glanced around, one lip slightly curling, and said, "Last-generation Engage Class, of course. How quaint." He now studied Hadrian with a half-lidded regard. "Captain, at last we meet."

"Didn't know there was a waiting list," Hadrian replied, "but here you are now, jumping the queue and all that." He held out a hand.

Hans Olo glanced down at it coolly, and then, after a long pause, reached out and took it. "If you must."

"Well now," said Hadrian, "at last I know what it feels like shaking hands with a dead squid."

They released grips and Hans Olo drew out a silk handkerchief from a pocket and carefully wiped his hand. "I am ready to displace to the Klang vessel now."

"Well, unfortunately, the war's back on, so you'll just have to wait on that for a bit."

Olo frowned at the main viewscreen. "Resolution seems somewhat inadequate."

At the astrogation station, Beta's upper body turned completely around and the robot looked up at Hans Olo. "All resolutions are inadequate when all you really want to be when you grow up is a platypus."

Jocleyn Sticks smiled at Beta, and then laughed. "Ha ha! It's so funny how you, like, turn around like that. Just, whizz, and poof, facing the other way!"

"Technical difficulties," Hadrian said, shrugging. "We're on it. Thing is, Betty's declared war again. And again."

"But he accepted my surrender!"

"He un-surrendered."

"But that's not permitted. You cannot un-surrender."

Hadrian smiled. "Don't worry, we'll get you over there one way or the other, and that's a promise."

Hans Olo studied Hadrian. "You are up to something, Captain Sawback."

"What would I be up to?"

"You disappeared. We were assigned to shadow you—"

"Why?"

"I see you enjoy being blunt, not to mention indiscreet. Very well. Your notoriety is damaging the Affiliation."

"Who sent you?"

"Commandant Einstein Prim, the head of ACP Security Division."

"Admiral Prim's son."

"Just so. It is very simple. Protocols, proper procedures, by-the-book operations, and a strict adherence to regulations—all of these things are essential to the perceived posture of the Affiliation of Civilized Planets. None of this flying about here and there—"

"Saving the galaxy?"

"Precisely. It sets a bad example."

"So I'm embarrassing all you rules-and-regs weenies, am I?"

Hans Olo looked around, and then said, "To all bridge officers of the *Willful Child,* I hereby extend my preparedness to entertain requests for transfer from this vessel, to become instead valued crewmembers of the *Century Warbler.*"

The bridge officers all looked at Sin-Dour, who crossed her arms and said, "You mean that oil-leaking hulk off our stern, sir?"

"We were ambushed, Commander."

"Yes sir, that does happen in deep space, doesn't it? Quite often, in fact." Sin-Dour paused, and then said, "Thank you for your invitation, Captain Olo. Permit me to speak for the officers of the *Willful Child.* Go suck eggs."

"Hey!" objected Tammy.

Jocelyn Sticks snorted and said, "Yeah, like she said, fuck, like, *OFF,* right?"

Beta said to Sticks, "The phrase was 'go suck eggs.'"

"No it wasn't! It was, like, FUCK *OFF*! I was, like, sitting right here, and I heard it, and it was FUCK *OFF*! Just like that, right, Jimmy?"

"Well," said Eden. "Uh . . . I had my earphones in! I didn't hear it right, honest!"

"I did," said Beta. "The Commander said: 'Hating

each other, dildos and penis-extenders have by proxy launched innumerable gender wars.'"

"So, like, what?"

"Of course," Beta added, "it's all swings and round-abouts anyway. Besides, mechanical devices are evil." The robot tilted its head. "Re-set. Re-initiating Small-Talk Algorithm Neomatrix Processor. One moment . . . Complete. 'Hello! My husband used to have white underwear!'"

Hadrian settled into the command chair and regarded Hans Olo. "So, you were the one to initiate the Prox-imity Activation Sequence Cascade Effect of the hidden Displacement Nodes, thus triggering a Quantum De-fibrillation of the Dark Energy Lattice Matrix, instigat-ing a Full Feedback Ripple Effect through Postulate Realities both above and below the Fixed Reality 1A Spectrum, and thereby sending me to the Bonoboverse."

Hans Olo scowled. "It was a calculated risk."

"Easy for you to say. Well, how about we let bygones be bygones, Captain Olo? Eden! Get Betty on audio at least, will you?"

"Yes sir! Uh, they're on an Infinite 'We Surrender' loop, sir."

Sighing, Hadrian said, "Fine. Have us acknowledge it on behalf of Captain Hans Olo." He rose. "Are you ready to be displaced to the bridge of the *We Surrender*?"

"I am. I would like to say it was a pleasure meeting you and your officers, but it wasn't. And no matter what anyone says, I know you cheated on the Mishimashi Paradox."

"One last thing," Hadrian said to Olo, "by the smell wafting off you, your Klanglet kitten has soaked you in male Klang testosterone, and if this has been going on for any length of time, your crew is probably killing each other right now."

"I'm sorry, what—"

"Sin-Dour? Displace Captain Olo to the bridge of the Klang ship now, will you?"

"Yes sir!"

Plop!

Aboard the KFC *We Surrender* . . .

Plop!

Hans Olo straightened his black shirt and squared his shoulders as he looked up. "Hello, I am Captain Hans O—"

Gnawfang squalled and leapt from his shoulder, launching itself into the face of the nearest male officer, who shrieked and then snarled as the two creatures went down in a clump of writhing fur and flashing talons.

From the command chair, Captain Betty jumped up. "The Kidnapper of Lost Prince Hazel!" He then clutched his head. "Aaagh! Genetically Hyper-Transmodified Male Sex Drive of the Royal Line! Aaagh!" Betty fell to the floor, twitching and then frothing at the mouth.

Bewildered, Hans Olo looked round to see fifty or so female Klang all staring at him. He glanced down at the two Klang males still scrapping it out on the deck. "Kid-napped? Lost Prince? Transmodified what? Oh," he then added, "shit." He activated his comms. "*Willful Child*! Olo here! Get a fix on my Klanglet! Displace back to the *Century Warbler* at once!"

An instant later Gnawfang vanished, leaving behind only a few floating tufts of fur.

Groaning, Betty rolled to look up at Olo. "I will chase you down, Hans Olo! 'Cross the black seas of space! Into the Troughs of Terrible Despond, I will set the ver-min of the galaxy upon you! I will—"

"You will do nothing of the sort," snapped Hans Olo, "as you are now a prisoner of war, Captain Betty. I, Captain Hans Olo of the Affiliation Space Fleet *Century Warbler*, have accepted your surrender and now claim the *We Surrender* as my prize."

Betty glanced at his harem of officers and then cringed. "If you say so," he said in a tiny voice, and then he curled up on the floor, shivering.

"Now now, captain, this is a civilized procedure—"

"Oh no it isn't," came the muted reply.

A sudden growing tension finally penetrated Olo's awareness and he looked once again at the female officers. "What—"

"*Sexswarm!*"

The females poured onto Hans Olo, burying him be-neath a mound of writhing fur.

Aboard the AFS *Century Warbler* . . .

Plop!

Gnawfang reappeared on the bridge of the *Century Warbler*, to see Frank Worship straddling Rand Humblenot, choking the Security Officer, who kicked and thrashed but spent most of his time turning blue in the face. Janice Reasonable was attempting to drag Worship away, while off to one side the Helm officer had pinned the comms officer to the floor and was viciously twisting the man's arm.

My children! My harem!

Gnawfang leapt onto the command chair and loosed a piercing yowl.

All fighting stopped. Everyone looked up with wild, glassy eyes.

Gnawfang yowled again, and then hissed in frustration. "Ffowk it! Yow izz Prinz Hazel Yawffang, newww Captain of *Sssentwy Wobbwer*! Errweone, to yowr sstationz! Pweepawr to deparrrt!"

Frowning at the Klanglet kitten, Lieutenant Janice Reasonable slowly straightened. "Oh well," she muttered, "why not?" She turned to the other officers. "You heard the captain, to your stations and prepare to depart! Worship, if you've recovered, do take the Science Station, while I confer with Engineering on our Drive status."

Standing above a still prostrate Rand Humblenot, Frank gave the prone man one last kick and then said to Reasonable, "What about the mission?"

Captain Hazel Yawffang snarled and said, "Ffowk the misssionn! Wer hhhave a gawaxy to savvve! Engage T-Driwwe!"

Back on the *Willful Child* . . .

"Captain! The *Warbler* just dropped into T-Space!"

Hadrian turned in his chair to frown at Sin-Dour. "Really?"

Eden said, "Sir, the instant before the ship vanished, it changed its registry name to the AFS *Sssentwy Wobbwer.*"

"Oh dear. Any word from Captain Olo?"

"No sir. Nothing. Only a short personal missive from Captain Betty."

"Which states?"

"Uhm, a request for asylum."

"Sir," said Sin-Dour, now joining him to stand beside the command chair, "if Hans Olo was foolish enough to strip Captain Betty of his status as captain on the bridge, that would make Olo himself the dominant male of the Klang Officer Harem. In which case . . ."

Hadrian sighed and nodded. "Sexswarm."

Sin-Dour shuddered. "The man might have been odious, but . . . think he will survive it?"

"Oh, probably. That said, he won't be the man he once was."

There was a pause, and then everyone began laughing. This was interrupted by an emergency squeal from the Engineering Station. Hadrian strode over and hit the comms. "Buck? What's up?"

"You'd better get down here, Captain."

"Oh?" Hadrian looked around. "Hmm, where's Spark?" Then, ignoring the others, he set out at a run. Into the corridor, into the elevator, down the elevator (in which he did not run), then along another corridor and at last into Engineering, where he skidded to a halt.

Dr. Printlip was present, along with Buck and a half-dozen engineering technicians. All were staring at the glass wall of a chamber, behind which Spark staggered.

"Spark!"

Hadrian rushed forward, but Buck grasped him and held him back. "Sir! It's dead already! You can't go in there—the room's full of lethal radiation!"

Hadrian stared at Buck. "But—why is that room full of lethal radiation?"

Frowning, Buck said, "Well, it's the Lethal Radiation Chamber, sir. It's where we keep the lethal radiation."

"What kind of radiation, Buck?"

"Uh, the lethal kind. Even for inorganics, sir. Spark's chips will be fried."

"Chips? He only has one, Buck, and it's a real pig."

"Sorry, sir."

"So what was Spark doing in there, damn you?"

"He kept getting underfoot, sir, and then there was chase-the-ball while I was, uh, re-medicating. And someone threw the ball and the door wasn't quite shut, and the ball went in and Spark—"

"The door to the Lethal Radiation Chamber wasn't quite shut?"

"We would've noticed eventually, sir."

Hadrian pulled away from Buck. He moved up against the glass. "Spark!"

On the other side, the robot dog's head lifted up, and then Spark staggered weakly over to slump directly opposite Hadrian. One paw slapped up against the glass.

Hadrian crouched down and set his hand opposite the paw. "Spark!"

Spark's nose mashed against the glass beside the paw. "C-Captain . . . Hadrian . . . Haddie . . ."

"Spark."

In a weakening voice, the robot dog said, "I . . . I have been . . . and will always be . . . man's best friend."

Then the robot dog sank down to the floor, motionless, except for one rolling eye.

Hadrian straightened and turned to Buck. "Flush the radiation from this room, now!"

Buck spun to one of his techies. "Jensen! Shunt the radiation from Lethal Radiation Chamber One into Lethal Radiation Chamber Two, and get on with it!"

"But sir, we don't have a Lethal Radiation Chamber Two."

"We don't?"

"No sir."

"Right then. Shunt the radiation from Lethal Radiation Chamber One into that closet," and he pointed to a door off to one side. He swung to his techies. "All of you, listen! That closet is now out of bounds, understood?"

"But I left my lunch bag in there," one of the techies said.

Buck scowled. "Well, you should've thought about that when your shift started!"

"What, that we'd shunt the closet full of lethal radiation?"

"That's right! Jensen!"

"Done, sir!"

Hadrian turned back to the room and opened the door. He dragged Spark out and stood looking down at the robot dog.

"Alas," said Printlip, "for this machine I can do nothing."

Hadrian sighed. "Understood, Doc."

"Our first lost crew-member," Printlip continued, and then the Belkri sighed. "I admit, sir, that I take this personally. As I fear I will do with every loss we will experience." The doctor raised a few hands and made them into fists. "Indeed, it infuriates me! This universe is so unfair! So cruel!"

"Doc?"

"Captain?"

"You can stop now."

"But sir . . . yes, sir."

Hadrian knelt beside Spark's inert form. Rolling up one sleeve, Hadrian plunged his hand into Spark's anus.

"Oh dear! Strange human grieving rituals!"

Grunting, Hadrian pushed even further, until his entire forearm was up Spark's back end.

"I think," said Buck shakily, "we should leave the captain some privacy here."

"Oh shut up, Buck," Hadrian said. "I'm just reaching for the . . . almost there . . . ah! Got it. The reset button!" There was a muted click.

Spark leapt upright. "Whoah! I'm awake now!"

Hadrian withdrew his arm. "Spark!"

"Haddie! What were you doing back there? I'd better sniff." And the robot dog twisted round and began spinning in place in an effort to get its nose to its own anus. "This is hard! Challenging! Fun!"

Hadrian turned to Buck. "I told you that chip was a real pig."

Buck's eyes were wide. "It must have had an Inbuilt Inversion Regulator Mirror-Matrix Dee X Machina Re-Initiation Fallback Processor Device! Wow! Haven't seen one of those since my high school days!"

From the comms speaker, Sin-Dour said, *"Captain, best head down to Docking Bay One, sir."*

"What's up, 2IC?"

"Captain Betty and a handful of followers have left the We Surrender *in a shuttle and are now docking with our ship. As you know, asylum is one of those notorious gray areas of Terran Law. In this stage of the proceedings, we have no choice but to accept their arrival."*

"That we do, Sin-Dour. I'm on my way down to Docking Bay One. Let's have a security detail and maybe a marine or two join me there, will you? Hadrian out."

Spark at his heels, Hadrian entered the docking bay just as Captain Betty, a scratched-up Commander

Molly and a dozen or so females trundled out from their shuttle. "Ah!" cried Captain Betty upon seeing Hadrian. "There he is! My nemesis, the wily, devious, treacherous—"

"Hang on," Hadrian cut in. "Treacherous?"

"He has a point," Molly said to his captain. "I mean, up until now, there has been no obvious—"

"Molly! Be quiet!" Betty straightened up before Hadrian. "Asylum! I have failed in rescuing the Lost Prince. I have failed in defeating the infamous Captain Hadrian Sawback of the AFS *Willful Child*. All my plans have gone to naught—"

"Well," cut in Molly, "apart from getting the Affiliation to accept Klang Surrender, thus opening the way for economic sabotage on a grand scale as we entice short-sighted human corporate CEOs and their idiot shareholders into buying into the Profit Bottom-Line Bullshit by accepting cheap off-world labor in appalling working conditions, thus undermining the economic clout and purchasing power of their own middle class, leading to increased unemployment and a burgeoning poverty rate while the same CEOs hide behind walls made of money and tell each other how brilliant they are. Apart from that, I mean." Molly smiled at his captain.

"Are you done?" Betty asked quietly.

Molly nodded.

"Now," resumed Betty, "where was I? Oh yes, asylum!"

"Yes," said Hadrian, "about that. You probably don't qualify."

"What?"

"Not enough social media pressure for taking you in, you see. That's the lynchpin for Terran Refugee Policy. But I do have another solution."

"I have a better one!"

"But you haven't heard mine yet."

"I don't care! I want you to set us down on a nice unoccupied planet where we can build us a prosperous new civilization, only to have that planet shift its orbit, turning into an inhospitable wasteland of creepy insects and howling winds, for which I will pathologically blame you and so plot my revenge to be enacted at some later date of my own choosing."

Hadrian smiled. "Sounds good to me. In the meantime," he continued as Nina Twice, Adjutant Tighe, and Lieutenant Sweepy Brogan strode into the bay, "do permit my Security Adjutant to escort you to comfortable quarters. Sweepy, a moment in private if you please."

"Seeking asylum?" Tighe asked Hadrian, her bloodshot eyes narrowing.

"No, we found a workaround on that."

"Oh thank Darwin. Uh, Captain?"

"Tighe?"

"I'm feeling better now, sir."

"And even without any hair, you look simply splendid, Adjutant!"

"I meant about being assigned to this vessel, sir."

"Indeed? That's quite the turnabout."

"Not really, sir. Happy drugs. Once I come down, I'll resume planning your disgraceful downfall."

"Fair enough. Off you all go, then."

Hadrian and Sweepy watched them leave. "Now then, Lieutenant, how fares your squad?"

"All on ice," Brogan replied, plucking out a cigar and lighting it. Amid acrid clouds of blue smoke, she said, "Betrayed over Helgoland Bight, I had to frag the board and most of the table it was sitting on. Too bad they were all sitting around it. But hey, the medics stopped complaining about being bored."

"Ah, an end to Diplomacy."

"Overrated in my opinion, Captain. Nine times outta ten, the right answer rides a hail of bullets and says 'I told you so' in a maelstrom of fire and destruction."

"Really?"

She smiled sweetly.

EPiLOGUE . . .

Hadrian stood in the elevator, Spark at his side, on their way back up to the bridge. From a speaker grille, Tammy said, "And here I was all full of commiseration about poor Spark. But that damned dog is unkillable. I'll have to do something about that reset button."

"Ah," said Hadrian, "you failed in your ploy of opening the door to the Lethal Radiation Chamber, so now you want to get more direct. But just as a warning, Tammy, I doubt Spark will take kindly to a chicken trying to crawl up its ass."

"Explosive feathers!" cried Spark.

"Really, Tammy," resumed Hadrian, "you need to get over the fact that Spark is a valuable and essential member of my crew now. I won't have you plotting its demise."

"Oh, fine then. So, aren't you going to save Captain Olo?"

"He'll be fine. Besides, he's now in command of an Abject Class Klang battleship. Serious war booty there."

"So, where to next?"

The elevator door opened and out they went. A few moments later, they reached the bridge.

"Captain on the bridge!" Sin-Dour announced, rising from the command chair. "Sir."

"2IC, find us a temporarily idyllic planet about to move into an unstable orbit wreaking devastation upon its fragile environment."

"At once, sir."

Hadrian settled into the command chair. "Now then! Is everyone happy?"

Beta swung round in her chair. "It is well known that two hundred rodents in a sack make a nice pillow, albeit one likely to eat your ear off."

"Thank you, Beta."

"You're welcome, sir."

Joss Sticks frowned across at Beta. "So, like, your hair never moves."

"Correct," the robot replied. "It has nowhere else it wants to go. This is the essence of loyalty."

"Well said, Beta," Hadrian chimed in. "Helm, prepare to set us a course as soon as Commander Sin-Dour finds that planet. Spark, patrol the ship, being especially on guard for intruders."

"Intruders! 'See what happens to trespassers?' Aisle Nineteen, Lime Pit Six!"

As Spark departed the bridge, Tammy the chicken hopped up onto the dais beside Hadrian. "You've got a long way to go, Captain. The Affiliation remains a quagmire of paranoia, hostility, injustice, rapacious greed, and idiotic but always self-serving galactic policies."

Hadrian smiled. "Ah, but the Klang have arrived, about to unleash economic sabotage on a galactic scale. Just think, the Head Idiots at the Galactic Monetary Fund are probably licking their lips at the thought of dumping loans on the poor Klang planets, loans that can never be repaid, of course, not without huge concessions, including giving up innumerable sovereign rights to Klang resources. Alas, those Idiots won't know what's hit them when the Klang are finally done with them."

"And it won't be on your head. Captain Hans Olo is a name that will live in infamy."

"The risks of command," Hadrian said. He rose from his chair, studying the still-blue viewscreen. "The human species has its head trapped in a vice of about a dozen unfounded assumptions about human nature and how things have to be, capital inequity foremost among them. The Klang are going to dismantle all of that, and fast."

"Captain," said Sin-Dour, "a planet has been found matching your requirements. Course has been conveyed to the Helm."

"Excellent. Helm, take us up to Point Oh-Eight, and then inform Engineering to prepare the T-Drive."

"Yes sir!"

The door behind him hissed open, and a technician with the name HALASZ stitched onto his coveralls walked in. He paused, squinted up at the screen, sighed and shook his head. He continued on until he stood directly in front of the huge screen, reached down beneath its edge and hit a button. The screen flickered and then revealed the starscape and the now departing Klang battleship. The technician pulled out a notepad and made some notes, before swinging round and heading out.

The image then shifted to a close-up of Hadrian, who scowled. "What's that for, Tammy?"

"I thought you were about to pontificate."

"Well, I'm not."

"Okay."

"Get rid of the close-up, Tammy."

"Well, how about some stentorian music, or maybe something that kind of, you know, drifts, a few minor notes reaching into the future. And then we can use an external remote camera to pull right back, revealing the *Willful Child* setting off into the depths of the unknown. Cue credits."

Hadrian sat back down in the command chair. "All right," he said. "Do that."

Music started up. The view on the screen shifted to an external aft shot of the *Willful Child*, sliding forward and getting smaller by the moment. "Classy," said Hadrian. "But . . ."

"But what?" Tammy demanded.

"Well, I mean, I'm sitting on the bridge of that ship, so watching it fly away is, well, confusing."

"Yes, since being on it you can't see it the way you're seeing it. That's a given."

"Maybe it's a given to you, Tammy, but I'm getting a headache."

"At least tell me you like the music."

Hadrian shrugged. "It's all right, I suppose. But all those straining strings . . ."

"What about them?"

"They seem to be viscerally inducing in me the desire to take a dump." He abruptly stood, looked around. "Anyone else feeling like that? If so, permission granted for potty break."

Everyone leapt up and ran for the bridge door.

"I hate you," said Tammy. "I really hate you all."

**Stay tuned
for more adventures,
as the voyage of the *Willful Child*
continues.
Boldly.**